PENGUIN BOOKS
LETTERS TO A LOVE RAT

Letters to a Love Rat

NIAMH GREENE

PENGUIN BOOKS

PENGUIN BOOKS

Published by the Penguin Group
Penguin Books Ltd, 80 Strand, London WC2R 0RL, England
Penguin Group (USA) Inc., 375 Hudson Street, New York, New York 10014, USA
Penguin Group (Canada), 90 Eglinton Avenue East, Suite 700, Toronto, Ontario,
Canada M4P 2Y3 (a division of Pearson Penguin Canada Inc.)
Penguin Ireland, 25 St Stephen's Green, Dublin 2, Ireland (a division of Penguin Books Ltd)
Penguin Group (Australia), 250 Camberwell Road,
Camberwell, Victoria 3124, Australia (a division of Pearson Australia Group Pty Ltd)
Penguin Books India Pvt Ltd, 11 Community Centre, Panchsheel Park,
New Delhi – 110 017, India
Penguin Group (NZ), 67 Apollo Drive, Rosedale, North Shore 0632, New Zealand
(a division of Pearson New Zealand Ltd)
Penguin Books (South Africa) (Pty) Ltd, 24 Sturdee Avenue, Rosebank, Johannesburg 2196,
South Africa

Penguin Books Ltd, Registered Offices: 80 Strand, London WC2R 0RL, England
www.penguin.com

First published by Penguin Ireland 2009
Published in Penguin Books 2009
2

Copyright © Niamh Greene, 2009
All rights reserved

The moral right of the author has been asserted

Printed in England by Clays Ltd, St Ives plc

ISBN: 978–1–844–88208–3

www.greenpenguin.co.uk

Penguin Books is committed to a sustainable future
for our business, our readers and our planet.
The book in your hands is made from paper
certified by the Forest Stewardship Council.

Prologue

Dear Charlie,
You are invited to my birthday party. It is on Wednesday at three
o'clock in my house.
*   You are the only boy coming but you don't have to wear a dress.*
Mummy says hitting is not allowed. I would like a doll.
Love
Laura x

Dear Charlie,
Mummy says I have to write and say thank you for the doll. But you
cannot come to my house ever again because Daddy says you are a holy
terror.
Love
Laura x

1989

Hi Charlie,
Jenny said she saw you kissing Susan Vine at the school disco last
week when I had chickenpox. I don't believe her, but why did you
ignore me at the bus stop? I know I still look a bit spotty, but I'm not
contagious any more.
Helen x

Charlie,

*I saw the hickey on Susan Vine's neck. I hope your you-know-what
falls off.*

   I'm going to snog Patrick Maher on Friday. I hate you.

Helen

1999

Dear Charlie,

*I love you more than life itself. More than I have ever loved anyone
before – even Jimmy Nolan. I can't believe I've found my soulmate at
last. I love you, honey lips.*

Kate xxxxx

*P.S. I've been thinking what we should call our future children. How
about Jack for a boy and Jill for a girl? Wouldn't that be adorable?
Love you xx*

Charlie,

*You are a self-centred, heartless asshole. I cannot believe you have done
this to me. I have burned all your pathetic love sonnets – they mean
nothing now that I know the truth about you. I hope you rot in hell.*

Kate

2009

To: Charlie
From: Rex
Re: You fat bastard
Hey Charlie, you fat bastard,
Sorry about tying you to that telephone pole on your stag night,

but it was pretty funny. Who was that bird you were talking to in the club? Can you get me her number? She had a great rack.
Rex

To: Charlie
From: Lulu
Re: You
Hey naughty boy,
Hope you enjoyed your stag night . . . If you want to get naughty again, give me a call . . .
Lulu xx

Molly

I squeeze my eyes shut against the sun streaming through the window and try to pretend that it's not morning yet. I don't want it to be morning. Or anywhere even close to morning. Because if it's morning it means I have to get out of this warm, cosy bed and face the real world. I have so much to do today, I really ought to get up and get going. But the trouble is, two blissful weeks of a honeymoon spent lolling by an aquamarine seawater pool doing nothing but sip exotic cocktails has made me chronically lazy and I just can't bring myself to move. All the hardcore relaxing (interspersed with a few half-hearted trips to see worthy cultural stuff) has finally proven to me what I always suspected: I'm perfectly suited to a life of idle leisure. If I ever win the Lottery I now know for sure that I will not be one of those people who keep the day job, just in case they get bored with all the five-star resorts and private planes. You know the type – they say things like 'Money won't change me' or, even funnier, 'Money can't buy you happiness.' After fourteen days at an all-inclusive couples-only resort I now know that money *could* buy me happiness and that if I ever do win wads of cash I'd be very content to lounge by a pool for ever and be waited on hand and foot. I'd throw in a few devoted servants to fan me down with giant palm leaves and rub suntan lotion into my back too, given half the chance.

I'm so annoyed I've even woken up – I'd been having such a delicious dream about the day Charlie and I got married. Maybe if I snuggle under the duvet some more and try really, really hard I'll be able to get back to it. I clamp my eyes shut and try to concentrate.

Where was I? I was past the part where I'd floated down the aisle clinging to Alastair's arm. Al had been thrilled to give me away. When I asked him if he'd take Dad's place on the day, he burst into tears. I was really touched. We've been friends for so long I didn't think he'd be that surprised that I wanted him right beside me, but he was. Sometimes of course I think that getting to be in all the official photographs was the *real* reason he was so delighted – centre stage is Al's favourite place to be.

I'd skated over the part where mad Aunt Nora had caused a bit of a scene by shouting and roaring about my ex-boyfriend David just as I reached the altar – I didn't want to dwell on that, not even in a dream. I was past the bit where my sister Tanya had taken my bouquet from me – even the part when she'd fumbled and almost dropped it – and I was right at the wonderful point where Charlie and I had just said 'I do'.

That part had been so *romantic*. At that moment, when Charlie looked deep into my eyes and promised to love and cherish me for ever, I knew that I was doing the right thing. All the doubts melted away. All the niggling little worries that we hadn't known each other long enough, that we were rushing into things, that we might regret it – they all disappeared and in that second I knew that everything would be all right. I'd found the One and now we were going to live happily ever after, just like characters in a chick-lit novel with a pretty pink cover and swirly gold lettering on the front. When Charlie slipped the slim platinum band on my finger I realized, right then and there, that I had found my fairytale ending. I wasn't going to die alone and lonely. I wasn't going to end my days as a bitter old woman who didn't believe in love. Even after everything that had happened, how close to the edge I'd come after Mum and Dad died and David and I broke up. It was all going to be all right.

If only I could get back to that dream, even for a few minutes. If I squeeze my eyes tightly enough maybe I might, just might, be able to drift off and recapture it. I shuffle under the goose-down duvet and try to concentrate, but it's no use – it's not working. The sun is too bright and now I can hear the noise of traffic drifting up from the street below. I'm going to have to get up. But maybe not just yet – maybe I'll have time for a quick cuddle with Charlie first. After all, isn't that supposed to be one of the perks of married life? You have love on tap whenever you want it. Things were a little quiet on that front when we were on honeymoon, but perhaps that's not so unusual – after all, I was busy organizing the wedding and then we were both completely shattered afterwards ... and work kept calling him every five minutes on his BlackBerry, so he was a bit distracted. But now that we're back home we probably won't be able to keep our hands off each other. Not that we're one of those couples who are all over each other all the time – we're a bit more restrained. Over the top Public Displays of Affection just aren't our thing – Charlie says our connection is more cerebral. And that suits me just fine, because passion is all very well and good but it can never be sustained. Once you get over the snogging-till-your-face-hurts stage at the start, lust usually fades away and all you're really left with is companionship and the ability to tolerate each other's bad habits. Passion never lasts – except with David; we'd never lost our lust for each other – but I'm not going to think about that now, because that would be completely inappropriate.

7

Anyway, having a cerebral connection with someone isn't as boring as it sounds – it can come in really handy. For example, Charlie's a mine of knowledge on current affairs and history – all the stuff I'm not very good at – which means that he helps me along if I get stuck. He's very good at prompting me to say the right thing, so that I don't seem too silly at dinner parties. Sometimes it can be a little embarrassing – like the time he teased me for not knowing how many states there were in America and everyone cracked up. I did try to tell him that of course I knew how many states there were – it's one of the facts I *do* know; after living in San Francisco for a year I ought to – but it was too late. Everyone thought it was hilarious, so I let it slide.

But it's so lovely to wake up with him as my husband. Imagine if I'd never gone to those media awards? I'd never have met him. I wouldn't be a happily married woman and we wouldn't be Mr and Mrs Charles Adler. What makes it even stranger is that I really didn't want to go. The only reason I was there at all was because my editor, Minty, had bullied me into it. Being the features editor/general skivvy at *Her* magazine isn't the worst job in the world, but going to boring awards dos is my least favourite thing. I only caved in because I thought I might get a goodie bag or a few free passes to the movies. For that, I was just about willing to sit through the agony of long speeches and very bad food.

When I got there, I noticed Charlie almost immediately. It was hard not to: he was sitting right opposite me and everyone at the table seemed to be hanging on his every word. He was charming and authoritative and very handsome, and so when he started to talk to me after the awful speeches I was intrigued. He certainly wasn't my type: unlike David, who'd always looked a bit scruffy, Charlie was well groomed and polished. And he was so attentive. He seemed to think that

8

everything I said was witty and hilarious – he even told me he loved my curly hair. It was like something out of a romcom movie: I was Julia Roberts in my blue full-length satin dress, and he was Pierce Brosnan in a well-cut tuxedo. All his smooth talk was very flattering, and after a few glasses of wine I started to believe him when he said I was the most gorgeous creature he'd ever seen. He spoke like a swashbuckling hero from the Mills & Boon novels I used to read at school; it was heady stuff. He said 'creature' quite a lot. And 'ravishing'. And 'intoxicating'.

When I was leaving he begged me for my phone number but I wouldn't give it to him, so instead he wrote his on my wrist and made me promise to call. I just laughed and said maybe I would and maybe I wouldn't, but really I had no intention of calling him – I was officially off men. Since David and I had broken up I hadn't dated anyone else and I didn't want to. I was happy by myself. Sure, sometimes I felt a little lonely when I was heating a frozen dinner for one in the microwave or curled up on the couch alone, but mostly I was pretty content and, anyway, work kept me so busy I barely had time to think. So I honestly never expected to clap eyes on Charlie again. I wrote off our meeting as a funny encounter that I'd tell Tanya about over a glass of wine – we'd giggle together about the charming stranger who'd been so flirty. But the very next morning he called to ask me out. *The very next morning!* It was practically unheard of. Because I'd refused to give him my number, he had called the switchboard at *Her* – he actually took the initiative. I got such a shock when he was put through and I heard his sexy velvety voice that I almost fell off my chair. I was so tongue-tied that Samantha and Penny in the office knew immediately that something was going on and proceeded to spend the rest of the day quizzing me about it. And now, six months later, we're husband and wife. I still can hardly believe that we're married. Really and properly married. Legally binding, no going back, till-death-do-us-part married. It's been such a whirlwind since we met, sometimes I find it hard to grasp that we're going to spend the rest of our lives together.

I snake my arm across to cuddle Charlie, but the sheet is cold and empty on his side of the bed. He must have gone for an early run – he's really into keeping fit. Which is fine by me as long as he doesn't press-gang me into going jogging any time soon. Although we could look really cute together if we bought matching Lycra running leggings and fleece tops. I think about this for a while. Maybe I could make an effort to get fit, develop some shared interests. I mean, obviously we love each other, but we probably should start doing stuff together more – that's the best way to keep the passion alive. We don't want to slide into being a settled married couple who have nothing in common. Then again, Lycra leggings are pretty unforgiving. And that seaweed wrap I got for the wedding didn't have any long-lasting results, so I'd have to go on a serious crash diet before I could even *think* about getting fit. And it's way too cold to go jogging so early in the morning.

Suddenly I wonder if Charlie put the coffee pot on before he left – I stick my nose out from under the cover and take a sniff. I can't smell a thing. Maybe he's going to bring me back a latte from the café on the corner instead. And some croissants to share. That would be fab. As long as he doesn't expect me to eat that awful organic porridge he loves so much. That stuff is vile – even worse than the smelly cheese he's so fond of.

I open one bleary eye to see what time it is – I really should get up soon. I'm going to need extra time to make myself look presentable. I have a bit of a tan from soaking up the sun while we were away, but the flight has played havoc with my complexion. I'll have to brush on extra bronzer and apply some of the tinted body moisturizer with the light-reflective properties that I treated myself to in the duty free – that'll give me the perfect finishing touch. And then there's my hair. All the sun and sand has left it so dry and brittle I could be the 'before' picture in a hair conditioner ad. I probably could squeeze in a hair mask if I'm quick. My bed head is legendary: it takes me a full hour to get it in shape sometimes. That's the curse of having thick, curly hair – you have to work extra hard to make it look halfway decent. Luckily for me, Charlie loves my wild hair almost as much as I hate it.

It's right then, just as I'm trying to remember where I left my hair straighteners, that I spot the sheet of paper on Charlie's pillow. He's left me a little love note – how cute. That's the first time he's done that. I'm really touched by his thoughtfulness.

I stretch out one arm and bring the letter close to my face so I can read it – he's probably told me he adores me and can't wait to get back from his run to do all sorts of naughty things to me. My insides warm at the thought. I'm definitely going to seduce him when he comes in. I'll have to ask him to have a shower first of course – all that sweat from running may look sexy and manly, but it can pong a bit.

But first I'll read his note – that'll get me in the mood. Prising my eyes apart is quite hard, but I really want to savour every special word, so I rub the gritty sleep away and try to focus on the page.

Dear Molly,
I'm sorry, I just can't do this. Please don't hate me.
Charlie

P.S. The bins are put out on Tuesdays. Try to remember to rinse the yogurt cartons before recycling.

Julie's Blog

11.03 p.m.
Right. This is it. Mr X is coming back. I have to come up with a plan. I can't continue my mad, passionate affair with him – having shag-fests with my boss would definitely be wrong. Especially when he's just back from his honeymoon.

11.04 p.m.
If only I could stop thinking about his strong, manly hands holding my face when we snog – he's so good at that.

11.05 p.m.
And the neck-stroking thing – the way he trails his fingers so slowly and so sensuously across my throat. That's almost impossible to resist as well.

11.06 p.m.
And of course there's that wrist-rubbing move he does. That's amazing . . .

11.07 p.m.
This isn't helping. I have to focus . . . I know! I'll make a list. That'll work.

Reasons to continue relationship* with Mr X:
  a) He's gorgeous
  b) He has really sexy toes – evenly spaced and no abnormally long ones

c) He has very little body hair (strongly suspect he has back, sack and crack wax on regular basis – once accidentally-on-purpose stumbled across his Visa bill on his desk and spotted beautician charges)

Reasons to end relationship* with Mr X:
  a) He just got married to his girlfriend
  b) He's my boss
  c) He just got married to his girlfriend

* 'Relationship' is defined as just-sex, no-strings-attached agreement. Absolutely no commitment involved.

11.10 p.m.

Right. So that's fairly clear. Mr X and I are over. Not that we had ever really begun. It was just sex. Really good sex. The best sex ever. But we can't do that any more, not now he's married. That would be wrong. Morally, ethically, terribly wrong. So that's it. The decision is made.

11.12 p.m.

But what if we can't help ourselves? What if all the animal magnetism between us is too much and we just can't resist? What if I see him and I want to rip his clothes off, shove him in the stationery cupboard and do unspeakable things to him? What if he gives me that special look, the one that says 'I want you', and I just melt?

11.19 p.m.

Maybe I should think about this in the morning when my head is nice and clear. It's late. Far too late to be thinking about this. And things always look better in the morning – I'll definitely know what to do then.

Open Forum

From Devil Woman: Hey, is this blog for real?

From Hot Stuff: I think so – I wonder what she'll do?

From Broken Hearted: Julie, take my advice and walk away. Continuing an affair with a married man will destroy you. Married men are a whole world of trouble and pain.

From Hot Stuff: I think it's romantic – Julie and Mr X are like star-crossed lovers who can't be together. Like Cathy and Heathcliff.

From Angel: Don't be ridiculous, they're not star-crossed lovers. And they're NOTHING like Cathy and Heathcliff – have you ever actually read *Wuthering Heights*? This Mr X is a low-life love rat – imagine how his wife will feel if she ever finds out what's been going on.

From Hot Stuff: OK, so I never read the actual book, but I saw it on telly – it was HOT.

From Devil Woman: Mr X's wife must be pretty stupid if she didn't suspect something was up before she married him. How could you not know your fiancé was having an affair? There must have been hundreds of clues!

From Sexy Girl: Maybe she did know – maybe she married him anyway.

From Angel: Why would any woman in her right mind do that? She'd have to be crazy. No way, she can't have known. He's obviously an adulterous liar – and so is this Julie.

From Devil Woman: All I know is that Mr X sounds gorgeous! Hey Julie, let us know what happens!

From Graphic Scenes: Do you think she'll describe any hot sex?

Eve

Dear Charlie,

Before I start, I'd like to make it crystal clear that it wasn't my idea to write to you. You will never read this letter of course, mainly because I'll never send it, but that's not the point. The point is that I want it to be known from the outset that this letter-writing thing is my therapist's idea, not mine. Yes, that's right, I have a therapist. Her name is Mary and she claims that, even though I believed I was over you, I actually have lots of unresolved issues about our break-up. Issues that, in her professional opinion, will significantly improve if I put pen to paper and express my innermost thoughts and feelings. I was really opposed to the plan at first – I was horrified at the idea of you reading what I might write – but I changed my mind when Mary explained that I didn't have to *send* the letters to you, I could just store them up and have one enormous bonfire with them at the end, when my mental health is fully restored. Mary says this may take quite some time, but I'm trying to stay optimistic.

A lot has changed in the two years since you left. I'm working from home now, which is great because there's no commute and I can stay in my pyjamas all day if I want to. It's going very well and I've been really busy. Sometimes I'm so snowed under with writing commissions that it's all I can do to keep up. Anna thinks I should get out more though – she says it's not natural to spend so much time indoors sitting at my computer. She's even started calling me the Hermit recently as a little joke. But just because my

17

social life is non-existent doesn't mean I'm unhappy. Tom and I have been very content pottering about together. Well, I say 'pottering', but really Tom just lies on the window ledge licking his bits and looking disdainful. He doesn't roam that much any more and he's even given up bringing dead mice into the kitchen and dumping them slap bang in the centre of the breakfast table. Mum says he lost the will to live when you left, but I tell her he just got older and more sensible and can't be bothered chasing rodents when he can simply concentrate on lying in the sun, toasting himself. That's not quite true of course – he did miss you at the beginning. He spent weeks ignoring me completely and turning away every time I tried to coax him out of his sulk with a head rub. It was like he blamed me for you leaving. But in the end he got used to it and I think he forgot all about you eventually.

I'd forgotten all about you too. Well, almost, that is. I'd *nearly* stopped thinking about you every day. I'd managed to train myself to allow you into my head only every *other* day, which was progress. Sometimes, if I was really lucky, I could block you out of my mind completely for three consecutive days at a time. Even I was impressed with myself when that happened.

So, you see, my life was fine. Quiet but fine. And then I saw your wedding photograph and it all fell apart.

I was in the supermarket when it happened. I was standing in line, waiting to pay for my basket of groceries, when I picked up the latest copy of *Hiya!* I wasn't going to buy it – I was just leafing through it to pass the time. You see, I knew I was going to be queuing for ages – the checkout girl had already taken four attempts to scan a tin of beans for the customer ahead of me – but I didn't mind. In fact, I was quite enjoying looking at the photos of all the Very

18

Orange People with very white teeth in very short dresses grinning out at me from the pages. It was really entertaining. Especially the close-up shots where you could spot the streaky bits of fake tan round their knuckles or the chips in their nail polish where chunks of diamanté had fallen off.

But then, just as I was chuckling over a VOP's VPL, there you were staring back at me from page 47, your arms wrapped round a ravishing blonde in a couture-looking wedding dress, and in a flash I felt really strange. All light-headed and dizzy and like I was going to pass out. I don't know if it was the shock of seeing you and another woman looking so smugly happy and in love, or the fact that you were wearing a tuxedo. (Which, by the way, I don't think suited you all that well. You looked like you were about to serve a good Sauvignon Blanc or pass round a platter of hors d'oeuvres.) Either way, I came over all funny. I don't remember much of what happened after that, but apparently I threw the magazine stand to the ground and started dancing on your head, and then flailed about with my shopping bag, which caught the checkout girl on the cheek – accidentally, I'm almost sure. I vaguely remember a security man trying to calm me down (well, sort of getting me in a headlock and threatening to handcuff me to the sweet counter), but other than that it's all a blur. Mind you, the store captured it all on CCTV so my solicitor says I'll be able to watch the entire thing soon.

One thing I know for sure is that, in that instant, all the progress I'd made since you left was erased and I was right back to square one again. I just couldn't stop thinking about how happy you looked with your new wife in that photo and how things between us had gone so badly wrong, and before I knew it I was scrubbing the grout between the bathroom tiles and rearranging all my cleaning products alphabetically again, and you know I only do that when I get really stressed.

It was Anna who suggested therapy. She said I should be completely over you by now and that the supermarket incident proved what she had suspected all along: that I wasn't. And therapy *did* work a treat for her and Derek. Of course Derek attended the sessions with her so they could understand why he suddenly wanted to wear women's G-strings under his grimy work overalls, but still. I know you think Anna's an interfering busybody – isn't that what you called her at that dinner party all that time ago? – but she's incredibly intuitive and my oldest friend, so I value her advice. And she *has* been very supportive since you left. She was brilliant when you walked out – cutting out a photo of your face and pasting it onto a dartboard in my darkest hour made me laugh when I thought I would never laugh again. I never actually threw any darts at you, but it did come in handy in the end – it's the perfect noticeboard for keeping track of all my freelance assignments.

I have to admit that, even though I was cautious at first, Mary the therapist has been very insightful so far. For example, she says my obsessive cleaning means I'm trying to control some aspect of my environment and that it's simply not healthy to be so attached to the vacuum cleaner. I need to learn to let go, apparently – which means that if I finish a coffee I should let the dirty cup rest on the worktop for longer than five seconds before putting it in the dishwasher.

She's certain she can help me find healing, and she already thinks my inner rage is subsiding a bit, which has to be good news. I don't think I have all that much inner rage to be honest – not unless you count how I feel about people who skip the queue at the deli counter when I'm waiting to get a wedge of that fresh Parmesan you used to love so much. (Can you believe I'm still buying that? Force of habit, I suppose.) Those types really make my blood boil, although I didn't admit that to Mary – I was afraid she might think I was a bit unstable. Mary says you'd be very surprised at what lies beneath the surface of most normal-looking people, and I suppose she'd know – she's been a psychotherapist for twelve years. That's what the certificate in the waiting room says, and I'm quite sure it was genuine and not a good fake like you might have suggested if you'd been there. She says that even people who seem in full control of their faculties can go a bit bonkers given enough provocation, and that I am a classic internalizer, which means that outwardly I appear perfectly fine but inside I am boiling over and could explode any time – which is what happened in the supermarket when I saw that photograph.

Apparently, that was only the tip of the iceberg. It might take decades for *all* the negative emotions to bubble to the surface, and then the suppressed anger might come gushing out in a torrent of unstoppable violence and I could end up in a home for the bewildered before you could say cuckoo's nest. I did explain to Mary that it's been two years since you left and that really, if I had internalized all this rage, then surely I would have seen more of it by now. But Mary says that these things are unpredictable and that you never can tell when disaster will strike and it all comes pouring out. That makes sense, although I'm worried I may have to see Mary for the rest of my life. Maybe I should go and have a chat with the bank manager just in case, because if there's one thing she really knows how to do it's to charge for her advice.

Anna is encouraging me to keep going, though. She's more determined than ever to help me now, after what's happened: she's even concocting a plan of her own to distract me from my misery, and she says that all will be revealed shortly. I have to say I'm a little nervous about that. The last time Anna had a great plan she persuaded me to go skydiving with her to conquer her fear of heights. She could barely climb the stairs before then, but jumping out of a plane at 30,000 feet really cured her. I'll never forget the look on her face when she was flying through the air, strapped to her instructor – it was a mixture of pure terror and pure euphoria. I loved it too – the feeling of freedom was amazing. Of course it was spoiled a bit when I landed awkwardly and broke my arm in three places and had to have five different pins inserted and nearly six months of physiotherapy. Still, I'm sure her new plan won't be anything as dramatic, at least I hope not – I'm not that keen on taking unnecessary risks with my life.

On a more positive note, the editor at *Her* magazine has commissioned me to do a series of relationship quizzes. She saw some of my work in the *Gazette* and liked my style, so called me out of the blue. I did tell her that I don't have a psychology degree and that maybe I'm not qualified enough, but she said that didn't matter and that I can bluff it if I have to. I felt kind of uncomfortable at first, but it pays really well and the bonus is that with my tragic relationship history I certainly won't have to do any research. I've attached my most recent example – it might ring a few bells with you.

Eve

Is He a Cheater or a Keeper?

According to recent research, 50 per cent of all men cheat on their partners. Would you know if your man was playing away from home? Take our simple test and find out!

Your man calls and says he has to stay late at the office to prepare an important presentation. Do you:
 a) Tell him he's working too hard, then whip up his favourite meal and pop it in the oven to keep warm. The poor guy'll need feeding up when he makes it home.
 b) Call a girlfriend and head out for a night on the tiles. It's a pity he has to work, but it's certainly not going to affect your social life.
 c) Pull on your biggest shades, jump in the car and race round to his office to make sure he's where he says he is. Excuses about working late could be the first sign of infidelity.

You find a receipt in your man's pocket for a sexy underwear store. Do you:
 a) Go get a bikini wax immediately. He's obviously going to present the set to you tonight and you want to look your best for him.
 b) Presume he's gone and bought another gift for his ungrateful mother. He's way too kind to the old bat.
 c) Hear alarm bells. The last time he bought you sexy underwear was years ago ... when you were actually having sex with each other.

Your man keeps getting mystery texts in the middle of the night. Do you:
   a) Suspect he's organizing a surprise birthday party for you – he's such a rascal!
   b) Wonder if he's ever going to cut those apron strings, and then roll over and go back to sleep.
   c) Try to get your hands on his phone – you have every right to read his messages.

Your man has been losing weight. Do you:
   a) Feel proud of him. It hasn't been easy cutting back – you really admire his discipline.
   b) Ask him how he did it. Maybe if you lost a few pounds that hunky waiter in the Italian wine bar would finally sit up and take notice.
   c) Suspect he's up to no good. He never minded being porky before now.

Results
Mostly As: Your man could have a dozen women on the side and you'd still be oblivious. You have to wise up.

Mostly Bs: Your man is probably playing away from home, but it's unlikely you are bothered. He's not your type anyway.

Mostly Cs: You're suspicious and with very good reason. This guy is making a fool of you – dump him now!

Molly

I'm sitting paralysed on the living-room floor, exactly where Tanya and Alastair found me when they arrived. I know I must have called them and asked them to come over, but I can't remember doing it. Everything is such a blur that I don't even know what time it is. All I know for sure is that I have already been handed at least four cups of very hot, very sweet tea, which Tanya insists is the only thing to drink in emergencies. That and brandy. But seeing as we don't have any brandy, hot, sweet tea will have to do.

Al and Tanya are good in emergencies. Correction: Al and Tanya are *mostly* good in emergencies. Sometimes they can be hopeless, like the time the chip pan caught fire – they were both completely useless then. Al panicked and threw a saucepan of water over the blaze to put it out (a very bad idea), and Tanya grabbed the pan from him and ran through the open door to chuck it into the garden (the worst possible thing to do, as the air just fanned the flames). But they have been great in other life-or-death situations. Like the day a few years ago when I was still with David and the four of us somehow decided that going for a hike would be the perfect way to spend a sunny Sunday afternoon. I was exhausted in less than twenty minutes, so David lugged my backpack all the way up the mountain for me. Then he tripped, fell awkwardly and broke his ankle. I'll never forget how good Al and Tanya were. Tanya morphed into some sort of Super Nurse and insisted that David keep still, while Al whipped a miniature bottle of brandy from his inside pocket and fed

David little sips to ease the pain. I was no use to anyone – in fact I was a sobbing mess – but that must have been because of the altitude: we were pretty high up. Whatever it was, by the time the emergency services came I was so hysterical and paranoid that I was convinced they'd have to amputate David's leg. I didn't even protest when Al got a bit over-enthusiastic trying to give him mouth to mouth.

A fleeting picture of David floats through my mind and I shake my head – I can't be thinking about my ex-boyfriend when my husband has just left me.

'Charlie has obviously gone mad,' Alastair says matter-of-factly, interrupting my thoughts. 'Stark raving mad.'

He takes a drag of his menthol cigarette and blows the smoke out his nose, then he splutters a bit and tries to cover it up by taking another drag. He's a hopeless smoker. He looks exactly like a skinny teenage boy trying too hard to be cool at the back of the school bike shed. Except instead of wearing a polyester pullover and too-short trousers he's wearing a clingy Prada knit and Gucci sunglasses perched on the highlighted hair he gets 'seen to' by a top stylist at Toni and Guy every three weeks.

Usually I wouldn't let Al smoke in here, but I'm too shell-shocked to protest so he's chain-smoking to his heart's content – this is his third cigarette in less than twenty minutes. I can't bring myself to tell him off. I'm finding it hard even to speak – I can't believe that Charlie has left me after a couple of weeks of marriage. This can't possibly be for real. There must be some sort of innocent explanation for this mix-up. If only I could think of what it could be.

'Alastair,' Tanya says, frowning at him, 'do you have to smoke? It's so gross.'

Tanya is vehemently anti-smoking. She has been ever since she saw that 'Smoking is not Cool' video at school –

the one where they split a diseased lung in half and all the black goo dripped out. Tanya threw up in the front row partway through the video, and she never really lived it down.

'All cigarettes are disgusting, but menthol cigarettes are *vile*.' She coughs and shifts away from him on the sofa.

'Sorry,' Al says, shrugging apologetically. 'But smoking is cool again, so I have to do it. And menthols are really hot – they're so retro.'

'Smoking *isn't* cool,' Tanya sniffs, 'and if I get cancer because of your idiotic lifestyle choices I'll kill you.'

'Haven't you heard about smirting?' Alastair sighs. 'You're no one if you haven't flirted with a total stranger in the outside smoking area.' He inhales again and tries to blow a smoke ring. 'I don't like it any more than you do, but I have to practise if I want to get any action. Do you think I look sexy enough?' He angles the cigarette from his fingers and pouts suggestively at her.

'Smoking isn't sexy.' Tanya glares at him. 'It's *disgusting*.' She turns away from Al and leans in close to me, as if she doesn't believe that she could have heard me right the first time and needs to listen again carefully, just to make sure. 'Now, Moll,' she says, 'take a deep breath and tell us what happened – start over from the very beginning.'

I inhale and feel my chest shudder. I won't panic. I need to stay calm. I'll take a few big cleansing breaths – that'll help. That's what the feature in *Her* advised last month, and that advice was given by someone who really knew what she was talking about: the freelancer I commissioned to write it was trapped alone in a store toilet for ten and a half hours when the security man locked her in overnight by mistake. I don't know what would be worse: being trapped in a store toilet all night or being so close to all the gorgeous designer goodies on the shop floor and not being able to get to them. Butter-soft leather handbags with dangly padlocks and buckles so big you'd get whiplash just from lifting them, one of a kind handcrafted jewels you'd have to employ a personal bodyguard to wear in public – that sort of stuff.

But I can't think about handbags right now. Right now I need to concentrate on not having a heart attack. OK, so heart attacks are probably rare for women in their early thirties, but I'm sure they can happen. Especially if you've just had a massive shock, like I have. I could keel over any second. It definitely *feels* like my heart is about to burst out of my chest. And my arm ... there's a stabbing pain in my left arm – isn't that one of the first signs of cardiac arrest? Maybe I should take an Anadin, that's meant to help – or is that for blood clots? I can't remember.

I try to breathe in and out as slowly and evenly as possible. There, I feel better already. I'm fine. Now all I have to do is remember to keep breathing. How hard can that be? I've been doing it for thirty-three years without even thinking about it. In, out, in, out, there's nothing to it. I try to ignore the way my heart is violently hammering or the way my head feels like it's going to explode. This is surreal. Charlie can't have left me – we only got married a few weeks ago. We're *newlyweds*, for goodness sake. We were happy ... weren't we?

'Molly?' Tanya softly prompts me to speak. 'Can you tell me what happened?'

'I woke up,' I hear myself croak, 'and that note was next to me.' I gesture feebly at the note that Al has managed to prise from my fingers.

'OK ...' Tanya chews thoughtfully on her lip. 'And Charlie hadn't said anything to you before that? About, um, being unhappy?'

'No, I don't think so.' I feel myself start to shake again.

It's so strange – it's like I'm floating above my body and looking down at myself on the floor. From up here I don't look like a deserted wife; I look perfectly normal. This can't be happening. This must be some terrible nightmare and I'll wake up any minute. I don't deserve this. I'm a nice person. I brush my teeth, I say my prayers. OK, so I don't exactly say my prayers, but I do donate to charity and I have a standing order to help a poor family in a Third World country – that has to count for *something*.

'I'm telling you,' Alastair says, 'he's gone mental. Maybe he's had a nervous breakdown. They're considered quite sexy now. All the best people are having them.'

He takes another drag and exhales elegantly through his nose. I know that in his head he's pretending to be Rhett Butler from *Gone with the Wind*. He loves that movie – he watches it every three months or so and then spends the next week speaking like a Southern belle and trying to decide if growing a Clark Gable moustache would make him more handsome.

'Let me see the letter,' Tanya says. She's using her 'calm and in control' voice. It makes me feel even sicker because it means she's taking this seriously.

Al passes it back to her and she scans it again.

'No, this isn't the letter of a madman,' she says eventually. 'The spelling's too good. If he'd gone mad his writing would be more scrawly – you know, spidery and kind of sinister.'

'Yeahhhh.' Alastair nods. 'Like a *proper* mentalist.'

'Exactly,' Tanya says.

Then she takes my hand in hers and I feel her soft, beautifully moisturized skin against my clammy palm. Tanya loves to moisturize – she carries hand cream with her everywhere. She says it's vital to massage it into the cuticles because they are an important indicator of a person's self-worth. Her cuticles are smooth and translucent. I start to feel wobbly. This is really happening. I'm not having some awful nightmare – I'm not going to wake up soon.

'Was Charlie acting strangely?' Tanya asks slowly. 'You know, out of character maybe?'

I try to think, but everything's a blur. Maybe the jet lag is kicking in, maybe that's why my brain feels like it's stuffed with cotton wool.

'I don't think so,' I say, and shake my head. But what if I'm wrong? Maybe he *was* acting strangely and I just didn't see it.

'Wasn't there *anything* unusual? Even the smallest thing?' Tanya's blue eyes search my face. She's wearing her extra-lengthening mascara. It's funny the things you notice in a crisis.

'He might have been a bit quieter than usual when we were away,' I suggest eventually. 'But we *were* unwinding. The wedding was so hectic, we were exhausted.'

I think I see Al and Tanya exchange a knowing glance, but I'm not sure.

'Yes, the wedding was certainly eventful, I'll give you that,' Tanya says, smiling at me.

I know exactly what she's talking about. The day *had* been pretty eventful. First there had been mad Aunt Nora, who'd successfully reminded anyone who hadn't already noticed that I wasn't marrying David, my ex, that I was marrying Charlie instead. The guy I'd just had the whirlwind romance with. The guy who had popped the question after just a few weeks of dating. That was a little awkward. And then the photographer forgot to recharge the battery on his digital camera and we had to reshoot most of the official photographs. It may have been a teeny mistake on my part to hire the photographer from *Your Animal* magazine, but I only did it because the staff photographer from *Her* was on holiday in Miami. How was I to know he was incompetent? His portfolio looked fine – even if it was mostly of cats. Anyway, it all worked out in the end – he even got a photo of us in *Hiya!* to make up for the inconvenience.

Then there was the meal. The soup was cold – and it wasn't supposed to be one of those trendy chilled soups that you sometimes see being made on cooking programmes either – but who could have foreseen a power cut in the hotel kitchen? And the music was problematic because the swing band was a bit late. By an hour and a half. It really was so unfortunate that the lead singer got his willy caught in his zipper in a petrol station toilet on the motorway and had to be rushed to A&E.

So, yes, there were a few little hiccups, but it was a beautiful day nevertheless. I can still remember how Charlie looked at me when he said, 'I do.' And I can still remember our first kiss as man and wife – no tongues, just chaste, closed lips, as we had agreed beforehand. French-kissing like teenagers in front of all our friends and family would have been too mortifying, despite Alastair's attempt to convince me that all the best celebrity couples got down and dirty on the altar after being declared man and wife and if we wanted to add an extra pizzazz to the proceedings we should snog like it was going out of fashion.

I can, in fact, remember every single detail like it was yesterday. It's all seared on my brain and it will be for ever. OK, so I suppose it's not like time has had a chance to dim the memories – we're only just back from our honeymoon. We haven't even eaten the leftover wedding cake yet. Mind you, I don't like fruit cake all that much. It's the sultanas that make my stomach turn – they're so *slimy*.

Sometimes I think I should have stuck to my guns and got the chocolate fudge cake I really wanted, but Alastair persuaded me that it wouldn't be traditional so I caved in. Tradition is vital – especially when it comes to the most important day in your life.

'Did you have a row maybe?' Tanya strokes my hand gently, like I'm a child again and she's the kind big sister helping to pick me up after I've fallen and cut my knee. She was always really good at looking after me whenever I hurt myself. Mind you, she liked to give me the odd sly bruise as well, just so she could play nurse.

'No, we didn't,' I say, clinging tightly to her hand. I see her wince. I realize I'm digging my nails into her skin.

'Are you sure?' Al gazes into my eyes. He's doing the 'I can see into your soul' thing that he likes to think he's so good at. Ever since he did that night course on psychic abilities he thinks he's got 'the gift'. He claims to have predicted the whole skinny jean phenomenon.

'Maybe there's something you're blocking out?' Tanya asks.

I try to remember. Had something major happened and I've forgotten? I can't think of anything. Surely I would remember something really serious, like him wanting to run out on me? I couldn't have missed those signs, could I? That couldn't be possible.

'Let's go back,' she says soothingly. 'What was the last thing you had an argument about?'

Alastair pauses mid-drag and looks at me expectantly.

I try to think.

'He wanted to watch a documentary about the ozone layer,' I say eventually in a small voice. 'I wanted to watch *EastEnders* instead.'

Charlie is really passionate about the environment. He's

32

always going on about reducing, reusing and recycling. I'm not that eco-friendly, to be honest. I did buy one of those 'I'm not a plastic bag' bags though, so I do try. I know it was only a fake one, but to get a real one I would've had to queue for hours, and standing in the pouring rain and freezing cold didn't strike me as a fun way to pass a morning. The truth is, I've never been that good at the recycling thing, and since meeting Charlie I hadn't needed to keep pretending that I was any more, because he started taking care of it all – the washing out of jam jars and making trips to the bottle banks: really boring stuff like that. Of course, we don't usually have that many jam jars – I never could stand the way the little seedy bits get stuck between your teeth and you can't get them out for days, even with floss. But I always have quite a few bottles, especially if Tanya and Alastair come to visit – then it can be more than a few. I used to hate going to the bottle bank because I'd had so many embarrassing incidents trying to shove all the empties into the great big tank while everyone stared at me. I always knew what they were thinking: that I was a total alco, personally responsible for most of the binge-drinking in the country. One time I tried to explain to an old lady who was looking at me in disgust that the bottles weren't all mine, that Tanya and I had been keeping Al company because he'd had a fight with his boyfriend. But she turned her head away like I was scum and she couldn't bear to be anywhere near me. So it was dead handy when Charlie took over complete responsibility for the environmental stuff. He even tried to get me to start using eco-friendly washing-up liquid, but I wouldn't do it because I like the way the supermarket brand bubbles up and keeps your hands soft – that's what the ad says, and why would advertisers lie? Maybe I should have listened to him, though. Maybe if I'd agreed to switch to an ecologically friendly product he wouldn't have left me. Perhaps I should change. Perhaps I should go out right now and buy that eco washing-up liquid. Who cares if the grease is left on the frying pan or the glasses are still grubby? I probably won't even notice. Not unless I get food poisoning or MRSA from the dirt of course. But I could do with losing some weight anyway. And I'll get really good at recycling too. I'll start that compost heap thing he's always talking about. It will be smelly and disgusting, but I'll put up with it because we'll be together again and that's all that counts. I'll get wellies and wear a woolly jumper and pretend I really care about the planet. I'll even give up hairspray. Charlie is always going on about toxicity and the ozone layer. I never really listened before, but I'm willing to listen now. I can just wear my hair in a ponytail every day so no one need ever know how grimy it really is. Who needs hairspray anyway? Well, maybe I won't go that far. I mean, my hair gets really uncontrollable if I don't give it a good coating occasionally. But otherwise I'll be a green warrior — an eco angel. I'll be the perfect, environmentally friendly wife.

Tanya blinks slowly. Al coughs and splutters on his cigarette.

'What? What is it?'

Why are they looking at me like that?

They exchange another glance.

'Um, arguing about watching a show on the ozone layer is hardly very . . . passionate, is it?' Tanya says slowly.

'I can't help it if we don't have blazing arguments,' I say. 'We don't really fight that much.'

'Well, you should try it. The sex is great afterwards,' Al pipes up.

'Oh yeah . . .' Tanya's face lights up. 'Last week Connor

and I had a massive row about who should get the toy in the cornflakes box. Then we ended up bonking on the kitchen table – it was *amazing*.'

Her eyes go all dreamy.

'Oooh saucy!' Alastair says, nudging her and giggling.

Then they see my face and compose themselves again.

'Sorry, Molly.' Tanya clears her throat. 'So, after you found the note you called his mobile . . .'

'And it went through to answerphone,' I finish. We've been through that part already. I've called a dozen times, but Charlie's not answering. I've left messages asking him to call me back, to tell me what all this means, but so far nothing.

'So you have no idea what time he left?'

'No.' I realize this is true.

'He could have gone in the middle of the night for all we know,' Al suggests. 'You know, under cover of darkness and all that.'

'This isn't a spy movie, Alastair,' Tanya says. 'He'll probably be back in time for tea. Perhaps he just felt a little panicky and had to have some breathing space.'

I feel a ray of hope bubbling inside me. That sounds good – that sounds plausible. Maybe this is nothing to worry about. Maybe it's just a little blip in married life. One of those things that happen to everyone.

'I'm not so sure about that,' Al interrupts. 'I mean, really, you two should still be in the honeymoon period. It's meant to last for a few months at least. Unless,' his eyes brighten and he visibly perks up in his chair, 'unless you're having a celebrity marriage.' He flicks ash from his cigarette and misses the saucer he's using as a temporary ashtray by a mile.

'What do you mean?' I ask.

Is that good? Does that mean that everything will be fine in the end?

'You know, you get married after knowing each other for a few weeks – you got that part almost right – then you split up and get divorced in the space of six months, sometimes less. It's all the rage. You might swing an annulment if you're lucky.'

He stubs his cigarette out in the saucer.

I feel weak. Divorced? We can't get divorced. We're barely married. We have wedding gifts to open. The remains of our three-tier cake are still in the fridge, for God's sake.

'Let's face it,' Al goes on, 'everything happened so quickly. How well do you know Charlie really? I mean, it's not like it was with you and David. You knew *him* inside out.'

Tanya gasps and suddenly the room is still and silent. It's so quiet I can hear myself swallow. So quiet I can hear air rushing in my ears. I feel as cold as ice. Almost as cold as that time Charlie and I went ice-skating in Central Park.

That was such an amazing holiday – it was the trip when Charlie proposed. We'd only been dating for four weeks when he'd sprung it on me out of the blue. He was treating me to three days in New York just before Christmas – I'd been sick with excitement when I'd found out. I'd never been to New York before, but I just *knew* I was going to love it. It was going to be so *romantic*. Charlie and I were getting on brilliantly, and now we were going to the Big Apple together. We'd be just like Ross and Rachel in *Friends*, drinking skinny lattes and sharing hotdogs on street corners. We were going to stay in a gorgeous Park Avenue Hotel, take horse-drawn carriages through Central Park and go on shopping sprees in Bloomingdale's. Of course I was a little nervous: it was a long way to go with someone you didn't know that well. For one thing, I was going to have to do my 'business' in the en-suite bathroom while he was in the bedroom. That scared me. What if he could hear me weeing? That'd kill any mystery I was trying to preserve.

But I was also excited. I needed a break and Charlie was handsome, charming and had one of those black American Express cards, the kind you only get when you don't have any trouble paying your bills at the end of the month. In the four weeks I'd been dating him I'd discovered that he really knew how to show a girl a good time. He was generous and flamboyant and sent massive bouquets of flowers to the office all the time. And he was totally smitten with me – he seemed to think I was the best thing since sliced bread. He kept telling me how amazing and unique I was and, thing is, I was starting to believe him. He said he'd never felt this way about anyone before, that I was special, that he was in love with me. It was intoxicating. So when he asked me to go to New York I hesitated for about half a second before throwing my arms around his neck and shouting yes! And the added advantage was that going to New York at that time of year meant I'd be away for the anniversary of Mum and Dad's deaths, and that had to be good. Because maybe if I was in Manhattan with a gorgeous man I would be able to forget what had happened, maybe if I was in a foreign city I could blank the date and all those painful memories from my mind.

And I was almost right. New York was exactly as I had imagined. Everything *was* perfect. In fact, it was beyond perfect, especially when Charlie got down on one knee at the top of the Empire State Building and proposed, completely out of the blue.

I was shocked at first – we didn't know each other that well, after all – but then when I thought about it, it started to make sense. When you know, you know, right? Well, maybe

I didn't exactly know that he was the One when I first met him. There wasn't that instant chemistry thing like there had been with David, that sensation you get when you look into someone's eyes and feel like you've come home. But how often does that happen? Once in a lifetime, if that. And when I blocked David from my mind and concentrated on Charlie properly, I realized he was perfect for me. He obviously adored me and now he wanted to take care of me for the rest of our lives. It's true I didn't know his shoe size or even his middle name, but he was proposing on top of the Empire State Building – that has to be one of the top ten places in the world to ask someone to marry you. Maybe it was a sign – a sign that we were made for each other. So, after staring at him with my mouth open for what seemed like an eternity, I accepted and he whisked me off to buy the ring. I never thought I wanted a diamond engagement ring, but Charlie was absolutely insistent that we get something really special, so somehow I found myself in Tiffany's sipping champagne and trying on enormous rocks in a private curtained area while a skinny saleswoman simpered round me and Charlie looked on, beaming. In no time at all, I really got into the spirit of things (lots of champagne can have that effect) and when he finally slipped a massive solitaire onto my ring finger I was genuinely over the moon.

But now he's left me. Maybe Al is right – maybe I didn't really know him at all.

'Molly? Are you OK?'

Tanya is still talking to me. She rubs the fleshy part of my palm with her thumb and I realize I'm twisting my massive solitaire engagement ring round and round.

'Listen, don't worry. I'm sure this is nothing. Let's make you another cup of tea and we'll figure it out. You just relax.'

She helps me off the floor and up onto the sofa, tucking a blanket round my legs.

Then she and Al disappear into the kitchen and the kettle is switched on again. I lean back against the seat and try to breathe. If I concentrate on breathing then maybe my chest will stop feeling like a massive weight is bearing down on it, crushing my lungs.

If Tanya is right, Charlie will be back soon and all this will be nothing. Nothing at all. But what if she's wrong – what if he's not coming back? What if he's gone for good?

Julie's Blog

9.05 a.m.

Mr X is due in at any minute, so I have to devise my plan *immediately.* Like right this second.

9.06 a.m.

Impossible to concentrate. All the UCs (useless colleagues) are driving me crazy chattering about pointless press releases and publicity opportunities for self-obsessed authors. Some two-page spread on a new chick-lit writer has them foaming at the mouth with excitement. Banter is doing my head in – who cares if a brainless bimbo has shot straight to number one in the book charts and wants to tell us all about her perfect life and gorgeous children on the pages of the national papers? Not me. Anyway, I know for a fact that she hates her husband, employs two nannies and has a secret Vicodin problem.

9.08 a.m.

UC One is trying to claim full responsibility for new chick-lit bimbo's success – she's now passing round her special-recipe home-baked muffins to celebrate the two-page spread. They're all talking about sales going through the roof, breaking industry records, blah, blah. UC One keeps saying in a very smug voice, 'I just *knew* the *Gazette* would love the kids angle – a two-page spread is almost impossible to get, you know. I really think she might be the next Carla Ryan.'

As if! Every female writer wants to be the next Carla Ryan, queen of chick lit, but most of them don't stand a chance. The only one who comes close is that brassy blonde Noreen Brady, and that's only because she's always happy to wear low-cut tops in photo shoots.

Just caught UC Two making stabbing signs behind UC One's back. Ha!

9.10 a.m.
Oh God, God, God. He's going to be here *any minute*. Feel a bit hot. Maybe I should turn up the air conditioning. I'm starting to regret wearing this tight red top now, even if it is Mr X's favourite.

9.11 a.m.
I know! I'll email N and R for advice. They're my oldest friends and I trust their opinions – they'll tell me what to do. Just hope they don't tell me anything I don't want to hear – like that it's immoral to bonk your boss in the stationery cupboard.

9.13 a.m.
Email from N:
> He's hot – you fancy him – what harm can it do? He's not cheating on *you*. Why don't you give him a proper welcome back – I would! Fill me in later – I want every single detail and don't you dare leave anything out! Great idea to wear that sure-thing tight red top – that'll drive him wild!

N has a very good point. *I'm* not cheating on anyone. *I'm* not married. Or living with anyone. Or even dating anyone. So, in theory, I have nothing to worry about. Except my conscience. And my black soul and eternal damnation.

9.15 a.m.

Email from R:

> He's MARRIED, end of story. You have to stop this now. Pretend it
> never happened. Or, even better, resign – then you'll never have to
> see him again. Either way you have to put a stop to it. BTW, tell
> me you're not wearing that tarty red top.

Bloody typical of R to overreact. I can't resign from a
perfectly good job just because I had a fling with the boss.
Plenty of people have affairs with their co-workers – it
doesn't mean they have to throw away their careers. Maybe
she is right though – maybe I should act professional and
pretend nothing happened. I could just stare vacantly at him
every time he passes by, or smile vaguely at him in meetings,
as if I simply can't remember that he ever unfastened my
bra with his teeth or photocopied my bum for fun after
office hours.

9.17 a.m.

He's back. He's baaacccckkkkk . . . I can't breathe. I CAN'T
BREATHE.

9.18 a.m.

OK – I'm breathing. Will just have a little look at him.

9.19 a.m.

Oh God, he looks really sexy. Has very dark tan and hair is
all shaggy and dishevelled, like he's just strolled off a tropical
beach. Which of course he almost has – he only flew home a
day or two ago. Think I can actually smell coconut oil floating from his golden skin and wafting across the office. Have
insane urge to stalk across the room, throw all the files from
his desk and lick his chest. Will not do that of course. Will

be poised and professional and pretend I am unaware of his existence, just like R advised.

UCs are flocking round Mr X's desk to welcome him back – it's pathetic. UC One is practically *drooling* on him and trying to force-feed him a home-baked muffin. I, on the other hand, haven't even looked in his direction. Am very proud I'm doing so well. Maybe this will be easier than I thought. Of course I haven't done any official work as such, except for updating this blog ... but I can't be expected to multi-task so soon. The main thing is, I can manage to be in the same office as Mr X and feel completely indifferent to him. Obviously now that he's married my intense physical desire for him has simply fizzled out. Thank you, God!!!

9.25 a.m.
Have composed two whole lines of a press release – not bad going, considering. Just have to finish it and then devise a brilliant media strategy to ensure optimum press saturation and therefore massive sales for my client Mr Dick Lit.

Am sure it won't take long – I'll just copy the same old template as always.

9.28 a.m.
Still pretending to work. Really observing Mr X from behind two-line press release. Cannot see any visible tan lines anywhere on his deliciously chiselled body. In fact, the colour of his silky smooth skin is completely even all over, as if he rotated himself on a spit every few minutes while sunbathing. Or else he has applied bottle tan very carefully. Although his skin is mahogany brown, not orange or streaky in any way, and there are no telltale lines on his palms.

Maybe he used latex gloves? Or could it be spray-on? Cannot imagine him in a booth wearing goggles and a thong, but it is possible.

Mr X's hair is curling round his collar. He looks exactly like Orlando Bloom in *Pirates of the Caribbean*, all sweaty and gorgeous. Am trying very hard to ignore him and continue to be poised and professional, but do feel a bit hot and flustered. Really wish I'd put a stick deodorant in my bag. Maybe I should splash some water on my face. Or get a drink from the water cooler. Or maybe not – the water cooler *is* right beside his desk. I don't want him to think I'm trying to get his attention when I'm actually trying to do the opposite.

9.35 a.m.

Hmmmm ... Mr X is fiddling with his wedding band a lot – keeps twirling it round and round his finger, like it's irritating him in some way – very interesting behaviour.

9.37 a.m.

Mr X has just taken off his wedding band and tossed it onto his desk, *like it means nothing to him*. And I've just noticed that there's no white mark on his ring finger – which means he must have been sunbathing *without it on*. Very, very interesting. Wonder if his new wife is aware he has been removing his wedding band already – *while on honeymoon in fact*. Possibly while she went indoors for a nap and he flirted with the cocktail waitress. Not that I care if he was – it's nothing to do with me, he can flirt with whomever he wants, we're both free agents. Well, he's not of course, he's a married man. But I'm a free agent. Completely and totally free. As a bird. So if I wanted to flirt with anyone, I could. Except not with him any more. Which is fine. Completely and totally fine.

9.38 a.m.
God, I'm really, really thirsty. Parched actually. Maybe I'll just saunter casually over and get a drink, no big deal.

9.41 a.m.
Back from water cooler – managed to look completely casual. Even snuck in a sideways glance to see if Mr X was secretly watching me but ... he wasn't. He had his head buried in paperwork. He didn't even acknowledge my existence.

9.42 a.m.
Of course, maybe he's trying to be discreet.

9.43 a.m.
Yes, that's it – he doesn't want to raise suspicion of UCs by talking to me.

9.44 a.m.
Still, he could have said hello. That wouldn't have killed him. What did he think I was going to do – leap across his desk and rip his clothes off?

9.45 a.m.
Right, that's it. Two can play at that game. I won't speak to him either. That'll be perfect, actually. He won't speak to me, I won't speak to him – no confusion. No saucy banter, no illicit snogging. This is ideal.

9.49 a.m.

Just caught Mr X looking at me. Could feel the heat of his eyes on my face so glanced up and our eyes locked for a split second – it was electric. Crap.

9.51 a.m.

Email from Mr X:

> I need to speak to you urgently. Meet me in the stationery
> cupboard in five minutes.

What's that about? He can't think I'm going to give him a welcome-back shag the second he walks back into the office from his honeymoon? Even I'm not that crass.

9.53 a.m.

Then again, he does look amazing. His skin looks so ... buttery.

9.55 a.m.

But I won't give in. He can't just ignore me one minute and then expect me to fall all over him the next, that's not the way it works. And there's something else as well, there's another reason I can't give in ... what is it again? I can't think – the way he's staring at me from across the room has made my mind go blank.

9.57 a.m.

Oh yes. He's *married*. I *knew* there was something else. How could I have forgotten that – even for a split second? It's just so strange to think that he's a husband now. I have to keep repeating it in my head: doing it with a married man would be very, very WRONG. Maybe I should stick a Post-it note on my PC to remind me.

10.08 a.m.

Oh. My. God. Mr X just told me in the stationery cupboard that

  a) he loves me

  b) he made a big mistake getting married

  c) he has left his wife

  d) he wants to move in with me

Then he threw me across the photocopier and kissed me passionately before I could say a word. He wants to come round after work with his stuff. He says he can't wait to begin his new life with me and that we're going to be ecstatically happy together but that we have to keep it quiet for a little while because people might be shocked if they knew.

People might be shocked? *I'm* shocked! I had no idea his feelings for me were so strong. All this time, when I thought we were having a sex-only, no-strings-attached affair, he was really falling in love with me! And now he's left his wife for me. I can't believe it. It's so romantic. But it's also so ... unexpected. We never discussed him leaving his wife. If I think about it, we never discussed much of anything at all except how much we wanted to rip each other's clothes off. Now he wants us to live together. In my flat. And see each other. All the time.

10.11 a.m.

Feel all trembly and weak. Can't decide if I'm happy or terrified. Think I might be about to faint. What do you do if you feel faint? Put your head between your legs? Can't do that here – UCs would know something was wrong. Maybe I could discreetly breathe into a paper bag – there has to be one around here somewhere. UC One definitely has some under her desk – she always carries her homemade muffins in them – but I can't ask her, she'd be bound to notice I was hyperventilating and want to know why.

10.13 a.m.

UC One just asked if I was OK – I *knew* it wouldn't be long before she spotted something was wrong. She said I look green round the gills. Then she laughed that awful braying laugh of hers. Told her my blood sugar level was probably low because I hadn't eaten anything yet, and she presented me with one of her special-recipe home-baked muffins and told me to tuck in. Have hidden the muffin in my drawer – her special recipe smells uncannily like vomit.

10.16 a.m.

Email from R:

> So, have you kicked him to the kerb then? I think forgetting all about him is the right thing to do – cut all ties and pretend your affair never happened. This is a fresh new start for you – who knows what could happen! You could meet the man of your dreams and be living in bliss with him this time next year!

Oh God. Have to lie to R. If she finds out that Mr X has left his wife and wants to move in with me then I'm done for.

10.18 a.m.

Just thought. If Mr X *was* to move in with me, we could have as much hot sex as we like – any time we like. We wouldn't have to sneak around any more. We could get down and dirty whenever we want, however we want. That could be good. That could be better than good. That could be amazing. Maybe this *will* work. And, if I think about it, what he's done *is* very romantic – he loves me so much he can't bear to be another second away from me. It's like something out of a Carla Ryan novel. Maybe I should send him a quick email, just to let him know I'm happy about everything. Now the nausea has passed I'm almost sure that's how I'm feeling.

10.20 a.m.
Email to Mr X:
Hey you, can't wait to see you later . . .

10.22 a.m.
Email from Mr X:
Meant to say earlier – it's probably best if you don't send me any 'personal' emails for a while, just in case.

What's he talking about? What will I do with my time if we can't even email each other? Emailing him and updating this blog are the only things that get me through the day! Not that I would ever admit that, of course.

10.24 a.m.
Email to Mr X:
Right.

10.25 a.m.
Email from Mr X:
It's not that I can't wait to get my hands on you, but we have to be more careful now. Just for a while, until we can tell everyone. Can't wait to do unspeakable things to you tonight at your place . . .

Feel all hot and bothered now, just thinking about that. Can't believe we're going to be alone together every single night!

Crap. Just remembered. Left the flat like a bomb site this morning. It took so long to find anything decent to wear that in the end I emptied almost everything I owned onto the bedroom floor in a panic. And I don't think I did the washing up last night. Or the night before. But that's only because I was so busy watching TV. I'm not usually so untidy. I'll just shoot home at lunchtime and sort it out. Mr X has never seen where I live and I don't want him to think I'm a slob. Come to think of it, I may have slightly exaggerated the size and general grandeur of my apartment to him, but I'm sure he won't notice – will keep the lights dimmed just in case.

Open Forum

From Devil Woman: Oh my God – can you believe it!!!

From Hot Stuff: Imagine: he's just back from his honeymoon and he's leaving his wife for her! It's just like a romance novel!!

From Sexy Girl: Yeah, a very bad novel! This can't be for real.

From Broken Hearted: He's a pig. Julie, if you're reading this, don't even consider resuming this affair – this man will destroy your life. Get out now, while you still have the strength.

From Devil Woman: It could be fun though! Tell us more about him, Julie! He sounds cute! Does he really look like Orlando Bloom?

From Angel: Adultery is immoral – Julie, if you have sex with a married man you will go straight to hell – and so will he.

From Devil Woman: Don't be so uptight, Angel – you only live once!

From Broken Hearted: Don't be fooled. Yes, he may be sexy, yes, there may be heat between you, but it won't last. He will destroy you. Walk away now.

From Hot Stuff: He sounds divine – just like a Mills & Boon hero!

From Angel: Don't listen to her. Adultery is a mortal sin – nothing good can come of it.

From Sexy Girl: Get a grip, Angel. If this is real, you go for it, Julie girl. Life's too short to worry about morals! If he does look like Orlando Bloom I wouldn't throw him out of bed for eating crisps – do you know what I mean?

From Angel: It doesn't matter who he looks like. Adultery is wrong in all circumstances.

From Devil Woman: Get a life, Angel. Do you mean to tell me that if Orlando Bloom wanted to have his wicked way with you you'd turn him down?

From Angel: Yes, if either of us was married then I would.

From Devil Woman: Well, I wouldn't!!! I'd do Johnny Depp as well if I got the opportunity!

From Hot Stuff: Oh yeah – he's gorgeous!

From Cupcake: Hi, Julie. Do you have the recipe for those homemade muffins by any chance? They sounded delicious.

From Graphic Scenes: When's the hot sex gonna happen?

Eve

Dear Charlie,

I woke up this morning feeling quite perky. Well, perky may be an overstatement – I don't think I've been like that since I was a hormonal teenager – but I definitely felt more upbeat. I was almost starting to think that maybe things were looking brighter. Maybe, I thought, writing that last letter to you had actually done some good. Maybe this whole idea of pouring out my feelings on paper wasn't a ridiculous plan that didn't have any merit. Maybe I was going to work my way through this twelve-step programme – or whatever Mary the therapist had planned for me – and come out the other side a stronger, happier person. A person who didn't feel completely crushed by life.

I think it helped that I had actually slept quite well: for the first time in ages I didn't jerk awake at 3 a.m. and then spend the rest of the night tossing and turning, checking the clock every five minutes and then drifting off again just before the alarm went. I nodded off almost immediately and when I finally opened my eyes I felt good   all peaceful and calm and just like the Dalai Lama probably does every day – minus the flowing robes and bald head obviously.

But then, just when I was starting to be at one with the universe, I spotted the organic porridge you used to love so much on the shelf and, before I could stop myself, I was crying again. All I could think about was that you were waking up beside your new wife and probably snuggling up together under the covers and doing unspeakable things to one other, and then I was howling on the kitchen table and mopping my eyes with a blue and white check tea-towel. Poor Tom didn't know where to look – he scampered into the bathroom and hid behind the shower curtain until I managed to calm down and compose myself.

It's so ironic – it used to drive me crazy that you made porridge from scratch every morning and refused to even touch the microwavable stuff, but now I'd give anything for you to be burning the bottoms of saucepans like you used to. I really don't know what's come over me. I mean, I thought I'd moved on from you – from us. I cried for so long when you left two years ago – I've probably gone through enough waterproof mascara to last me a lifetime. None of those worked, by the way – obviously the formulas were never properly road-tested by truly heartbroken women before they hit the production line.

Mary the therapist has been teaching me ways to calm myself when I'm feeling stressed, so, once I'd dried my tears and pulled myself together as best as I could, I tried to do the set of visualizations that she had shown me to increase positivity and centre myself for the day. It was impossible though, because what with all the commotion coming from next door, I couldn't exactly get in the zone. It's very hard to get to a quiet place when Johnny the plumber and his new girlfriend are going for it at full pelt and I can hear every scream and moan through the wall. You know what Johnny's like when he has a new woman – he's so eager to impress that he uses every single trick he's learnt from his sizable porn collection in one night. He's working his way through all the manoeuvres from *Debbie Does Dallas* at the moment – I'm starting to know every move by heart. I shouldn't complain really – he *is* very sweet. He always picks the lock for me when I forget my keys (which has been quite a lot recently), and he unblocked the toilet when it over-flowed that time. I'm glad he's got a new girl though because he was going through a really dry spell for a while and you know how he gets if he's single. He came on to me again last month, said he'd be willing to keep me warm at night if I liked. I tried to be pleasant when I turned him down. He's not the worst guy in the world, but I think he's for-gotten that he asked me for advice about genital warts last year.

Anyway, I gave up on the visualizations in the end because Anna hammered on the door and destroyed my concentration. She'd come round to tell me all about her new plan.

It's fairly straightforward: I have to find a new man ASAP to exorcize your ghost once and for all. Anna says it's abnormal that I haven't had a date since you left, and I need to have a few one-night stands to get my mind off things. She couldn't believe it when I admitted that I'd never had sex with a complete stranger just to fulfil a physical desire. According to Anna, every woman of a certain age should have had at least a dozen lovers. I didn't like the way she referred to me as a woman of a certain age, but I suppose she could have a point. I've only ever had two serious boyfriends – you and Connor Maguire, and he didn't really count. We were only together for a month before he told me I wasn't sexually adventurous enough for him. He constantly wanted to do it on the kitchen table of all places. I just couldn't stand all those cornflake crumbs getting in every tiny crevice. I hear he's going out with a girl called Tanya now – a real high-flier by all accounts.

Anna says that if I don't dip my toe into the mating pool soon I will shrivel up and die a lonely old crone and I'll only have myself to blame. All I have to do is tart myself up and get down the local – that's how she met Derek, and she maintains that if that approach was good enough for her then it should be good enough for me. She says sitting in on a Friday night reading a book simply isn't acceptable when everyone else is out getting pissed and having sex with random people they meet at nightclubs. I told her that didn't sound all that much fun and that I'd be too self-conscious to loiter at a bar and hope a single man would talk to me, but she said that was no excuse and that there are loads of other ways to snare a man if I am that socially inept. Internet dating is huge – apparently there are millions of no-hopers in chat forums looking for love, so by the law of averages I have a very good chance of meeting someone normal. I just have to create an online persona that bears no relation to the real me. Anna said I could call myself Sexy Writer and pretend I'm mad for it and then post a fake photo of myself online and leave lots of saucy information on my profile. It's very important that I suggest that my chest is at least twice its real size and that I'm a fun-loving person who is absolutely up for it. Anna says pretending to be something you're not works a treat to get a man interested, and that it doesn't matter if you lie – everyone does it. She says I could even create a blog. She's reading a brilliant one at the moment about an office worker having an affair with her married boss – loads of people she knows are addicted to it. But I told Anna I don't want to have to pretend to be sexy in cyberspace; if I was interested in meeting someone new, and I'm not sure I am, then it would be a nice man who likes me for who I am. Then Anna said that I needed to lower the bar *a lot*, and that finding a nice man who likes me as I am could be a very tall order – most men aren't keen on six-foot beanpoles who won't put out on the first date. She said that her plan was going full steam ahead – whether I cooperate fully or not – and that she knew I'd refuse to sort something out myself, so she's already set me up on a blind date. If I don't go then she's washing her hands of me and will accept no responsibility if I turn into a sad no-hoper with no future. She said she's sorry for being so harsh but that she only has my best interests at heart and she simply won't take no for an answer. You know how determined she can be. Derek had an underwear relapse recently and she told him that if he didn't get over his G-string fetish pronto, she'd be throwing him and his thongs to the kerb.

My blind date's name is Cyril. He's a successful accountant who's been unlucky in love (Anna says it's not true that he's been rejected by every woman in the Northern hemisphere) and is two years younger than me (but I'm trying not to let that put me off). We're meeting in the Sheldon Hotel lobby for lunch – Anna said the date should take place where there are lots of people, 'just in case'. I asked her what 'just in case' meant, but she wouldn't elaborate. She says she'll call me half an hour in and if it's a complete disaster I'm to pretend that my very ill grandmother has had a bad turn, make my excuses and leave. I told Anna that Cyril would see right through that excuse and we'd have to come up with something more original, but she said that he'd fall for it hook, line and sinker. I'm starting to suspect that Cyril may not be all that bright, even if he is an accountant with his own practice and a two-bedroomed flat in the city.

I've been trying to think of topics of conversation that might be suitable. So far I have come up with very little. Maybe I could bring my tax return along and get him to take a look. It might be a good way to break the ice – and a bit of free advice about my finances wouldn't go amiss either. Things have been a little tight since I started my therapy sessions, although writing those relationship quizzes for *Her* has helped. I'm going to have to keep churning them out if I want to keep seeing Mary. I saw her driving round in a convertible sports car the other day – no wonder she charges so much for a session. Mary herself said that Anna's plan could be very helpful, as long as the man wasn't a psycho who shatters my confidence and impedes my progress towards emotional balance. Once I told her that, according to Anna, Cyril didn't have much confidence of his own so there was no way he could dent mine, she seemed much happier and gave me the thumbs up to proceed. She says it's definitely a good idea to become more socially active. She even said that working from home and mostly communicating with the outside world by email may not be that healthy and I might consider switching to a more traditional office environment. I ignored that bit though – working freelance from home suits me, and not having to field awkward questions about my love life from curious work colleagues suits me even more.

Anyway, Anna is very excited about my blind date. She's convinced that all I need to snap out of things is a good shag, and hopefully Cyril will deliver. Trouble is, it's been so long since I had sex that I wouldn't know where to start. Maybe I *do* need to stop being so old-fashioned and live a little. Anna certainly seems to think so.

Eve

Are You an Old-fashioned Gal or a Free-living Woman?

Take our quiz and find out!

You've just had your first date with your new man. It went really well and you realize you fancy the pants off him. Do you:
a) Give him a peck on the cheek and nothing more: you have a no-sex-for-three-months rule.
b) Kiss him passionately but leave him at the front door: you have a no-sex-until-the-third-date rule.
c) Drag him upstairs and get down to it: you have a why-waste-time rule.

Your new man calls to ask you for a second date. Do you:
a) Screen the call and then don't get back to him for a day or two. A man should have to do lots of chasing.
b) Tell him you'd love to meet again and make a date for the following week. You know you should probably play hard to get but you really like him.
c) Cancel a movie date with your girlfriends to meet him that night. They'll understand – they'd do the same for a hot guy.

You are out to dinner with your man. When the bill arrives, do you:
a) Politely thank the waiter and then wait for your lover to pay. Gentlemen should always pay for everything.
b) Pretend to look for your wallet in case he thinks you're a tightwad, but take your time. You spent

far too much on shoes last month and your credit card still hasn't recovered.

c) Shove the bill across the table and tell him bluntly it's his turn to pay. You covered the Chinese meal last week and you're not going to be taken advantage of.

You've been dating your man for a year and really want to move things on to the next level. Do you:
  a) Keep quiet and wait for him to realize what you want. It would be unladylike to force him into something he's not ready for.
  b) Drop hints that you'd like to become more serious, such as giving him a key to your place and suggesting you have one to his.
  c) Tell him straight up that you want to move in together. What's he waiting for – a handwritten invitation?

Results

Mostly As: You are an old-fashioned gal who likes to play by the rules, but this isn't the Stone Age, honey. Sometimes you have to speak up and be heard!

Mostly Bs: You know how to play a good game of cat and mouse, with enough give and take to keep things interesting. Well done, sister!

Mostly Cs: You're upfront, in your face and don't take prisoners. But the direct approach can be abrasive – you need to soften it up!

Molly

I'm at work, pretending to be a deliriously happy newlywed instead of a shell-shocked mess. Turns out I'm a pretty good actress because I've already managed to describe our idyllic honeymoon in Technicolor detail. I've even fabricated romantic moonlit walks on the beach, with warm waves lapping at our bare feet. And so far no one suspects a thing. Everyone believes I'm floating on cloud nine, and that's the way it's got to stay. It would be too mortifying if people knew that I'd only been married for such a short time before my husband decided to run away from home. I've got to keep that to myself, because if it gets out I'd die of shame. I'd be known as the woman who couldn't even hang on to her husband for a month. People would start calling me 'poor Molly'. I would never, ever live it down. Anyway, once I speak to Charlie I'm sure it'll all be fine, so really there's no point in creating a big fuss. Once we talk, everything will be OK again. Trouble is, Charlie still hasn't contacted me and I'm running out of reasons why that could be. If he'd had a panic attack, shouldn't he be over it by now? Shouldn't he have already turned up with his tail between his legs and the biggest bunch of flowers available to man? Shouldn't he be begging me for forgiveness for his stupid mistake? Shouldn't he at least have called me to explain? He's still not answering his phone – I know this because I've tried calling him at least a hundred times.

The strain of pretending that everything is fantastic is enormous. When I walked into work and everyone swarmed all over me I thought I was going to burst into tears. Well, it was really only Samantha, the secretary, who did the swarming. Penny, the advertising manager, just scowled at me like she wasn't all that thrilled that I was back and I haven't seen my editor, Minty, yet. But Samantha made up for it. She's been fussing round me all morning and, even though I usually find her a bit grating, it's been quite comforting listening to her rabbit on. It's helping to take my mind off things, and I've only had the chance to think about Charlie once or twice. I can almost pretend that finding his letter was some sort of bad dream.

'So, how's your hunky husband?' Samantha says now. 'Still treating you like a princess, I bet!'

She beams at me and I can feel myself going red. I've done well covering up so far, but I know I'm starting to crack. Samantha loves Charlie – she's always harping on about how gorgeous and talented he is. Every time she meets him she tells me how lucky I am and how any woman would love to get her claws into him. She's genuinely fond of him, and it feels all wrong to deceive her. But there's no way I can tell her what's happened.

'He's great!' I say brightly, hoping she won't notice that I'm lying through my teeth.

'Isn't love wonderful!' she sighs dreamily. 'You two are so perfect for each other. This is such a special time. You should make the most of it.'

'Yeah, while it lasts,' Penny mutters.

'Don't be so cynical, Penny,' Samantha lectures, wagging a finger at her. 'True love is a wonderful thing to be treasured. I should know.'

Then she snaps her headphones on to take some dictation and Penny makes a face at me behind her back.

'She's still writing to that jailbird, Steve,' she hisses to me. 'The deluded fool thinks he's going to propose soon.'

'I thought he'd broken up with her,' I hiss back, horrified. Samantha has been writing to Steve – a death-row prisoner in Texas – for over a year. She's even saving up to go visit him. But last I'd heard he had written to say that he felt their relationship had run its course. Which had to be the worst break-up line in history considering he is seriously low on other options.

'I dunno.' Penny shrugs. 'But if even a condemned prisoner doesn't want you, things must be bad. She lives in a fantasy world.'

I glance over at Samantha. Her eyes are half closed and she's typing swiftly on the keyboard, like she's in a trance. I feel bad that I'm pulling the wool over her eyes. But I can't admit that Charlie has left me, even if it is temporarily. She'd be devastated. And I definitely can't confide in Penny. She'd use it as another reason to add to her list of why all men are bastards. She hates men. Mind you, she has good reason: her boyfriend left her at the altar. Literally at the altar. Just before the priest proclaimed them man and wife he sprinted down the aisle and was never seen again, like in some really bad movie. She spent the weeks before Charlie and I got married telling me I was making the biggest mistake of my life. Looks like she might have had a point, although at least Charlie made it through the ceremony.

I go back to clearing my in-box. There are still 683 emails waiting for a response. That has to be some kind of a record. I'm quite obviously indispensable – maybe I should think about asking for a pay rise. OK, so quite a few of the emails seem to be asking if I want to thicken my men's appendage or make it stay harder for longer, but still, the volume of correspondence is there, that has to count for something. I *deserve* a pay rise – I've been on the same measly salary for years. It's about time my achievements were recognized. It's not easy persuading high-profile contributors to write for a two-bit magazine – not when other glossies with much higher circulation figures are fighting tooth and nail for their opinions too. And as well as being responsible for features, I also do lots of other stuff that's not in my job spec – such as anything that Minty asks me to. You see, Minty doesn't believe in job specs. She prefers to throw people in at the deep end and see if they can sink or swim. It's her favourite hobby.

'Earth calling Molly! Come in, Molly!' A shrewish voice interrupts my thoughts.

It's Minty. She's standing over me. How long has she been there? It's so spooky the way she can creep up on people like that.

'Sorry, um, Minty, did you want me?' I peer up at her.

'You're back.' It's a statement, not a question.

'Yes. I had a great time!' I start to gush.

'Yeah, yeah, OK. Spare me the details. It's good you're here.'

Wow – Minty's being nice, I can't believe it. She's actually glad to see me back at my desk. She's taking a personal interest in me. Maybe this means I *am* going to get a pay rise.

'Thanks Minty . . .' But before I can finish she interrupts again.

'Yes, it's good you're back because we need to firm up next month's issue. We're way behind thanks to you being off.'

'Well, I *was* on my honeymoon, Minty . . .' I start.

'Whatever.' Minty ignores me. 'Be on top of things by tomorrow. Samantha can help – just make sure she doesn't fuck up.'

Then she sweeps away. I can hear Penny snorting with laughter on the other side of the partition.

Great, that's all I need. Samantha has a heart of gold but she's really hopeless at anything other than dictation. Having her help me out could prove more of a hindrance than anything. I look over at her now. She's still typing happily, mouthing along to her headphones, her eyes half closed.

There's no point in dwelling on it now though. Once Minty has decided something there's no changing her mind, and I know Samantha will at least try her best. I'll just have to make sure I keep a really close eye on her.

I go back to checking my email and in my in box I spot a mail from Lee Merkel, the senior publicist at Embassy Publishing. I'd written to her requesting a 'Day in the Life' feature on one of her authors, chick-lit queen Carla Ryan.

I click on it quickly and grin when I read her response: she's agreed to it. That's bound to be major brownie points for me – Carla Ryan is notoriously wary of the press. Ever since a former PA provided the *Gazette* with explosive behind-the-scenes details of her alleged temper and secret binge-eating episodes a few years back, she's been really media shy. Not that all the juicy revelations harmed her sales: they trebled in the weeks after that. If I pull off this exclusive it'll be a real scoop. But I'd better keep it quiet for a little while longer, just until it's in the bag. I still haven't lived down the time I told everyone that Hollywood A-lister James Law was going to give me a tell-all interview. James and his ex-wife Angelica were locked in a bitter divorce and custody battle over their only son, and bagging an exclusive scoop was going to be the highlight of my career. It was all set up and then his people pulled out at the last minute. I was so embarrassed.

Suddenly Penny looms into view.

'Great news about Samantha!' she sniggers. 'Lucky old you!'

I wince. I hope Samantha didn't hear that: I don't want to hurt her feelings.

'By the way,' Penny goes on. 'I know your big secret.' She leans right across the partition and looks me straight in the eye.

'What?'

My stomach lurches. How can she know about Charlie? I thought I'd been doing a brilliant job of pretending to be fine. How will I persuade her not to say anything? I really don't want anyone to know. Maybe I could appeal to her softer side. She's been through heartbreak before – there's a chance she'll be sympathetic. Or else she'll want to track down Charlie and kill him as slowly and painfully as possible. I haven't forgotten the time she got drunk at the Christmas party and described to me, in horribly graphic detail, what she planned to do to her ex-fiancé if she ever caught up with him. I still can't look at liver pâté in quite the same way.

'Yes, I know ALL about it. What's it worth to you for me to keep quiet?' She's smiling but she definitely has an evil glint in her eye. Mind you, that could be her peripheral vision problem. She had surgery for that last year, but I'm not sure it worked. She still squints quite badly.

I try to think what would persuade her not to pass on the gossip of the decade to everyone else.

'I'll buy you a latte every day for a year?'

She snorts. 'Good one, Molly.'

'Lattes and KitKats?'

Surely that will do the trick. Penny loves her KitKats. She keeps a bag of mini ones in the fridge in the kitchenette and counts them every morning to make sure that no one has been rifling her stash.

'No way.' She snorts again.

Oh God, she's not going for it. Penny is going to tell everyone that Charlie has walked out on me. I gulp for air. What will stop her from blabbing and save me from the worst mortification of my life? My mind has gone totally blank.

'Aw, I'm just messing with you,' she says, and then guffaws. 'I suppose I should congratulate you really. It's a first, that's for sure.'

'Congratulate me?' I knew Penny had a warped sense of humour, but that's cruel, even for her. How can she congratulate me because my husband left me?

'Yeah,' she continues, 'I mean, getting an exclusive with Carla Ryan is pretty big for *Her*. Although God knows why she's so popular when she writes such drivel – even I could do better than that! I mean, who believes in all this happy-ever-after bullshit any more?'

Carla Ryan? What's she on about? What does Carla Ryan have to do with Charlie leaving me?

'I spoke to Lee Merkel. She told me all about the "Day in the Life" thing – that's quite a scoop. Hey, are you OK? You don't look so hot.'

I exhale. Penny hasn't been talking about Charlie; she's been talking about my exclusive with Carla Ryan. She doesn't know about Charlie; she hasn't got a clue.

'Yes, I'm fine,' I gasp. 'I just have a bit of a headache – maybe the jet lag is getting to me.'

I'm so relieved that Penny doesn't know the truth that I want to cry.

'Are you sure?' Penny looks over her shoulder to make

sure she can't be overheard. 'If you need a little pick-me-up, you can have some of these.'

She reaches into her pocket and pulls out a small clear bottle full of pink pills.

'Three of these little babies and you won't be feeling a thing, do you know what I mean?'

I look at Penny and realize that her eyes aren't squinty like I'd thought – they're more glassy, as if she's popped one pink pill too many.

'Um, thanks, Penny,' I mumble, 'but I think I'm feeling better already.'

'OK, but keep it in mind.' She winks at me and then disappears behind her desk.

That was close. For a minute I thought Penny had cottoned on to what was happening. I really thought she knew.

Out of the corner of my eye I can see Samantha bounding up to me. Why can't everyone just leave me alone? I'm starting to think it might be safer to hide out in the toilets.

'Oh my God!!' Samantha's squealing and clapping her hands with excitement. 'Minty just told me I'm going to be your assistant. I'm sooooo excited!'

'Well, you won't exactly be my assistant,' I say weakly, trying to smile. Samantha is always so overly enthusiastic about everything. It can be exhausting.

'Don't be so modest, boss!' she says, grinning. Then she stops in her tracks and cocks her head at me, like an over-excited spaniel who suspects his master might be under the weather. 'Hey, are you OK? You look very pale.'

'I'm fine, thanks,' I manage to reply, even though my heart is racing and I feel like I might throw up. Thinking that Penny knew my big secret has really rattled me. This nightmare is all starting to feel far too real.

'Are you sure?' Samantha looks like she doesn't believe me. 'You don't think you're, you know . . .' She points at her stomach. I realize she's trying to ask me if I have morning sickness, if I'm looking pale because I'm pregnant.

'No, definitely not,' I say firmly. My God, that's the last thing I want people to think.

'Going to have some alone time first, are you, before the kiddies arrive?' she asks. 'I think that's a good idea – the marriage has to be rock solid before you go introducing babies into the equation, right? That's what Steve and I have decided too. It makes a lot of sense.'

'Um, yeah,' I mumble. 'Er, I'd better get back to this, I have so much to do . . .' I gesture vaguely to my screen. I have to get her away from me before she asks any more awkward questions.

'Of course, I'm sorry. I just can't wait for us to work together. It'll be brilliant!' Then she punches my arm playfully, bounds happily back to her desk and snaps her headphones back on.

If only she knew the truth. I can't have alone time with my husband, because I don't know where he is. He's hightailed it out of my life before we even had a chance to discuss having children. It simply doesn't make any sense. We just had the perfect picture-book wedding. Well, almost perfect. This cannot be happening to us. We have to sort it out.

My hand shaking, I reach into my bag to get my phone. If he won't answer my calls, maybe he'll respond to a text message. He wrote me a letter after all. Maybe texting would be an easier way for him to tell me what's going on in his head and why he's suddenly decided that I'm not the intoxicating, ravishing creature he kept telling me I was.

I root around in my bag until my fingers close on something. I recognize its shape instantly. It's not my phone, it's the tiny photo frame of Mum and Dad I carry everywhere with me. I pull it out and hold it in the palm of my hand. They look so deliriously happy in it. It's obvious the shot was taken when they had no idea they were being photographed. Neither of them is looking at the camera – they're gazing at each other, oblivious to everyone else around them, lost in their own little world. Mum's hair is whipping messily around her face and Dad is curling a tendril of it round her ear, a look of perfect tenderness on his face. It's such a beautiful picture, just looking at it gives me a physical dart of pain in my chest.

Charlie, please call me

I text quickly. Then I say a prayer to Mum and Dad and press Send. If they can't help me sort out this mess, no one can.

Julie's Blog

Am exhausted. Spent most of last night helping Mr X unpack his stuff – it took AGES. It wasn't that he had all that many clothes, it's just that he wasn't happy to throw them on the bedroom chair until I found somewhere to put them, like I usually do when I can't cram anything else into my over-packed wardrobe. When I suggested that draping them across the back of the handily placed chair for the time being was the perfect solution to the storage problem, he laughed loudly like he thought I was joking, and said we had to do things properly and start as we mean to continue. So I ended up having to empty out half my wardrobe so he could hang up his entire collection of pinstriped suits in a neat, evenly spaced row. Secretly, I was a little annoyed about it, but I guess if we're going to live together then I need to make space for him in my life and be as welcoming as possible, not scowl at him because my Anna Sui black lace dress had to be shoved into the airing cupboard just to make room for his Thomas Pink shirts. He seemed a bit taken aback that my flat was so small, actually. Maybe I had exaggerated its size a bit, but I never thought he'd really see it. Our entire relationship has been conducted in the office, so I thought I was safe to imply that I had a massive apartment with great views and a walk-in wardrobe.

Once we got over the clothes blip, Mr X said we needed to celebrate. I was thrilled because I thought he wanted to take me out for a slap-up meal somewhere posh and very expensive – we'd never eaten out together before, unless you count lunch in the canteen with all the UCs – but then he said that maybe we needed to wait a while until we were seen in public together. In the end we got some takeout and wine. It wasn't exactly what I'd had in mind, but it *was* lovely to be able to lean across and seductively feed him some prawn sticks with my fingers. Thought it might lead to wild, steamy sex like in that movie *9½ Weeks*, but Mr X was so tired that he said he had to go to bed. Was a bit disappointed about that, but I suppose jet lag mixed with emotional upheaval can be really draining. Anyway, I'm sure we won't be able to keep our hands off each other tonight.

9.05 a.m.
Mr X just left a note on my desk.

> *Will we go food shopping later? We'll have to go out of town of course, in case anyone sees us, but we can't have takeout every night, can we??*

Eh? What's he talking about? Why can't we have takeout every night? I mean, we can't have *Chinese* takeout every night, but there's always Thai, or Indian or even pizza. Gianni's does a mean special.

9.14 a.m.
Crap. Just remembered I have a meeting with Mr Dick Lit at 9.30 to discuss PR strategy for his new book. Luckily I still have sixteen minutes to read the entire thing from cover to cover and prepare a comprehensive media plan.

9.24 a.m.
Then again, I could just read the blurb on the back of the jacket cover. That'll give me the general gist, surely. There's

no point wasting time on in-depth research when a brief overview will suffice. It's not like he'll notice the difference. And I can't be expected to read every book I publicize – that just wouldn't make logistical sense. I'll wing it and dazzle him with my brilliance.

11.30 a.m.

Meeting was excellent. Mr Dick Lit is very promotable (i.e. good looking and charming) and will be a dead-easy sell; the media will lap him up. Didn't tell him that of course. Told him the market was tough, times were hard and it's impossible to guarantee media coverage and sales unless he has famous contacts we can manipulate or dark personal secrets I can use as a hook. I think it worked perfectly. He'll be so grateful when this book does even better than his last one that he'll think I'm a genius. Only blip was when UC One burst into meeting, accidentally on purpose, then fawned all over him, saying his novel was genius and should be nominated for a Gold Dagger award. Then she actually started quoting passages verbatim. Luckily, I could tell that Mr Dick Lit could see right through her fake act.

Now just have to send completely professional email to Mr X to update him on the meeting and that will be another job well done. Will not engage in flirtatious innuendo, even if I really, really want to.

11.41 a.m.

Sent Mr X an email to say that the meeting went exceptionally well and Mr Dick Lit's new book will be 'massive' and may even win a prize or two if we twist the right arms. Privately feel he probably hasn't a hope of winning anything, but there's no harm telling a little white lie to Mr X – he's still bitter that one of his authors was passed over at the book awards last year. Was really tempted to say that I knew something else that was 'massive' as well, but I didn't succumb to the urge – am really proud of myself. I've been thinking about what he said and he's right: now that we're together properly it's probably best if we stop the sexy banter thing we usually do via email and keep things purely professional between us in the office.

11.46 a.m.
No response from Mr X. What's he playing at? I know he read my email at 11.42 a.m. because I secretly ticked the message-read device.

11.47 a.m.
UC One just popped by my desk to give me a homemade chocolate and orange muffin. She says she used freshly squeezed orange juice in her secret recipe – which I can have if I'd like to try it out. She's up to something, I can tell. She guards those recipes with her life. The deluded fool still thinks she'll be offered a six-figure sum to publish them.

11.48 a.m.
Hate to admit it, but the muffin is unusually good – tangy but not too bitter. Maybe I've misjudged UC One a bit. She may be deluded but apparently she can cook. Might rescue that old muffin from my drawer: it's nearly stopped smelling of vomit now.

11.51 a.m.
Just got an email from Mr X. Mr Dick Lit isn't convinced I'm the right publicist to work on his precious book! He suspects I haven't even read it!! He thinks UC One may be a better fit for him because she seems to really know where

he's coming from!!! The nerve. Just because she was able to quote passages verbatim and told him he should win a prize, he thinks she'd do a better job than me. Well, they're welcome to each other as far as I'm concerned. And Mr Dick Lit isn't *that* promotable anyway: his front tooth has a chip in it that needs seeing to and he definitely needs a haircut. If his fringe flopped into his eyes one more time I might have taken a pair of scissors to it myself.

11.54 a.m.
Just thought. I can't have UC One stealing Mr Dick Lit. Her press coverage has been quite impressive lately. That new chick-lit author she's working with is getting a lot of attention in the media, and if she does the same for Mr Dick Lit then people might start to think she's actually competent.

I'll just have to persuade Mr Dick Lit that I am the woman for the job. I'll present him with a well-thought-out press plan – maybe I could even put together a few statistics to convince him that I can get results. Or I could stroke his ego a bit. Writers love being told how talented and special they are, even when most of the time they're nothing of the sort.

11.58 a.m.
Have sent smarmy email to Mr Dick Lit to ask him to reconsider. Really pitched it so it would appeal to his vanity. Said it would be an honour and a privilege to work on his book, that I feel he is a star in the making and I will dedicate all my time and energy to promoting his brilliant work and ensuring it bags a dozen awards, blah, blah. Am positive he will change his mind – they nearly always fall for the 'star in the making' line. Then I emailed Mr X to say I would do an excellent job, have a raft of brilliant publicity ideas and

could guarantee a top ten book-chart placing. He'd be a fool to turn me down.

12.54 p.m.
No response from Mr Dick Lit. Have decided to up the ante and send an express luxury gift basket to him – tropical fruit never fails.

3.00 p.m.
Just got email from Mr Dick Lit to thank me for fruit basket – result!!! I'm in!

3.01 p.m.
Oh. Just read last line of Mr Dick Lit's email – he's allergic to pineapple so he plans to donate the basket to the local hospital. Allergic to pineapple??? Who the hell is allergic to pineapple? Tosser.

3.05 p.m.
UC One is swanning about looking smug and self-satisfied. Can hear her talking loudly about Mr Dick Lit. Like she'd know anything about it – she hasn't had a dick in years. Feel like throttling her.

3.08 p.m.
Have decided that being professional is getting me absolutely nowhere. It's much more efficient to be flirty and physical – that's always worked for me in the past.

3.15 p.m.
Cornered Mr X in kitchenette as he was getting a cappuccino from the dispenser. Rubbed myself accidentally against him as I leaned in to get the milk, and asked him if he'd

reconsider me for the Mr Dick Lit job. Then I sucked my teaspoon for far longer than necessary, just for good measure. We were interrupted when UC Two walked in, but I think he got the message. From the reaction in his crotch area there was no mistaking how he felt.

3.19 p.m.
Email from Mr X:

That was very naughty of you. Bordering on sexual harassment in fact.

3.20 p.m.
Email to Mr X:

I have no idea what you mean.

3.21 p.m.
Email from Mr X:

I think you do.

3.22 p.m.
Email to Mr X:

I simply want to represent the client – and I think I am the best woman for the job.

3.23 p.m.
Email from Mr X:

You think you're the best woman for the job, do you? Do you want to prove that to me?

3.24 p.m.
Email to Mr X:

Hmmmmm . . . that's very flirty – I thought we weren't allowed to do that any more?

3.25 p.m.
Email from Mr X:

> I have no idea what you mean. I was simply referring to your
> professional prowess, nothing more.

3.26 p.m.
Email to Mr X:

> So, you'll let me keep Dick Lit?

3.27 p.m.
Email from Mr X:

> OK, but you better make sure you get the press coverage. You
> know the drill, if we don't get the press then the book won't
> sell. If the book doesn't sell then we're not happy. Make sure
> it works.

Yay!

3.28 p.m.
Email to Mr X:

> Of course it'll work.

3.29 p.m.
Email from Mr X:

> It better. Once people find out about us they'll be picking over all
> my past decisions. I can't be seen to favour you just because we're
> in a relationship – your performance will be judged by the sales
> figures. So get your nose to the grindstone and keep it there.

Eh? Does this mean that I'm going to have to start
proving myself to be better than everyone else here? What's
the point of sleeping with the boss if there are no special
privileges?? Not that that's why I'm with Mr X of course.

I'm with him because I like and admire him. And I love the way he gets that little crease on the bridge of his nose when he's concentrating. And the way his chin crinkles up when he frowns is so sexy. And of course I like his personality too – it's not just his body I crave. That would be very shallow. We have lots in common. Lots and lots.

3.35 p.m.
And I want to prove how good I am at my job – not to impress Mr X though – to annihilate UC One. She's getting far too big for her boots and it's time I took her down a peg or two. All I have to do is fax a press release about Mr Dick Lit's new book to every media contact I have and wait for them to get back to me. Simple.

Open Forum

From Broken Hearted: You see? The emotional games have begun already. One minute he'll ignore her, the next he'll be all over her like a bad rash – the guy is toxic – she needs to walk away.

From Shaz: Sounds like a sexual discrimination case to me. Julie, if I were you I'd start journalling everything now – could be useful if it all ends up in court.

From Hot Stuff: Hey, Julie, who's Mr Dick Lit? He sounds gorgeous!! I love guys with floppy fringes – that whole Hugh Grant look is hot!

From Broken Hearted: This is going to get messy. Things can only go downhill from here, you know. She might think she has it all under control, but she doesn't know what she's getting herself into, believe me.

From Devil Woman: He does sound pretty anal about his shirts.

From Broken Hearted: Before she knows it, he'll be taking her for granted and she'll be picking his smelly boxers off the floor and ironing his vests.

From Sexy Girl: Yeah, he sounds like a bit of a control freak to me – be careful, Julie!

From Hot Stuff: But isn't it so romantic? He loves her so much he left his new wife for her!

From Angel: It isn't romantic – it's immoral, and you'd do well to remember that, Hot Stuff.

From Broken Hearted: Imagine how his wife must feel. This is a total disaster and it'll all end in tears, mark my words.

From Hot Stuff: Hey, Broken Hearted, that sounds like something my mother would say!

From Broken Hearted: Mothers are usually right at the end of the day.

From Shaz: Julie, if you need legal advice, click on this link.

From Devil Woman: I can't believe you're hawking for business on someone's personal blog – that's really low.

From Shaz: I'm only saying – the girl might need legal advice and I'm here to help.

From Devil Woman: Let me guess, you can give her help for 500 euros an hour, right? You're scum.

From Shaz: Be careful what you say, Devil Woman – that's libellous.

From Angel: Yes, name-calling is offensive.

From Devil Woman: Not half as offensive as you, Angel.

From Broken Hearted: Listen everyone, we're losing track here. The main thing is, Julie needs to get rid of this Mr X, not have him move in with her.

From Hot Stuff: Well, I think it IS romantic – true love will win out in the end.

From Broken Hearted: The only person Mr X loves is himself.

From Cupcake: Hi, Julie. Those chocolate and orange muffins sound divine! Any chance you could post the recipe online?

From Graphic Scenes: Hey, everyone! Did I miss the hot sex part??

Eve

Dear Charlie,

Today was not a good day. I was walking back from the shop, munching on a mint Cornetto to reward myself for finishing another relationship quiz for *Her*, when I bumped into Mrs Clancy from three doors up. I had been trying to avoid dairy products because of my sinus problem, but Mary the therapist says it's important to be kind to myself, and what's a little nasal congestion between friends? In fact, I think her exact words were 'If you're not going to be kind to yourself, then who will?', which I found a little depressing quite frankly. I mean, I'd much prefer other people showering me with kindness than having to search through my small change for a Cornetto covered in freezer burn.

Anyway, I was strolling leisurely along the path back home, eating and trying to block out all thoughts of you and how much you used to love the tiny mint chocolate chunks on the top, when Mrs Clancy sprang out of the hedge, as if she'd been lying in wait to catch me. I was so busy trying to lick the dripping ice cream off my fingers that, before I knew what was happening, she was blocking the path and I would have had to leapfrog over her or throw her to the ground to avoid having some sort of conversation. It was exactly like the time that she hid behind the recycling bins and then pounced out and asked you to start a compost heap for her. I was caught completely unawares. She grabbed hold of my arm and said she'd seen your wedding photo in *Hiya!* and wasn't your new wife a lovely-looking girl? Didn't she just *glow* in the picture? And didn't you look so happy together? It was all I could do to stop myself from blubbing all over my Cornetto there and then. Thankfully I managed to just nod and grit my teeth in a kind of forced smile. I'm hoping she didn't notice that I didn't actually speak at all. You know her – she loves the sound of her own voice so much that replying isn't usually necessary. I held it together long enough to get into the house, and then I burst into tears in the hallway, because I knew she was right. You and your new wife *do* look so right together. Much better than we ever did in any of our photos. I'd put all of those away of course – I hid them in the cupboard under the stairs ages ago. But then I started thinking to myself – had we ever looked that blissful? Like we were literally glowing with happiness? I think it's one of the things that's been bothering me most since I saw your wedding picture – aside from the fact that you exchanged vows in a medieval chapel dripping in scented honeysuckle, that is. When we were together did we ever look that happy?

So, in a fit of unusual energy, I dug out the box of old photos and went through them, one by one. I had to search for quite a while before I found it – it was right at the back, wedged up against the wall beside the blue and red striped deckchairs that we bought in Brighton when we went to visit my brother Mike that time. I seized it like a gun dog pouncing on his prey (not that I would know what that looks like, but I can imagine), and then I went through every single snap, desperate to find a really good one of us. There was one of us at Anna and Derek's wedding – I look depressed and you look relieved and slightly drunk. There was another of us on that mini-break in West Cork when I asked the old fisherman to take a quick snap of us on the pier and you said you didn't want him touching your prized camera. The look on your face says it all – you're terrified he's going to drop it in the harbour by mistake. Then there was one of us with Tom. We'd set up the camera on timer to take it of all three of us, do you remember? He's curled up on your lap gazing up at you, you're looking down adoringly at him and I'm looking longingly at you. It's like the two of you are locked in your own secret world and I'm just a hanger-on, good for opening cans of cat food and pouring milk into saucers, but that's about it.

The only photograph that even came close to how you look in your wedding photo is that shot of us on the terrace of that restaurant in Cyprus. The sun is behind us and we're smiling into the camera like we haven't a care in the world (which we hadn't in fairness – we'd drunk at least three bottles of wine between us at lunch, and some cocktails as well).

In every other snap of the two of us together you look uncomfortable, as if you want to be somewhere else, and I'm sort of squatting behind you, doing my best not to look too tall. In almost all of them my shoulders are hunched up, I have a stupid grin on my face and it's really obvious that I'm trying hard not to lose my balance and topple over on top of you. I know you always denied it, but I do think you hated the fact I was so much taller than you, even in flat shoes. Looking at the photos now, it's so clear you weren't happy. Maybe I should have known something was wrong, just from the body language between us. Maybe your expression was saying 'I want to be anywhere but here' and I just didn't realize.

I was just putting all the photos away when Mum arrived. I knew it was only a matter of time before she heard about your designer wedding, but I thought I'd have another day or two to prepare for her reaction – she'd only just got back from her Caribbean cruise with the retirement society. I was starting to hope that she might take an extended break in Antigua – maybe fall for a toy boy and decide to stay there for a while – because I knew she wasn't going to take the news that you'd got married at all well. But then I should have known that Mrs Clancy would be itching to tell her everything. Turns out that, just after she accosted me, she'd dashed straight over to Mum's with the photo from *Hiya!* that she'd had the foresight to cut out and keep especially.

Even though Mum had only just arrived back, she immediately dropped her suitcase in the hall and raced over here to quiz me about it. She was still wearing her cruisewear – front-pleated linen Bermuda shorts and a cream-coloured straw fedora – when she burst through the door demanding an explanation.

She's absolutely furious of course, but not with you. She maintains that *I* am the one to blame for what she called 'an utter disaster'. You see, I brought it all on myself because I was foolish enough to engage in sexual relations with you before I had a ring on my finger. That, according to my mother, gave you the wrong impression. The impression that I had loose morals. And men do not want to marry girls with loose morals, or, as she said, 'Why buy a car that's already been round the block and could have engine trouble?' I wasn't sure what she was alluding to there, but I tried to tell her that this was the twenty-first century and that the idea that women should save themselves for marriage was a bit old-fashioned – men don't have to do that, after all. But she just said that the world would be a much nicer place if everyone kept their bits to themselves like they used to in her day, before sex was invented.

Then she said that, if I'd been thinking straight, I would have given you an ultimatum. I should have *insisted* that we get married. I told her that, as far as I could remember, you didn't want to get married so there was very little I could have done about it. (I am right about that, aren't I? Didn't you always say that we didn't need a piece of paper to prove to one another how we felt? That marriage was an outdated, old-fashioned institution that meant nothing and that we were already married in every meaningful way? I could have sworn that you used to laugh at other people's wedding plans. In fact, I'm sure you once said that a white wedding was a middle-class expression of vulgarity and that you wouldn't be seen dead in a morning suit – or did I imagine that conversation? It's hard to tell. Sometimes I think that this whole thing might be just a dream and that I'll wake up like Pamela Ewing did in *Dallas* and discover Bobby singing and soaping himself in the shower.)

But Mum said that was not the point at all. No man ever *wants* to get married. It's the woman who must do the persuading and that's the way of the world. I tried saying that it would have been very difficult to persuade you, not unless I forced you to get down on bended knee against your will. But she said, judging by the current state of affairs, that your arm obviously could have been twisted and that if I had been a little more forceful then everything would have turned out for the better and she would have had the comfort of knowing that her only daughter wasn't doomed to be an old maid and would be looking forward to becoming a glamorous grandmother when the time was right (just not before she was at least seventy-five – she wouldn't have anyone call her Granny before then). I said that surely if I had to twist a man's arm to marry me then it wouldn't be an equal partnership, but she said partnership didn't come into it and that if she had been concerned with that she never would have got Daddy up the aisle. I knew it was useless to point out that getting divorced from Daddy ten years later meant that her theory was flawed – there's no point antagonizing her when she's in that kind of mood.

Sometimes, though, I do wish I had just told her the truth about what had happened from the very beginning, instead of saying that we'd broken up because we'd simply drifted apart. Maybe then she'd be easier on me. But at the time it just seemed wiser, because I knew that if I told her the real reason you left me she would have hunted you down. I still remember the time she found the dog poo on her front lawn – she wouldn't rest until she caught the perpetrator. Imagine what she'd do if she knew that you'd had carnal knowledge of another woman for most of our relationship.

Mary the therapist thinks I should come clean about it all. She says that not telling people the truth about why we broke up was a mistake and symptomatic of my lack of self-esteem. Which is fine in theory, but I can't be expected to have much self-esteem when I find out, all in less than an hour one rainy afternoon, that not only has the love of my life been cheating on me, but he's leaving me too. There was no way I could have told people that. It was far better to say that it was my idea to split and that there was no third party involved. We'd grown apart, but we were still great friends – that was the line I used and everyone seemed to believe me. Only Anna knows the truth, and that's because she wrangled it out of me after one vodka too many. Mum would die if she ever found out. Mind you, she might stop telling me I was a fool to let you go if she knew that I had come home early from work one day to finish an article in peace but instead found you and a busty brunette under my best Egyptian cotton covers. The Egyptian cotton covers I had so painstakingly ironed to perfection before I'd changed the bed linen that morning. And everyone knows how tricky

Egyptian cotton can be to get crease-free, even if it is of superior quality. Yes, Mum might change her tune about how wonderful you were if she knew the truth, although I can't be totally certain of that because she really was crazy about you – everyone was.

Anyway, I tried to distract Mum from her rant by asking her about the cruise. She had a wonderful time, dining at the captain's table, playing boules and reading beside the seawater pool. Do you remember her cruise buddy, Leona Merkel? Well, it turns out that Leona's daughter, Lee, is a book publicist now, so Mum's got her hands on an advance copy of Carla Ryan's steamy new bonkbuster, *Second Chance at Love*. Mum highly recommended it – she even agreed to lend it to me once she calmed down. I've never read anything by Carla Ryan – chick lit isn't really my thing – but then again the book looks like the closest I'll get to sex for a while, so I really can't afford to be picky.

I almost told her that Anna has set me up on a blind date – that would have cheered her up, especially because he's an accountant. Mum loves accountants. She says they're the last bastion of good sense in a nonsensical world. I know she says that because, when Dad left, her own accountant uncovered the stash of cash that he'd squirrelled away in a secret bank account. He had to hand half of it over, and Mum's been an ardent admirer of the accounting profession ever since. In the end, I decided against mentioning it. I think it's best to see how it goes before I raise her hopes. When she left I was so tired that I couldn't even finish putting all those terrible photos of us back where they belong – under the stairs.

Eve

Do You Have a Picture-perfect Partnership or Does Your Body Language Mean Your Relationship is Doomed?

Do our simple quiz and find out!

When you're watching TV together, do you:
a) Snuggle up as close as possible, wrapping your limbs round each other.
b) Sit comfortably close together, occasionally touching.
c) Sit on different seats, sometimes in different rooms. His fidgeting drives you crazy.

In photos of you as a couple you are usually:
a) Looking lovingly at each other, completely oblivious to the camera.
b) Standing angled close together, smiling widely.
c) You don't have any couple photos. You're never in the same room for long enough.

If people comment on your appearance as a couple, they usually say:
a) You could have a stylist, you look so well matched in every way.
b) You could be brother and sister, you look so much alike.
c) You can't be a couple. You look like complete opposites.

In bed, do you:
a) Lie welded together. You love the feel of his skin against yours.

b) Lie close together, side by side. You love the comfort of being with your man, but you don't need to constantly touch him.
c) Lie with your backs to each other. You're thinking about moving into the spare room – his snoring makes you want to scream.

Results

Mostly As: Your body language screams passion and romance – you're in the first flush of love! Try not to panic when things settle down a bit.

Mostly Bs: The passion between you has dimmed a little, but that's all right with you! You've moved to a deeper understanding of each other. You know you don't have to be all over each other like a rash to prove your love – bravo!

Mostly Cs: According to your body signals, you can't stand the sight of each other. Maybe you need to reconsider your future together?

Molly

'OK, so the theme for the next issue is "True Love". Capital T, capital L. We're talking romance, we're talking true blue, we're talking TOGETHER FOR EVER. Are you with me?'

I flinch as Minty's voice booms round the room.

Samantha and I are locked with Minty in her office to 'brainstorm'. Minty loves to brainstorm, mostly because she is the only one ever allowed to speak. So far, I've told her that Carla Ryan has agreed we can shadow her for a day, but that's all I've managed to say. Minty did a very good impression of not caring that I've bagged an exclusive with the queen of chick lit, but I could tell she was pleased – she's scowling less than usual, which means she's in quite a good mood.

Right now, I'm only half listening to what she's talking about. Really, I'm thinking about Charlie and why he still hasn't contacted me. There's been no response to my last text and I'm starting to panic now. Tanya and Alastair think I should turn up at his office, demand an explanation and force him to talk to me. A showdown in front of all his work colleagues is the last thing I want, but I'm running out of options. The feeling that this isn't some sort of silly mis-understanding that we'll be able to laugh about when we're old and grey is growing stronger every minute, and it's getting harder and harder to shake the awful feeling that he's actually serious about leaving me.

But I'm trying not to think about that. Instead, I'm

pretending to take lots of notes in my jotter, to make it seem like I'm hanging on Minty's every valuable word. Samantha is copying me; she looks as if her hand is about to fall off, she's writing so fast. Maybe I shouldn't have told her about the time Minty caught an intern picking at her nails instead of paying attention and then made the poor girl's life a complete misery. Minty has a unique take on employee rights: she doesn't believe in them. If you work for her she thinks she owns you – and you're supposed to be glad about it. In fact, you're supposed to lick her size-eleven wedges as well as her skinny ass as much as you humanly can or she will make your life a living hell of cappuccino-making and photocopying.

'I'm thinking old-fashioned love story.' Minty is now waving her hands about to show that she is being creative and inspiring. As she speaks, she twirls her trademark chiffon neck scarf – the one she thinks makes her look distinctive and everyone else knows is a decoy to hide her sagging turkey neck.

'We want love in a bucket. Boy meets girl, boy loves girl, boy and girl live happily ever after. No second wives, no brats and no *complications*.'

Minty hisses this last bit. She married for the third time last year and rumour has it her adult stepchildren refuse to be in the same room as her – not that I blame them. I'd refuse to be in the same room as her if I didn't work here.

'I'm thinking straightforward, pure, uncomplicated. Are you with me?'

Samantha and I nod simultaneously like we both understand exactly what she's talking about, even though my husband is a runaway and Samantha's boyfriend is a death-row prisoner she has never met. Straightforward, pure and uncomplicated don't exactly apply to us.

Not that we can tell Minty that, because as far as Minty is concerned we don't have lives – not ones that exist outside of these office walls anyway. I could never tell her what's happened, because she has zero tolerance for people who bring their personal problems into the workplace, and anyone who has ever made the mistake of doing so has lived to regret it. Like that time when Michelle from Accounts's boyfriend was caught sex-texting his old teacher, and poor Michelle was found sobbing her eyes out in the Ladies: Minty marched Michelle into her office and told her that if she didn't get a grip quick then she could pack up all the cute teddy bears and love-heart photo frames littering her desk, go straight home and not bother coming back. Thinking about it, if Minty knew how well I was hiding the shambles that is my life from everyone, she might be quite impressed.

'Now, which no-hopers are looking for some self-promotion this week?'

Minty looks disdainfully through the paperwork in front of her, raking her sharp, pointy fingernails down the list of possible contributors and flicking violently through perkily worded press releases from fawning publicists as she goes. Getting writers who have a new book to promote to pen a piece for the magazine is a cheap way to fill the pages of *Her*. We mention their new book; they write the article for free. Everyone's happy. It helps to get 'names' of course – writers who have strong media profiles add cachet to the magazine, and having cachet is what this business is mostly about.

'Bonnie Banks? She's got a new book out. What's she like?' Minty says.

I like Bonnie Banks. She's a crime novelist who writes one book a year, every year. She's done features for the magazine before and they're always punchy. She also delivers on time, which is rare for an author of her calibre. But I don't say any of that, because Minty is not really asking me what I think. Her question about Bonnie is purely hypothetical, and I know better than to say anything. The only opinion that matters in the room is hers.

'Hang on.' Minty narrows her eyes. 'Isn't she the bitch who did that piece on office politics last year? That was horseshit.'

I sigh ... but only on the inside. I can't let Minty see my reaction. I should have known she'd veto Bonnie after that brilliant piece she did last year on bosses who bully. Rumour has it that it was based entirely on Minty's antics.

'The girl wouldn't know good writing if it came up and bit her on the ass,' she goes on. 'She's dead to me.'

Out of the corner of my eye, I see Samantha diligently write 'DEAD TO ME' beside Bonnie's name in her notebook.

This is one of Minty's favourite expressions. She talks like she's a big-shot American magazine editor, even though she's only the editor of a mid-market glossy that struggles for readership and advertising. The truth is, she's only ever been to New York on long-weekend shopping trips (rumour has it that she used to fly over just to stock up on shoes – they have a much better selection of extra-large sizes over there). She gets most of her 'witty' Americanisms from *Sex and the City*, which, at the height of its popularity, she watched religiously every week. In fact, her *SATC* addiction used to be so bad that whatever eccentric mishmash ensemble Carrie Bradshaw wore onscreen on a Monday night Minty would be rocking on a Tuesday morning. Gaudy flower corsages were huge for her. At one stage she wore one almost every day. Now she sticks to the infamous chiffon scarves.

She glares at Samantha, who beams back.

I remind myself to tell her not to smile too much in editorial meetings. Minty doesn't like it: it interferes with her creative flow.

'Joanne Tisdale? She's not bad.' Minty twirls her neck scarf again. 'Hang on, she's a dyke, right?' She sighs dramatically as if Joanne Tisdale decided to be homosexual purposefully to annoy her. 'Scrap her. We can't have a raving lesbo write about boy meets girl.'

I see Samantha carefully write 'DYKE' beside Joanne Tisdale's name and then underline it.

Minty is starting to throw more and more paper around. I can tell she's getting frustrated because she also starts to pick her nose. She does this to help her concentrate and she has no problem going for it in plain view of us. She couldn't care less that we can see her shoving her ring finger up there and rooting around furiously. I lower my eyes and force myself to look at my jotter. God only knows what life-size buggers are up her nostrils waiting to be given their moment to shine and I really don't want to see them.

'What about David Rendell?'

I almost swallow the pencil that I'm pretending to chew thoughtfully.

'Yeah, David Rendell . . .' She says his name again and the room starts to spin. She's talking about David, my David, my *ex* David.

'Where has *he* been?' she asks no one in particular. 'Not that I care of course. Well, according to this badly written press release, he has a new book to promote. Let's get him to do something for our Love issue. It's always good to get a man's perspective, even if we totally disagree with it, right?'

She cackles madly, and Samantha cackles along to show she thinks Minty's hilarious.

David has a new book coming out? How on earth did I miss that? I usually keep such a close eye on his writing career, even more so since he's become a best-selling author.

'Molly. Earth calling Molly.' Minty is still talking to me, except now she's using her really sarcastic voice – even more sarcastic than usual, which is very bad news.

My tongue feels like it's swelling in my mouth and slowly suffocating me. I have to say something.

'Sorry, yes?' My voice comes at last. I whip up my jotter again and grip my pencil so I look like I'm ready and eager to take even more notes.

'David Rendell?' she sneers.

'David Rendell, right.' I write his name down, as if it isn't already branded on my memory.

'Hang on . . .' she drawls. 'Didn't I hear that you used to have a thing with him a few years ago?'

She leans back in her custom-made leather chair and assesses my reaction. She's enjoying this, I can tell.

'It won't be awkward, will it – now that you're *married*?'

Samantha swivels to look at me, her eyes wide. This is all news to her. I've never told her about David. I'm not sure how Minty even knows. Then again, Minty seems to know everything about everyone.

'Awkward? With David?' I gulp. 'Of course not!'

Then I smile as convincingly as I can, even though I think my breakfast is about to reappear. I can almost taste the cream cheese bagel that I wolfed down before this meeting inching its way back up my gullet.

'OK . . . perfect,' Minty drawls, trailing her neck scarf slowly through her fingers and smiling slowly. 'Well, in that case, let's go full throttle. Scrap his feature – let's do a lead interview with him instead. I want his thoughts on true love. Does he believe in love at first sight? Has he met his soulmate? That sort of shit. Get a half-decent photo and he might even make the cover. From what I remember he's quite the hottie.'

Samantha writes 'HOTTIE' in her notebook beside David's name. Then she draws a love heart and a smiley face beside it.

I swallow. This cannot be happening.

'So you're OK to do the interview?' Minty smirks at me.

'Of course!' I stutter. 'This is *great*!'

That is a big fat lie. This is not great. This is terrifying, but I'm trying not to let that show. I'm still smiling – well, I'm more or less gritting my teeth, but Minty probably won't notice the difference. What on earth will I say to David? How will I even begin to have a normal conversation? Because he wasn't just a fling, he wasn't just someone I used to have a thing with a few years ago, as Minty put it. He was the love of my life. I can still vividly remember the first time I saw him in that crowded Lesson Street nightclub. Tanya had persuaded me it would be a good idea to go clubbing. It wasn't really my thing, but another unsuitable man had just broken up with her and she had declared that dancing was the only thing that would cheer her up. I didn't want to disappoint her. So I went and tried to pretend that getting jostled around a hot, packed club was my idea of a great night out. But then a sleazy guy who'd had one too many beers and whiskey chasers pinched Tanya's bum and she retaliated by throwing her gin and tonic in his face. She wasn't in the habit of doing things like that, especially not when paying ridiculous nightclub prices for minuscule drinks, but because she'd been dumped again she was in a spectacularly bad mood. And so she decided that *no one* was touching her bottom without her express permission, least of all a sweaty, overweight drunk who could barely stand or see straight. But getting a drink in his face didn't deter this guy, it only spurred him on. When he groped her again, Tanya threw *my* gin and tonic in his face. And that's when things turned nasty. The drunk's mood changed and he started screaming abuse at Tanya, shouting that she was a dick tease and a slut and all sorts of awful names. I was starting to get scared, and I could tell that even Tanya was getting nervous – this guy had us backed into a corner and he was furious. I quickly realized that he wasn't just a bit drunk – he was way past that, and probably capable of anything. And that was when David stepped in. In less than a minute, security was hauling the drunk away and David was buying us new drinks to replace the ones Tanya had wasted. Tanya downed hers in record time – she wouldn't admit it, but she was really rattled. And so was I, but not by the groping drunk – by David. The minute I looked in his liquid brown eyes I felt this huge connection to him. It was like something I'd only ever read about in trashy romance novels. I felt like I knew him, knew the bones of him, and we'd only just met. It was that powerful.

Within days we were inseparable. Within weeks I had moved into his poky little flat, where the water was always cold and the radiators never worked but it didn't matter. It didn't matter a bit because we were utterly, blissfully happy together. We were madly in love but we were also best friends who could make each other laugh until our sides ached. And the sex – well, the sex was like I'd never experienced before. Sometimes madly passionate, other times slow and tender, but always, always amazing.

I had never been happier. I adored David and I wasn't the only one. Tanya and Alastair loved him too – and so did Mum and Dad. Everyone did. He was kind and generous and so sweet natured that he never had a bad word to say about anyone. I often came home from work prattling on about some silly drama I'd had to deal with that day and he'd just nod calmly and ask if I wanted a cup of tea and then he'd listen to all my woes until I felt better, which sometimes took a very long time.

And he was brilliantly talented – he'd already written three critically acclaimed thrillers and he wasn't even thirty yet. Of course he liked to joke that being critically acclaimed didn't pay the electricity bill and that he'd have to give up the starving writer gig if the books didn't start selling in big numbers, but he didn't mean it, we both knew that. Writing was his passion. Sometimes he would become so engrossed in front of the screen that I would leave for work and come back again and he would still be there, tapping away at the keyboard, having not moved the entire day. It was one of the things I loved most about him – his commitment to his craft. And that commitment had paid off because his last novel had been a massive success and he was tipped for very big things.

And now he has a new book on the shelves and I'm going to have to see him again. I feel myself start to shake at the thought. How am I going to interview him? What on earth will I say?

'Well, get a move on then,' Minty snaps, interrupting my thoughts. 'I need it, like, yesterday.'

'OK.' I pretend to write something very important in my jotter. I really spell out 'HELP' in big capital letters. And then I underline it at least six times.

'Um, can I make a suggestion before we go?' Samantha is speaking.

Minty raises an eyebrow. Samantha is going to be running up and down the stairs for days, just like that poor intern, if she says anything even remotely stupid.

'Seeing as you want to take a traditional look at true love for this issue,' Samantha says, 'which I think is a very sweet approach by the way –'

Minty raises her other eyebrow.

'– do you think we should do something on marriage?' She pauses and smiles playfully at Minty.

'Marriage?' Minty's voice raises a decibel. I can tell she's not sure if Samantha is having a sly dig at her. After all, her latest marriage is her third attempt at wedded bliss.

'Yes.' Samantha is still talking. 'You know, why people marry now when there's no real pressure from society for them to do it any more. What drives them to walk up the aisle – it must be true love, right? Um, capital T, capital L.' Samantha glances at her jotter to make sure she's got that bit right, and then smiles again and shakes her hair back.

Minty's eyes narrow and her unusually large nostrils start to flare. I can spot a bogey inching its way down and dangling enticingly just inside her nasal cavity. If we're really unlucky, Minty will wrench that one out of its hiding place and give us all a good look at it any minute now.

'Why people marry ...' She pauses, whirling her specially commissioned hand-made pen in her fingers, the one with her name engraved on it in gold lettering. 'I like it.'

I gasp. Minty liking anything is unheard of.

Samantha smiles as if she knew she was on to something.

'Molly?' Minty looks straight at me.

'Yes?' I can feel my lips say the word, but my voice sounds very far away.

'You got married recently. Why?'

'I, um ...' I can't think of anything to say. 'Why?' I squeak, hoping she won't notice that I've just repeated her question back to her. My head floods with possible answers.

Because I wanted a nice dress?

Because I wanted a big party?

Because I never got over David and this was the only way I could be certain to forget him?

Before I can answer, Minty interrupts.

'Look, it doesn't fucking matter – I couldn't care less.'

She bares her teeth at me. I can see she's had some sort of omelette for breakfast – the remains of it are still on her veneers.

'I want 700 words from you on why you walked up the aisle. And, by the way, I've emailed Eve what's-her-name for more of her quizzes – they're not bad. Now get out.'

I scramble from the room behind Samantha, my head spinning. How can this be happening? Not only do I have to interview David about true love, but I have to come up with 700 words of my own on why marriage is still a relevant institution, when I can't even track down my own husband. It would be funny if it wasn't so terrifying. How am I going to do either? I'll never pluck up the courage to speak to David, not after the way I ended it. And how can I write about a happy marriage when my own marriage is a disaster zone? It doesn't bear thinking about.

'Shall I organize the David Rendell interview?' Samantha says, her face hopeful. 'Would that help?'

'Sure,' I croak. 'Good idea.'

The less I have to do with this whole process the better. I'll let Samantha speak to the publicist and set up an interview location. I have no idea who David's publicist is now anyway – his publishers have merged and re-merged so many times since we broke up that I've lost track. If Samantha does the legwork then all I have to do is the interview itself. That won't be so bad. But even as I try to convince myself, I know it's not true. Seeing David again *will* be bad. In fact, it'll be worse than bad, it'll be awful, but I have no choice. I have to do it.

Julie's Blog

9.01 a.m.
Email from R:

> Long time no hear. How are things? Are you OK since you ditched
> Mr X?

Crap. Can't come clean with R. She'll never speak to me
again if she finds out that not only am I still seeing Mr X but
that he's moved in with me. If only she wasn't such a good,
wholesome person she might understand how complicated
everything is. I'll have to lie to her. Just a little lie. Just until
I can tell her the truth. Not sure when that will be, but hopefully it'll be soon. Tomorrow. Well, maybe not tomorrow.
Maybe the day after. Or next week. I'll just tell her a little
white lie now and then fix it later. On some unspecified
date in the future. The last thing I need is for her to find out
that Mr X has moved in and taken control of the remote. I'm
still in shock that he likes the Discovery Channel! Who,
under the age of ninety, likes the Discovery Channel? I
couldn't believe it! It was bad enough that I had to pretend
to eat some God-awful organic stir-fry that was only half
cooked (eating vegetables almost raw keeps the nutrients
intact apparently), but then we had to watch some boring
documentary about a primitive tribe living in the jungle –
who wants to know about that? Not me. Not when I need to
watch *E!* to find out the latest celeb gossip. Didn't say anything to him though. Pretended that learning how to catch a
fish with just a rock and a stick was fascinating viewing, even

though I was really itching to find out the news about Brad and Ange. Maybe I should get another TV for the bedroom. Mind you, there's nowhere to put it any more, not now that he has covered every surface with his anthropology books. At least we had sex I suppose. Of course, it wasn't as hot and steamy as it used to be in the stationery cupboard, but maybe that's because we're both a bit uptight. We probably need time to ease into this new arrangement, settle into our new roles as cohabiting partners, then things'll heat up again.

Anyway, I'll just send R a quick email to throw her off the scent for a bit.

9.06 a.m.
Email to R:

> Hi there, sorry, just really busy at work! Will catch up with you soon for a night out. Xx

God, I feel awful lying to her like this. But I can't tell her the truth, she'd think really badly of me. And if she knew she might tell someone else, and if she did that then what would other people think of me? That I'm a marriage wrecker, that's what. That I'm a really bad person with no morals.

In fairness, it's not like I *asked* Mr X to leave his wife. I wasn't even sure I was going to continue the affair once he got back from his honeymoon, but he's in love with me now – what can I do? I can't tell him that I don't want him in my flat. Not that I *don't* want him there. Of course I do. It's amazing to think that he loves me so much that he's willing to throw away his marriage so we can be together. It's just … it's just that I wish he had talked to me about it first. Asked me if I agreed. Asked me if I minded. But I can't think about that now. I'll think about it tomorrow. Or the next day. Or maybe next week. Just not right now.

9.10 a.m.

Email from R:

> Great – a girls' night out would be fab!

She's right ... a girls' night out *would* be fab. But I better let Mr X settle in before I go out clubbing with the girls. I'm not sure I ever told him about my passion for clubbing – he might be surprised I like to dance till dawn as often as possible. I don't think I've ever seen Mr X dance. I'm not even sure that he can. I can't imagine him shaking his stuff under strobe lights, although he must have danced at his wedding. Probably something really naff like a waltz with his wife.

9.12 a.m.

I wonder how his wife is. She must be devastated. She's probably not sleeping. Or eating. God, I hope she hasn't done anything stupid.

9.15 a.m.

But it's not my fault if she has. I can't be blamed. I didn't ask him to leave her. I didn't expect him to. Thank God I don't know her – that would be awful. I know nothing about her – what she looks like, where she works, nothing. That was always understood between Mr X and me. I was very careful not to bring up her existence and so was he. Anyway, there was never time – we were always too busy getting physical to ever talk that much. The only thing I know is her name – Molly – and that's only because I had to sign the over-the-top flowery wedding card that UC One presented to Mr X before his big day.

10.29 a.m.

Email from Mr X:

Meet me in the boardroom at 11 a.m.

Hmmm ... what's that about? Why does he want to see me in the boardroom?

10.32 a.m.

Just thought ... maybe it's a coded message. We've pledged not to write saucy emails to each other any more, so maybe this is his way of saying he wants to get up to no good with me! He wants to make love to me on the boardroom table!!

10.34 a.m.

Hang on. If Mr X wants to meet me at 11 a.m. that means he's suggesting we have sex in the boardroom in *broad daylight*. That's very risky – we could get caught. Anyone could walk by and see us – there's no way we can do that.

10.35 a.m.

Just thought: maybe he's suggesting the boardroom because he wants to make the sex even more exciting by increasing the danger factor. This is more like it! Last night was soooooo dull in bed. Maybe he thought so too and now he wants to spice things up again between us! This is just like old times. Thank God I wore my best leopard-skin thong today. It's been cutting off circulation to my bottom, but that's all worth it now!

10.36 a.m.

Not sure I'd like co-workers to catch me in sex act though – could be very embarrassing. Maybe it would be safer to have hot, sweaty sex with Mr X in the failsafe stationery cupboard, where it's always pitch dark and no one ever goes.

10.37 a.m.
Then again, sex on the boardroom table could be good.

10.38 a.m.
Could be better than good – could be best sex ever. Could be mind-blowing.

10.42 a.m.
Email from UC One:
> Have you seen my press clippings this morning? You should take a look. How's your latest campaign going, by the way? If you need any tips on maximizing publicity, let me know!

Can see UC One smiling smugly at me from here. It's all I can do to stop myself from leaping across the desk and hitting her with my laptop.

10.49 a.m.
May nip to Ladies, just to tidy up and make sure I look my best before I meet Mr X. Will reapply cherry lip balm and brush highlighting powder across cleavage area to 'delicately accentuate bosom', like it says on the box. It's crucial that Mr X sees my chest looking all glowy and sparkly and finds me utterly irresistible. We can't start taking each other for granted just because we've moved in together. Keeping a spark alive is crucial.

Back at desk.

Did not have mind-blowing sex with Mr X on the boardroom table. When I sashayed in, three of my top buttons undone to highlight my sparkly cleavage, all the UCs were there, shuffling papers and sharpening their pencils. Was a bit shocked at first – surely Mr X hadn't turned into an orgy-loving weirdo? But then it transpired he had sent that email to *everyone*, not just me, requesting them to attend a meeting to discuss media strategies for new signings. He didn't want to ravish me at all. He wanted me to tell everyone my detailed media plan for Mr Dick Lit right there and then. If I didn't know better I would have thought he'd ambushed me.

Thankfully, *Her* magazine had just called to request an interview, so I sexed that up a bit. Well, what I actually said was that *Elle* was very interested in doing a two-page feature on him. Strictly speaking, *Elle* hasn't expressed any interest in Mr Dick Lit at all, but no one else needs to know that. *Her* isn't exactly the most prestigious title, so I *had* to exaggerate a bit. Could hear UC One sniggering loudly as I spoke, like she didn't believe me, but everyone else seemed really impressed, especially Mr X. I'm sure it's only a matter of time before *Elle* gets on board as well. Maybe I could send a fruit basket to the editor to butter her up. That's what PR is all about after all: building relationships and sucking up to people as much as humanly possible.

11.45 a.m.
Just thought: I'll tell *Her* that *Elle* are interested in Dick Lit when I call back to confirm. No harm spreading the word that he's in demand and they're lucky to have him.

11.47 a.m.

Email from N:

Hey there, sneaky girl, you've been very quiet . . . let me guess . . .
you're so busy shagging your boss you're too busy to email?

11.48 a.m.

Crap. Can never hide anything from N. She can always tell
in a millisecond if I'm lying, even online.

11.50 a.m.

Email to N:

Something like that, but don't tell R. Will catch up with you soon
and fill you in. x

11.56 a.m.

Email from N:

Sounds juicy! Chat soon x

12.01 p.m.

Email from UC One:

Congrats on the *Elle* interview – look forward to seeing it. What
date is that running?

Cow. She knows I'm bluffing.

12.03 p.m.

Email from Mr X:

Well done on your little presentation – it sounded great. Sorry if it
seemed like I sprang it on you, but like I said I have to be careful to
treat you just like everyone else, so I couldn't forewarn you. What
date is the *Elle* feature running BTW?

Crap. Don't tell me he believed that as well. I'll have to tell him the truth. Then again, he did say he can't treat me any differently from anyone else, so if I own up I could be in big trouble. Maybe I should keep that information to myself for a while and see how it plays out. He'll probably forget all about it anyway, especially if I seduce him properly tonight.

Open Forum

From Broken Hearted: You see, you see? Julie, wake up and smell the coffee – he's trying to assert his control in the bedroom *and* the office! This is a disaster!

From Hot Stuff: I'm so disappointed they didn't have sex on the boardroom table – that would have been like something out of a movie!

From Broken Hearted: Well, it isn't a movie, Hot Stuff. This is the real world and if Julie doesn't get rid of this guy soon he's going to ruin her life.

From Devil Woman: Hey, are you speaking from experience?

From Broken Hearted: I might be.

From Devil Woman: Go on, spill, we're all friends here.

From Broken Hearted: Well ... OK. I had an affair with my married boss too. He used me, promised me the world – then he went back to his wife.

From Devil Woman: Bastard.

From Shaz: Hey, Broken Hearted, if you need legal advice, click on this link.

From Devil Woman: Leave her alone, you creep. The girl's in real pain.

From Broken Hearted: That's OK – thanks.

From Hot Stuff: But maybe this is different? Maybe Mr X and Julie are meant to be together?

From Sexy Girl: Yeah, it's only a bit of fun!

From Broken Hearted: It's fun until she downs five bottles of pills and a litre of vodka in despair.

From Hot Stuff: Oh no, Broken Hearted – did that happen to you?

From Devil Woman: Well, of course it did, Hot Stuff. Otherwise she wouldn't have brought it up! Are you dense or what?

From Broken Hearted: It's OK, I'm over him now.

From Angel: It doesn't sound like that to me.

From Hot Stuff: Yeah, I agree. You really do sound heartbroken, just like your name.

From Sexy Girl: Well, I for one am so disappointed they didn't do it on the boardroom table. This is getting a bit boring. I don't think I'm going to read Julie's blog any more. There are loads of other blogs out there – ones with real drama.

From Hot Stuff: I think you should stick with it. You never know what's going to happen next. It could get really exciting!

From Sexy Girl: Like what?

From Hot Stuff: Who knows? Maybe his wife will storm the office and try to get him back!

From Sexy Girl: Maybe his wife doesn't want him back. Maybe she loves someone else. Maybe it was a big mistake getting married to him in the first place.

From Shaz: I hope you're right! He doesn't deserve either of them in my opinion.

From Angel: This so-called relationship is based on nothing more than primal lust.

From Sexy Girl: Don't knock lust – friendship doesn't keep you warm at night!

From Comfy Pants: Hello there, Julie. I was just wondering if you've ever tried hipster pants. They're much more comfortable than thongs.

From Devil Woman: Are you for real? The girl doesn't need advice on what pants to wear!

From Comfy Pants: I'm just saying – hipsters don't ride up like G-strings do. M&S do a great six-pack. I've never looked back since I started wearing them.

From Devil Woman: Girl, you need to get a life.

From Graphic Scenes: Can anyone tell me when the hot sex is happening?

Eve

Dear Charlie,

My blind date with Cyril the accountant was a complete disaster. I should have known things weren't going to go well when the only magpie for miles around flew straight past me while I was on the way there. You used to think I was silly to be so superstitious, but everyone knows that one magpie equals a whole lot of sorrow, and this bird almost mowed me down he was so intent on singling me out for special attention.

It had been agreed that we were to meet in the lobby of the Sheldon Hotel for lunch, and because it's not all that far from the flat I stupidly decided it would be a good idea to walk there. I thought walking would help to clear my head and get rid of the nerves that were fluttering in my chest. After all, this was going to be my first date in two years. It was a big deal. Who knew what could happen? Cyril could turn out to be perfect for me. Doubtful, as I still couldn't think of a thing we might have in common or what I could say to him, bar mentioning the trouble on the stock markets – not that I really knew what all that was about of course. But maybe he'd surprise me. Maybe he'd be charming and witty and not at all like the stereotypical picture of an accountant I had in my head. Maybe he'd fallen into accountancy because his parents had pressured him into it. Maybe numbers and spreadsheets and balancing books did nothing for him and he really wanted to be an artist. Maybe we'd look at each other and fall madly in love at first sight. It wasn't very likely, but it was possible.

Thinking about it all had made me really nervous, and that's why I decided to walk – I knew it would help calm me down. The trouble was, Anna had insisted that I had to make a bit of an effort to impress Cyril so I wasn't allowed to wear my favourite flat shoes. She said that if I wanted to look the part of a happy-go-lucky single girl about town then I was at least to put on some slutty high heels. She tried to persuade me to wear a low-cut top as well, but I drew the line there. I wore my failsafe wool polo neck instead – the one you once jokingly said made me look like a librarian, although I tried not to think about that.

Anyway, I forced my feet into my one pair of heels and set off, but the thing is, I'd forgotten how walking in anything more than an inch can be so treacherous. I've become so used to going everywhere in my trainers that I ended up tripping over my feet every few steps. I had to slow right down and sort of tiptoe along the footpath to avoid falling flat on my face. It's no wonder that magpie picked me out of the crowd – I must have stuck out like a sore thumb.

By the time I wobbled unsteadily into the hotel I was fifteen minutes late. I wasn't that worried though. Anna told me that you're allowed to be late for a blind date – in fact it's almost part of the deal. Arrive late in case your date hasn't shown up yet; don't sit at the bar looking like a total loser and craning your neck every time the door opens: those are the unwritten rules. But it turns out that Cyril didn't know about the rules, or if he did he'd decided not to abide by them.

I spotted him the minute I entered the lobby. He was the only one wearing a too-tight suit and reading the *Financial Times* while all the other red-blooded males were downing lunchtime pints and chewing open-mouthed on cheese toasties. He was holding the paper really close to his face, like he was short-sighted or trying to hide – I couldn't figure out which, and by then I didn't care. I was so relieved to have made it at all that I limped across to him, introduced myself and was just about to collapse on a stool and rest my weary feet when he looked me up and down, checked his watch, said he couldn't have a relationship with someone who wasn't punctual, folded up his beige Burberry trench coat and left without saying another word. I had just broken the record for the shortest blind date in history. So I wobbled home again, completely deflated.

Anna was really annoyed when I told her what happened. In fact, she wanted to call and threaten him with physical violence. It took me ages to convince her not to. She says I'm to forget all about him and that just because he wasn't the One it doesn't mean that I shouldn't persevere and keep looking for love – or a good shag at the very least. I said I never got a chance to find out if he was the One or not – he hightailed it out of the lobby too fast (and there was no way he was getting me into bed: anyone who wears a polyester suit is definitely not my type).

Anna said I can't give up and I have to put myself out there. I said I didn't particularly want to put myself out there – that 'out there' was far too scary and I was happiest where I was: holed up in my flat, not being rejected by complete strangers. Then she said I had to cop myself on and that she wouldn't be as happy as she was now with Derek if she hadn't taken a few chances on the way. I didn't want to tell her that ending up with a man who likes to wedge himself into my G-strings is not my idea of a successful relationship. But then who am I to judge? I haven't had any sort of relationship since you left – successful or otherwise. Perhaps sharing your underwear with a sixteen-stone man wouldn't be all bad. Perhaps I should try to take more risks.

If I'm honest with myself though (and Mary the therapist tells me that's part of my problem), I always knew that this blind-dating lark would never work. I'm destined to be alone for the rest of my life, and I think I'd be far happier that way.

I didn't tell Anna that, of course. She's so gung-ho on finding me true love that I couldn't tell her the truth. She's already talking about organizing another date for me. I'm dreading it after this disaster, but I know better than to say no to her — she's more determined than ever to find me someone new. So I lied and told her that I was looking forward to it. I'm not sure she believed me though: I'm not much good at telling fibs. If only I'd been more observant when we were together. You lied to me for so long that if I'd been paying attention I could have become an expert. Then again, if I think about it, I used to lie to you too.

Do you know that, secretly, I never agreed with you about the marriage thing? The reality is I used to fantasize that you'd change your mind about marrying me. I used to dream that you'd whisk me off my feet and I would get the chance to wear a meringue dress, have fifteen bridesmaids and dither between choosing chicken or beef for the wedding menu. Silly, I know. I hate chicken *and* beef, but fish is still not an acceptable option. That's according to the wedding magazines anyway, and they are the authority on all things bridal. I know this because I've been buying wedding magazines for years – that's another secret of mine. I started subscribing to three within a month of meeting you, which seems a lifetime ago. I have quite a collection now. In fact, if I wanted to I could pull off an intimate ceremony for ten or a grand affair for 400 without even batting an eyelid.

I have the flower arrangements, music and colour schemes all decided. I could get married tomorrow if someone proposed. But that's very unlikely to ever happen. Especially now that even complete strangers are rejecting me before I can utter a word.

Mary the therapist says I need to move on from this little setback. She says the process of healing will involve one step forward and one step back and that I'll eventually reach a peaceful place full of love and acceptance. Thinking about it, she spends quite a bit of time talking about the rocky paths I'll need to travel and the mountains I'll need to climb before I find the love-and-acceptance part, but she seems pretty positive it will all come good in the end.

She's suggested that it might be a good idea to paint the flat a nice, colourful shade to cheer myself up. I told her I was perfectly happy with the flat the way it is – beige suits me – but she said that bright colours can be a real mood adjuster and that coating everything in a sunny yellow would do wonders for my state of mind. I wasn't too sure about that. I mean, I know yellow is supposed to be a cheering colour, but I can't help but think of bananas when I see it and you know how I feel about those. I still have nightmares about being called Chimp at school because of my unusually long arms. I know I grew into them eventually, but all the teasing has never left me.

Anna thinks painting the flat is a great idea. She says it's a scientific fact that bright colours improve a person's mood. That's why she's now insisting that Derek wear blue and red all the time. She thinks if he starts to feel manlier he'll stop raiding her underwear drawer. She's convinced that wearing strong primary colours can make a man's testosterone increase, and she thinks that if Derek dresses like Superman then he won't want to try on her frilly knickers. I told her that there has to be more to it than that, but she says she's going to try it and if that doesn't work she's going to start him on hormones. Only problem is that Derek is needle-phobic, so she might have to knock him out before she can inject him. I'm hoping she doesn't want me to help; she kind of looked at me knowingly when she said that.

Anyway, I might give the colour thing a try. It can't do any harm, I suppose, and Anna says she has the perfect handyman for the job: Derek's friend Homer. Homer isn't his real name; his real name is Murray. Anna doesn't know why everyone calls him Homer, but I'm sure it must be because he loves *The Simpsons*. Anna says he's a great painter and decorator, but I have my doubts, especially if he's anything like his namesake. Anna also claims that once the flat is sexed up in a vibrant shade of yellow, I'll feel brilliant, but from the uncertain look on her face when she said it, I think she might have been telling a little white lie herself.

Eve

Are You a Fabulous Fibber?

We all tell little white lies, but are you more than economical with the truth? Do our quiz and find out!

Your best friend asks if she looks fat in her new dress. Do you tell her:
  a) She looks amazing – just like a supermodel.
  b) She might need to drop a pound or two – just to tone up.
  c) She looks clinically obese and you won't be seen in

public with her unless she does something about it – quick.

Your partner asks how it was for you. It was less than spectacular, but do you say the experience was:
a) Fantastic: the earth really moved.
b) Not bad, but maybe it'd be a good idea to try something new now and again, just to spice things up a bit.
c) Terrible: you fell asleep halfway through.

At the end of a disastrous restaurant meal, the waiter asks how everything was. Do you say:
a) Gorgeous: this place deserves a Michelin star!
b) Quite good, but maybe they could use less seasoning next time?
c) Awful: you feel like throwing up. And you're not paying either.

A salesperson undercharges you for that fabulous dress you've been lusting after. Do you:
a) Tell her immediately. You couldn't wear it in good conscience if you didn't.
b) Keep quiet, but make a donation to charity for the amount afterwards.
c) Say nothing – it's not your fault if she's stupid. And now you can afford matching shoes as well.

Results
Mostly As: Sometimes the truth hurts – but you need to get a backbone, sister!

Mostly Bs: Good effort. You're the diplomatic type, but in serious situations sometimes you may have to take a tougher stance.

Mostly Cs: Ouch! Try a more softly-softly approach or you'll have no friends left, girlfriend!

Molly

I'm in Gianni's Italian restaurant with Tanya and Al, eyeing a nine-inch pizza with all my favourite toppings: anchovies, pineapple and pepperoni. When Gianni himself slapped it down in front of me I fell on it in ravenous hunger, grabbing a large slice and stuffing it into my mouth as fast as I could. But it tasted like chewy cardboard and I couldn't swallow. In an instant my appetite vanished. Now I'm pushing the pizza round and round my plate, cutting off tiny pieces of doughy crust from the edges and then piling them up in the centre to keep my hands busy.

I look around me. The place is almost deserted except for the three of us and a loved-up couple in the corner. I haven't been here in a while, but it definitely used to be a lot busier at lunchtime. It *used* to be buzzing in here. Where is everybody now? Do they know something we don't? Maybe Gianni's has had some sort of hygiene scare we haven't heard about. Maybe it's been raided by the health and safety authorities and it's going to be closed down. Maybe my pizza is drenched in teeny rat droppings that are invisible to the naked eye – that might be why it tastes so awful. I push my plate away and try to erase the image of a rodent nibbling pepperoni slices from my mind. I'm starting to regret coming here at all. It sounded like a good idea when Tanya called to suggest it, but now I know it's been a mistake.

'Does this pizza look funny to you?' I ask Tanya, who's busily shovelling pasta carbonara into her mouth like she hasn't eaten in a week.

'I don't think it's the pizza, Moll,' she replies.

'Really?' I ask, wondering if maybe I should order a salad instead. That might be safer. Rats don't like lettuce, right?

'I think it might be your ... situation.' She chooses her words carefully. 'It's completely natural to lose your appetite when something like this happens. Do you want some of my pasta?'

I look at her creamy pasta dish and my stomach flips. I feel queasy even looking at it; I definitely don't want to taste it. Usually I love pasta, but these are unusual times.

'No thanks,' I say. 'I might just have another drink.' I look around to see if I can catch Gianni's eye. I don't usually drink alcohol at lunchtime, but I've already downed a glass of wine – and I want another.

'Yeah,' Al says, tucking into garlic bread. 'Like when Dougie dumped me, remember? I couldn't eat a thing. Of course then I progressed to phase two. That was even worse.'

'What's phase two?' I ask, trying to get Gianni's attention. He's too busy flirting with the busty teenage waitress in a miniskirt to notice me. I need some more wine, and fast.

'That's when you can't stop comfort-eating,' Al says. 'You'd gnaw your hand off if you thought it would numb the pain.'

I look at my chapped hands, at the chipped nail polish and ragged cuticles. They don't look very appetizing. They look like the hands of an eighty-year-old woman – one who hasn't moisturized in fifty-odd years.

'Yeah, you usually put on at least a stone, but it varies ... depending on the circumstances.' He eyes me across the table. 'Someone in your situation could easily put on two, maybe more.'

I try to imagine myself two stone heavier. I'd have to kiss

goodbye to skinny jeans and start wearing full-length tent dresses, great big billowing ones that would hide me and my massive behind. That might be no bad thing: skinny jeans are a crime against womankind in my opinion.

'I think we should change the subject,' Tanya interjects, frowning at Al. 'Molly doesn't need to listen to this.'

But Al is on a roll. He can't be stopped.

'Then of course there's your skin. That's the next to go.'

'What do you mean?' I ask. Piling on the pounds after heartache I'd heard about before, but skin disorders as well? This is new.

'I always get boils on my chin after a break-up. I had to get one lanced once, don't you remember? The doctor said he'd never seen so much pus come out of one boil before. It was vile.' Al lifts a slice of pizza from my plate without asking and proudly takes a bite. The cheese oozes slowly out of the corner of his mouth.

'Oh God, yeah.' Tanya laughs in spite of herself. 'Didn't we give that boil a name?'

'Judy,' Al says, wiping his lips with the red paper napkin.

'That's right,' Tanya says. 'Judy! She was a shining star – just like Judy Garland!!'

Suddenly it all comes flooding back. I *do* remember it now. It was *David* who named that boil Judy. Al had just broken up with the latest in a long string of disastrous men, and David had cooked us all a delicious three-course dinner to take his mind off things. At some drunken stage of the evening we'd started talking about the massive boil on Al's chin and David had decided it was so impressive that it would be a sin not to name it. So we'd cracked open a bottle of champagne and christened it Judy – then we'd drunk some more until we all ended up in a heap of laughter round the table. It had really cheered Al up.

That was right before Mum and Dad died. Right before all our lives were shattered into a million different pieces.

It happened on a beautiful winter's day a year after David and I first met. We'd asked Mum and Dad over for a special lunch to celebrate our anniversary. David had been really keen for them to come. Of course, they'd met him loads of times before that, and they loved him to bits, but for some reason he was adamant that they had to join us that day. He said he had something special to say and he could only say it if Mum and Dad were there. I was curious, but I didn't question him too much: David liked surprises and I decided to humour him. So, I persuaded Mum and Dad to come with promises of lemon chicken and roast potatoes. Dad had joked that he hoped David was cooking, not me, because the last thing he needed was a bad bout of indigestion. Then Mum had told him off and said they'd be delighted and that they'd be there by one. But one o'clock came and went and they never arrived. They never made it because, on the way, a lorry came round a corner too fast and ploughed straight into their car and they were both killed instantly. Wiped out in the blink of an eye, just like that.

I knew immediately that it was my fault. If I hadn't invited them to come for lunch they wouldn't be dead. It was simple. If it hadn't been for me, they wouldn't have been at that exact spot in the road when the truck flew round the corner and lost control. It was my fault they were dead. I blamed myself and I knew Tanya blamed me too. She never said so, but how could she not think it? We had lost the best parents in the world all because of me.

I push my pizza away. Whatever appetite I'd had before, it's gone now. I see Tanya and Al looking at each other. I know they've just remembered exactly the same thing.

'So … no news from Charlie then?' Al says finally to break the silence.

'No,' I reply.

'You've heard nothing at all? Not even a text?'

'No.' My voice sounds very small. 'Nothing at all.'

'You need to talk to him, Moll,' Tanya says gently.

She's right. I know she's right. But it's not like I haven't tried to contact him. I can't *force* him to talk to me – so what should I do? Sit outside his office and wait to confront him? I can't bring myself to do that. I have *some* pride left, even if it's only a smidgen.

'Do you want *me* to have a word in his ear?' Al offers, puffing his chest out. 'I'll make him see sense.'

'Thanks, Al, but I'm not sure that's a good idea.' I smile gratefully at him. Truth be told, Al wasn't overly fond of Charlie to begin with. He never said so, but I know they only tolerated each other because of me. They were never buddies – not like he was with David. If I think about it, the same is probably true of Tanya. She was polite to Charlie, yes. But were they ever really friends?

I shake my head to clear it. I have to stop thinking about David. Trouble is, ever since Minty told me I have to interview him I haven't been able to think about anything else. He's everywhere I look – even here. Gianni's used to be a favourite haunt of ours. If I close my eyes I can see *us* sitting right where that couple is in the corner, holding hands and laughing over a bottle of Chianti.

'Molly, are you listening?'

I drag myself back to what Tanya is saying.

'We want to help you get to the bottom of all this,' she says carefully. 'We hate to see you upset.'

If only she knew what was really upsetting me. Because right now what's on my mind is not the fact that my husband has left me, but that I might be seeing David soon. And that can't be right, surely? Why am I obsessing about my ex when I should be concentrating on where my husband is and why? A therapist would have a field day with me, I just know it.

'Yeah, we want to help. So that's why we need to know how often you and Charlie had sex,' Alastair says, picking up another slice of my abandoned pizza and biting into it.

Tanya kicks him under the table. I know she does this because Al gives a little yelp of pain before glaring at her.

'What?' he asks. 'You said finding that out was crucial.'

'Can you, for once in your life, try to be discreet?' Tanya hisses, her eyes glinting dangerously at him.

'Moll –' She composes herself and then smiles at me again. 'We're just trying to figure out if you were still, um, close. You know . . .'

'Yeah, so can you tell us how often you and Charlie used to do it? On average?' Al looks at me expectantly.

'I'm not answering that,' I say firmly, hoping they'll get the hint. Some subjects are just off-limits. And my sex life is one of them. I don't want to discuss it – it's private. I'm not a teenager any more, I can't spend my lunchtime gossiping about this sort of stuff.

'Sex is an indicator of how a relationship is doing,' Al says. 'If you two weren't getting it on, it could be a sign that something was seriously wrong.'

'Well, obviously *something* was seriously wrong, Alastair,' I growl, my temper flaring. 'He's left me, or hadn't you noticed?'

Al's face falls and I instantly regret snapping at him. But what does he want me to say? That we were ripping off each other's clothes every night? That we were insatiable? That we couldn't keep our hands off each other?

That would be far from the truth. Because, if I am brutally honest, things had always been a little quiet between Charlie and me in the bedroom. He was very romantic in lots of ways, that was true, but he wasn't exactly passionate. He'd never lost control and thrown me to the floor in lust. He'd never grabbed me out of the blue and told me he had to have me right there and then. Sex between us was fine. It just wasn't . . . amazing.

At the beginning, I thought it was something that we could work on. OK, so maybe things weren't naturally explosive between us, but I was sure that if we put our minds to it, we could get it moving in the right direction. Perhaps we just needed a little help.

So, one day, I decided to take advice from an article I'd commissioned for *Her* about spicing up your love life. 'Put the Spark Back in Your Relationship' the article was called, and it described in minute detail what to do if things were a bit dull in the bedroom department. I was confident I could make it work. So I spent one whole lunch break choosing very expensive sexy silk underwear while a snooty sales assistant hovered around me as if she thought I was going to shove half the shop into my handbag and take off. I think she could tell I wasn't the fancy knickers type. And I'm not usually – I'm a white or black cotton underwear type. I don't do silk, I definitely don't do lace and I never do ribbons. But this was an exception. This was going to improve my relationship and finally light the fire of desire between Charlie and me. So I was happy to hand over my credit card to the snooty sales girl because I knew that the extortionate price was going to be worth it. These knickers were going to ignite the passion that was surely just under the surface.

I took them home and spent ages laying a trail of rose

petals to the bedroom, lighting candles and spraying musky scent around. Then I clambered into my fiddly knickers, spent about twenty minutes trying to tie the ribbons on the side and lay as seductively as I could manage on the bed, waiting for Charlie to arrive and ravish me. I'll never forget the look on his face when he walked through the door. It wasn't lust, or passion, or even curiosity. It was horror. It was only for a second, but it was definitely there and, just like they say in cheap thrillers, my blood ran cold. We both tried to pretend I hadn't seen his face and we went through the motions, but I could tell his heart wasn't in it. And when it was over he got up and went downstairs and I lay there wondering what was wrong between us and feeling very scared because the wedding plans were already in full swing. I tried to push it to the back of my mind and ignore what it might mean, but deep inside I knew what I was missing because I'd had that special spark before. I knew what it felt like to want someone with an intense passion that nothing could quell. To turn to jelly at someone's touch, to quiver with desire from just one look. I knew what it felt like, because that's what I'd had with David.

'OK, I'll give a guess,' Al says, interrupting my thoughts. 'You and Charlie did it twice a week – am I close?'

If only that were true. I say nothing and concentrate on fiddling with the pizza crust.

'I'm right, aren't I?' He punches his fist in the air and gives a little yelp of victory.

'Oh my God.' Tanya's mouth is open with shock. 'Is that all? Really?'

Tanya seems to think that having sex twice a week is shocking. What if she knew the truth? That we hardly had sex at all, even on honeymoon?

'That's not so bad, is it?' I say. I have to pretend we

were doing it at least that much or she'll have a coronary.

'Connor and I still do it five days a week – at least. We did it twice yesterday.' Tanya's smile is wide.

'Yeah, and I get *loads* – who could resist me? Have I told you about my new man? He's a prison officer called Butch, and let me tell you he really lives up to his name! This man has muscles in places you can only imagine!' Al giggles and then gives Tanya a little high five. They grin happily at each other. They're delighted with themselves.

Until they see my face.

'I'm sorry, sis,' Tanya says, looking uncomfortable. 'It's just that you're newlyweds. Surely you should be bonking each other's brains out?'

I know she has a point, but I don't want to think about it.

'Actually, Molly –' Tanya glances at Alastair and then clears her throat. 'We need to ask you something.' She looks at Al again and he nods at her to continue.

'What?'

What else can they possibly ask me? What our favourite position was?

She takes a deep breath.

'Do you think Charlie could be having an affair?'

'That's ridiculous,' I say automatically.

And it is. Charlie wouldn't cheat on me. He may have left for some unknown reason, but having an affair with another woman isn't one of them.

'We think it might make sense,' Tanya goes on slowly. 'It certainly explains what's happened, don't you think?'

'Yes, because if he's been shagging someone else behind your back, that's why he hasn't been shagging *you*, pet.' Al leans across and pats my hand.

Tanya kicks him under the table again and he howls with pain.

'What Al is *trying* to say is that all this is very weird. I mean, he just ups and goes, no explanation, no call . . .'

'But he can't be with another woman,' I say. 'He's not the type.'

We're only just married. He wouldn't have had *time* to meet someone else . . . would he?

Tanya looks at her plate but says nothing.

'Do you have another explanation for it then?' Al asks. 'Do you think he's gay maybe?'

Al looks like he thinks this mightn't be a bad thing. 'Maybe he wants to explore his sexuality?'

I try to think. There must be a reasonable explanation for all this.

'Perhaps . . . perhaps he's having a mid-life crisis,' I suggest.

He did ask me if he looked fat in his cargos a while back. And he's been doing all that running and working out.

'Yes, that's possible,' Tanya says, pouring water from the earthenware jug into her glass.

'Or maybe, just maybe, his mid-life crisis was when he proposed to you,' Al says. 'Maybe he proposed because he panicked.'

'Panicked?'

'Yes. He's nearly forty and he panicked because he hadn't ticked every box on his life's to-do list. So he decided to get married. To the first woman who said yes. That's you. Then he realized what a big mistake he'd made. So he bolted.'

I feel sick. Is Al right?

'Or . . . or maybe he married you on the rebound!! *That* could be it.' Al's eyes gleam as he changes tack.

'What?'

Tanya puts her head in her hands.

'Maybe he was in love with someone else, they broke up and he married you by mistake. It happens all the time.'

'I think that's enough theories to be getting on with, Al,' Tanya says, shaking her head at him to keep quiet. 'What we're trying to find out is how well do you really know Charlie, Moll?' Tanya takes my hand in hers. 'Everything happened so fast between you. What do you know about his relationship history, for example?'

I gulp. Charlie and I had never really discussed previous relationships. For lots of reasons.

'Molly, I know this is awful, but you have to think about it,' she goes on. 'Could he have had another woman? Was there anything to suggest that might be possible?'

I can't speak. Tanya takes this as a sign to keep talking.

'You have to face facts. Charlie has left you for no obvious reason. He might be cheating on you. It could explain why he went so suddenly.'

'Yes,' Al chimes in. 'He's having it off with someone else. Probably a blonde with big boobs.'

'That can't be true,' I manage to stutter.

'Why do you think that?' Tanya says.

I pause, grasping around for something convincing to say. 'Because, because . . . he's not a breast man.'

'Sorry?' they both say together.

'You said he's cheating with a busty blonde. He's not into boobs – he prefers bottoms.'

I have no idea if this is true. Charlie never really expressed a preference for either, but I can't say that now.

'Um, I was making a generalization, sis,' Tanya says. 'Maybe he's not into blondes with boobs, maybe he's into brunettes with big bums. The point is, you have to consider the fact that he might be playing away from home.'

'That's impossible.'

'I wish it were.' Tanya looks into my eyes. 'I *am* speaking from experience, remember?'

She's right. Nearly all her ex-boyfriends have cheated on her. She has officially had her heart broken five times.

There was:

a) The bloke who dumped her when she told him her real age (I can't tell anyone what that is: she has me sworn on pain of death never to reveal it. Besides, even though we're sisters, I can barely remember myself, she's been lying about it for so long).

b) The guy who broke up with her when his mother said she wasn't good enough for him (she was better off without him: he still brought his laundry home to Mummy every week).

c) The man who ran for the hills when she gave him a key to her flat (he said he had a fear of heights and her apartment was on the ninth floor).

d) The fella who jumped ship when she suggested a mini-break to Wales (he then emigrated to Australia with his next girlfriend).

e) The man she dated at work (he broke it off by internal email when she got promoted).

She definitely surpasses me in the heartbreak stakes – or she used to, until this most recent episode. Now I outrank her: a husband leaving you straight after your honeymoon definitely outstrips even her impressive record. And besides, she's been perfectly happy since she met her new boyfriend, Connor. She's calm and content – like I've never seen her before, in fact. Maybe it has something to do with the passionate nookie she and Connor are having on the breakfast table every five minutes.

But Charlie wouldn't cheat on me. Or would he? How

do I know what he's really capable of? I never thought he'd leave me, but he has. How well do I know him really? A chill runs up my spine and I shiver.

'Charlie isn't like that,' I manage to say. *I hope.*

Another look passes between them.

I struggle out of my seat and reach for my bag.

'I have to get back to work.'

'Don't go,' Tanya says. 'Have a coffee at least.'

'Yeah, and what about dessert?' Al pipes up. 'We could order some chocolate fudge cake to share?'

Chocolate fudge cake. That's the dessert that David and I used to split. He always used to tease me that I never could share fairly and that he only ever got a mouthful. Suddenly my chest aches. I have to get out of here – fast.

'I have to go.' I grab my things and then sprint out of the restaurant before they can say anything else. Because if they do I might just burst into tears.

Tanya and Al think Charlie is having an affair. They think that's why he left me. They actually believe he left because he was seeing some other woman. Having sex with some other woman. It sort of makes sense. An affair. Why didn't I think of it before? Most women would have jumped to that conclusion, but it didn't occur to me. Charlie could be having an affair. He could have a mistress. Do they call them mistresses any more? That's a bit 1980s bonkbuster, isn't it? Not a mistress then – a lover. Charlie could have a lover. And if it *is* true, then how do I feel about it? Sick? Repulsed? Betrayed?

No, none of those. It's something else, something I can't put my finger on just yet.

Suddenly I feel bile rise at the back of my throat. Could they be right? Could Charlie be having an affair – is that why he left so suddenly? Is he secretly in love with someone else?

But how can that be when he told me he adores me? That he can't live without me? He was the one who proposed so quickly, after all. It's not like I pursued him; he did all the chasing. So now that he's caught me, why has he run so fast in the other direction? None of it makes any sense. And there's something else niggling me as well, something about the thought of him having an affair that I can't quite put my finger on. That glass of lunchtime wine has made me feel a bit fuzzy. It's probably a good thing I didn't have a second.

Right then my phone beeps and I rummage in my bag to answer it. It could be Minty wanting to know where I am – we have an afternoon meeting I can't be late for. I should grab a strong coffee on the way back to the office: that wine has definitely gone straight to my head, and I don't want her to suspect that there's anything amiss.

'Hello?' I try to sound sober and together.

'Hi, Molly!'

It's not Minty, it's Samantha. I'd recognize her cheerful voice anywhere.

'Great news!!! David Rendell has agreed to the interview. He can do the day after tomorrow at twelve. I just had to call you when I heard – I'm so excited!!'

'Um, that's a bit short notice, I'm not sure if I can . . .'

My mind is racing. That's far too soon, I haven't even got used to the idea of seeing David again. I need to prepare. I need time, lots and lots of time. A week or two, at the very least.

'But you *have* to!' Samantha screeches. 'The publicist said *Elle* wants him as well! It's us or them!!'

'We'll take it,' I say quickly. I know I have no choice: Minty would skin me alive if we lost an important exclusive to a rival magazine.

'Great! We're going to meet him in the lobby of the Sheldon Hotel at noon – is that OK with you?'

'That's fine.' I feel sick. 'Thanks, Samantha.'

'See you back at the office!' Samantha sings.

I close my phone slowly, my head reeling. I'm meeting David. After two years of desperately trying to forget that he exists, I'm finally going to see him again.

Julie's Blog

5.00 a.m.

It is 5 a.m. and I can't sleep. I can't sleep because Mr X snores. He snores like nothing I have ever heard before. Like a rattling whistle, combined with a nasal gurgle and then a raspy tickle at the end. This is something I never knew. Mr X also hogs the duvet. He starts off pretending he's going to be fair, but within minutes of falling asleep he's tucked most of the duvet around him, hanging on to it with a vice-like grip. This is also something I never knew. Then again, how would I? We never shared a bed before. Not once.

I have been lying shivering on my side for the last two hours, listening to his snoring getting louder and louder and trying to prise the duvet from his hands. I tried poking him with my toe, then kicking him gently, then kicking him quite hard, but nothing would budge him or get him to stop. He was totally oblivious – he is a very deep sleeper. He sleeps the sleep of the dead – again, something I didn't know.

8.00 a.m.

At desk. Exhausted after the worst night's sleep of my life. But the office is completely deserted, which means that at least I'll get a head start on my brilliant PR strategy for Mr Dick Lit. I already have the *Her* thing in the bag, but that's not nearly enough, not when everyone is expecting *Elle* to be on board too. I'll have to get much more media coverage, and just as every good publicist worth her weight in tropical fruit baskets knows, the best way to do that is to exploit his personal life. I wonder if he has any deep dark secrets we could leak, accidentally on purpose, to the press? Not that it matters, because even if he doesn't have any skeletons in his closet, we can always make up something good and juicy. Something that will grab the public's attention and make sure his novel flies off the shelves. Or maybe we could get him on a reality TV show. I wonder if he's any good at cooking? Even better if he's not, the public loves an underdog. If I can pull some strings at one of the TV stations, we'll be minted.

8.04 a.m.
God, it's so hard to concentrate when I can hardly keep my eyes open. I'm wiped out after last night – and for all the wrong reasons. I'll just get a coffee from the machine in the kitchen. That'll wake me up.

8.10 a.m.
Can't believe it – the coffee machine is broken! How am I supposed to work in these conditions? Will have to email the janitor and get him to come up here and fix it quick.

8.12 a.m.
Email to janitor:
  Coffee machine is broken. It needs to be fixed ASAP.

8.14 a.m.
UC One has just arrived. She's sipping on hot water and lemon. She just called over that I should try it: it really clears her nasal passages and helps her focus. Tosser. I could help clear her nasal passages for good ... with one direct hit to her big hook nose.

8.16 a.m.
Email from janitor:
> A please would be nice – or can't you remember your manners
> until you have caffeine?

What a nerve. It's his job to make sure things like that
work. I shouldn't have to crawl all over him to get the job
done. And since when did he become so cheeky? He's such
a nerd he never usually answers back. He's always been so
quiet and easy to push around.

8.18 a.m.
Email to janitor:
> Just do it. Please.

8.45 a.m.
No sign of Mr X yet – he's probably still snoring in my bed.
Feel just a teeny bit resentful.

8.47 a.m.
Email from UC One:
> I couldn't help but notice that you were in early this morning. I'm
> usually the only early bird here! Is everything OK? If you're behind
> with some of your work then please do let me know – I'd be happy
> to help. I'm so organized I'm almost twiddling my thumbs. BTW,
> have you seen my latest press cuttings for my new chick-lit client?
> They're amazing!

8.58 a.m.
Just read UC One's press cuttings. Her new chick-lit author
has appeared in a 'My Favourite Room' piece for the *Gazette*.
Turns out her favourite room is her kitchen because 'rolling
pastry relaxes her' – yeah, right. The only thing that woman

is interested in rolling is money – and I bet she never eats, so why on earth would we believe that she makes complicated apple tarts with fiddly latticework? That's it – I'm going to blow UC One out of the water with my Dick Lit campaign. Maybe I'll take him to lunch, butter him up a bit. And of course I can put it on expenses, so I get a free meal too. I feel like Italian today ... yes, a special pizza at Gianni's would hit the spot. I just hope he's not still flirting with that waitress – he's old enough to be her father.

9.05 a.m.
Email to Mr Dick Lit:
> I'd be thrilled to take you for lunch today, if you're free. It could give us the opportunity to discuss the direction you'd like the press campaign to take. How about Gianni's at 1 p.m.?

This is a great idea. I'll charm him, get him on-side and let him think he's having a say in the PR. And hopefully a few glasses of wine will help persuade him that the more controversial and outspoken he can be, the better his book will sell.

9.15 a.m.
Email from Mr Dick Lit:
> OK, that might be a good idea. See you there.

Perfect! With any luck we'll bag *Elle* yet.

10.01 a.m.
No sign of Mr X. Where the hell is he? He can't *still* be asleep.

10.02 a.m.

Just thought: hope he hasn't got trapped in the flat or something – the lock on the front door can be a little tricky until you get used to it. Maybe I should call him.

10.06 a.m.

Mr X not answering his phone. Am starting to get worried. Maybe he slipped and fell in the shower. Maybe he slapped his head on the tiles and is lying bleeding and helpless on the bathroom floor. Maybe an intruder broke in and assaulted him. Feel a bit panicky. Perhaps I should go round and check he's OK.

10.08 a.m.

UC One just commented to UC Two that Mr X is very late today. UC Two said that he's probably having trouble dragging himself out of the marital bed – he is a newlywed after all. Could feel my cheeks burning. If only they knew the truth.

10.14 a.m.

Mr X just arrived. Am so relieved he isn't dead. He doesn't look like he had a bad fall or was attacked by an intruder. He looks . . . cheerful. And very well rested. Like he had the best night's sleep of his life. I'm sure he'll email me any second to let me know what happened.

10.16 a.m.

Any second now he'll send me an email to let me know where he was.

10.18 a.m.

I can't believe he's not emailing me. I can't believe that he's being so selfish. I was worried sick about him. I thought he had been attacked or was even dead, and there he is filling his cup from the water cooler and smiling at UC One like he hasn't got a care in the world. Right, that's it. I'm going to give him a piece of my mind. He can't have me crawling the walls with worry and then act like nothing's happened.

10.20 a.m.

Email to Mr X:

Where have you been?

10.23 a.m.

Email from Mr X:

I decided to work from home this morning.

He worked from home? He went back to his wife for the morning just to get some work done? What's he playing at?

10.25 a.m.

Email to Mr X:

You worked from home?

10.28 a.m.

Email from Mr X:

Yes, I got loads done – it was so quiet. BTW, you do know that you need to separate your plastics from your paper before you recycle, don't you? I think we need to get a proper system up and running or things will get out of control.

Of course. He means he worked from *my* flat – which he is now calling home. God, that's sort of freaking me out.

11.03 a.m.
Email from janitor:

The coffee machine is now fixed, m'lady.

Thank God. If I don't have a coffee soon my head will explode.

11.04 a.m.
Email to janitor:

It's about time.

11.05 a.m.
Email from janitor:

By which you mean thank you?

11.06 a.m.
Email to janitor:

By which I mean it took you long enough.

11.07 a.m.
Email from janitor:

You're welcome.

3.03 p.m.
Back from lunch with Mr Dick Lit. Things did not go exactly as I'd hoped. He has point-blank refused to co-operate with my brilliant publicity plans. He won't even *hint* that he might be recovering from a drug problem – even though that would guarantee huge press coverage. He seems to think that revealing details of his personal life is in some way sordid and that the book should stand on its own merits. Which is a sweet old-fashioned idea, but it'll never work. We need an angle. Readers need to identify with him

before they'll buy his book in droves, and how can they identify with him if they know nothing about him? He just can't seem to grasp that idea. He was even edgy about the *Her* interview. The minute I mentioned it he got all shifty and weird. It took me ages to convince him that he needs to do it for the exposure. I didn't tell him that I'd already agreed to it on his behalf – he didn't need to know that.

3.07 p.m.
Just thought: maybe we could pretend he's a recovering sex addict. That would be huge.

3.08 p.m.
Or he could have mental health problems. Some sort of split personality disorder? Or how about OCD? That would be great: 'Top Author Washes Hands a Hundred Times a Day'. The public would *love* it.

3.10 p.m.
Or we could go the old-fashioned route and concentrate on his looks. He's very attractive in a scruffy kind of way. Perhaps I could suggest one of the glossies give him a head to toe makeover – get his chipped tooth capped and his bushy eyebrows waxed. Readers love that sort of thing. It'd be even better if we could get a few shots of him in his underwear – he looks like he's quite fit under that corduroy jacket he wears. Will put the feelers out and see what I can come up with. Won't bother asking him first – what he doesn't know won't harm him.

3.16 p.m.
Feel a bit tipsy. Maybe I shouldn't have polished off that bottle of Chianti at lunch. Still, it would have been a shame

to leave it there, and Mr Dick Lit insisted on only having one measly glass – which really screwed up my dastardly plan to get him drunk and confess his deep, dark secrets to me. I just don't know what to do with him. I mean, really – what do these authors expect? That their books will just walk off the shelves? Have they no idea they're competing with celebrities who are happy to reveal all the intimate details of their gastric-band surgery or how they like to self-harm with hookers?

4.07 p.m.
Mr X is back at his desk.

4.08 p.m.
Might go talk to him – he looks a bit lonely. Can't say that of course. Need to come up with something professional I urgently need to discuss with him. Like ... my meeting with Mr Dick Lit. Yes, I'll tell him all about it. He might have some really good suggestions that will help me. That's an excellent idea.

4.11 p.m.
No, that's a very bad idea. Am definitely tipsy – could do something I might regret later. Like confess that I don't have an *Elle* exclusive at all, that all I've managed to drum up is a pathetic interview with a two-bit magazine called *Her* ... which he has probably never even heard of.

4.13 p.m.
Or I could do something even worse ... like sit on his lap and nibble his ear. That would be bad, especially when we're trying to keep our relationship a secret from everyone.

4.19 p.m.

But ... desperately want to talk to him. Maybe I'll just send him a quick professional email to ask his advice. That's perfectly acceptable. And hopefully he'll send me a sexy email back and we can have a bit of naughty banter like we used to.

4.22 p.m.

Email to Mr X:

Had excellent meeting with Mr Dick Lit – would you like to discuss?

4.25 p.m.

Email from Mr X:

Sorry, too busy, can't. Can you just email me an update?

What's that supposed to mean? He was never too busy to talk to me before.

4.28 p.m.

Email to Mr X:

Of course. I'm very busy myself.

Right. Will have to pretend to be snowed under with work.

4.47 p.m.

Email from Mr X:

Are you asleep over there?

Crap, maybe I did nod off for a split second. Drinking wine at lunchtime always makes me a bit drowsy.

4.49 p.m.

Email to Mr X:

> Don't be ridiculous! I was simply closing my eyes and trying to
> concentrate – I was mentally drafting a brilliant press release.

4.51 p.m.

Email from Mr X:

> Spoofer. You were snoring.

4.54 p.m.

Email to Mr X:

> No, I wasn't.

Oh God, what if I was? UCs acting normally around me,
but what if someone videotaped me snoring with my mouth
open on their mobile phone and I end up on YouTube?
UC One is definitely smirking.

4.56 p.m.

Email from Mr X:

> Yes, you were. It was sexy – your little nostrils were flaring. It was
> really cute.

Ah ... he thinks I'm cute. But must keep denying that
I was asleep, just in case he's bluffing. Can't admit to
cat-napping in the office.

4.58 p.m.

Email to Mr X:

> I've never snored in my life, unlike some people I know. Now,
> please stop harassing me – I'm very busy.

5.02 p.m.

Email from Mr X:

So I guess you're going to be late home tonight then?

5.05 p.m.

Email to Mr X:

Why would that be?

5.07 p.m.

Email from Mr X:

Because, according to your brilliant press plan, you're going to fax at least 300 publications telling everyone how marvellous Dick Lit is before you leave.

Crap – he expects me to do that straight away.

5.09 p.m.

Email to Mr X:

Yes, that's right.

5.12 p.m.

Email from Mr X:

It's great to see you're so committed. BTW, there's a problem with the system so you're going to have to fax them all the old-fashioned way, by hand. I won't wait up.

Open Forum

From Broken Hearted: Do you see what Mr X is doing, Julie? He tells you the way you snore is cute and then he reminds you that he's the boss. He's playing mind games with you. This is just the start of the emotional torture – wake up and smell the coffee!

From Angel: Julie, how can you justify trying to sell books to people by manufacturing hype? The publishing industry has sold its soul by giving six-figure deals to celebrities who secretly employ ghostwriters to do all the work! It's immoral for people like you to feed off this celebrity sickness.

From Devil Woman: If you object so much then why don't you stop reading her blog? No one is forcing you to!

From Angel: I'm just saying that there's real writing talent out there – talent that the public should be made aware of.

From Sexy Girl: Hey, Angel, have you had a novel rejected by a publisher by any chance?!

From Angel: Not that it's any of your business, but my writing tutor told me that my novels were all powerfully enlightening – and he's positive that a publisher will see their potential one day.

From Devil Woman: Maybe you should bed a pop star and get fake boobs – you'd probably get a book deal then!

From Angel: That is exactly the kind of depraved mindset that has ruined the chances of real literature ever seeing the light of day.

From Sexy Girl: Face it, Angel, people prefer to read about hot sex, not highbrow drivel. That's why we're all reading this blog – the sexual chemistry is explosive!

From Devil Woman: I agree! Hey, Julie, what's the janitor like? He sounds cute.

From Angel: You really are pathetic.

From Comfy Pants: Hi, Julie. I was just wondering if you tried those hipsters yet? They're on special offer this week.

From Devil Woman: Will you give over about the hipsters? This girl has more important things on her mind!

From Comfy Pants: I just wanted to let her know. It's buy one pack, get another pack free – that's pretty good value.

From Broken Hearted: Julie, do you see what he's doing? He's toying with you.

From Hot Stuff: I wouldn't mind him toying with me!!

From Devil Woman: And so say all of us, Hot Stuff!!

From Graphic Scenes: You know what, Julie? If you don't start describing all the hot sex soon then I'm not coming back to this blog.

Eve

Dear Charlie,

My brother Mike called today. He's in Texas with the school's basketball team, on some sort of cultural exchange. I know what you're thinking. Mike's a physical education teacher: he wouldn't know culture if he was slam-dunked by it. I still remember the time you tried to persuade him to read Kafka and he said he thought Kafka was a spreadable cheese. But he has improved a bit since then. He swears he's cut right back on those lads mags. Anyway, I think he's really enjoying Texas, in spite of the killer heatwave. Apparently things have got much better since they bought those little portable fans – they carry them everywhere now to keep cool. Mike says the heat's not too bad once you get past the fainting. And it sounds like they're doing much more than just playing basketball: they've arranged an entire schedule of activities for the kids. Although perhaps taking a group of teenagers to see death-row prisoners is a bit strange. I asked Mike if the visit was to teach the students that spirituality could be found even in the grimmest of conditions, and he said that was the official line all right ... but really the teachers were more looking forward to seeing the looks on the lads' faces when they met hardened criminals up close and personal. The boys have been getting very boisterous on the tour bus and Mike reckons that a good dose of real-life brutality should bring it home that bad behaviour doesn't pay. I might be wrong, but I got the impression that he wouldn't be unhappy if an execution was carried out when they were there.

I didn't tell him that you had got married and I was in therapy to come to terms with it. There's no point worrying him. After all, he has enough on his plate trying to keep thirty teenagers from running amok. Mum is up the walls with worry about him – not because of the death-row killers but because Stacey Holby, the school's religion teacher, is on the trip too. Mum says Stacey isn't a proper religion teacher at all – she's never been to Lourdes or even the shrine at Knock. I tried to explain that they don't really teach religion in the old-fashioned way any more, not now that so many schools are non-denominational. But Mum doesn't believe in non-denominational. She thinks it's only a fad. She's terrified that Stacey is going to lead Mike astray. I told her there was very little chance of that. Mike had been led astray long ago – we all know about his passion for busty platinum blondes. Then she said that it was perfectly natural for Mike to want to sow his wild oats, all young men did, but she knew Stacey Holby's sort. She was a conniving trollop – one of those girls who are determined to trap a man and get a ring on their finger, no matter how. I thought that was ironic, considering that's exactly how *she* trapped Dad, but I didn't tell her. Bringing that up would make it much worse, even if Mary the therapist thinks a lot of my problems can be traced back to Mum and Dad's flawed relationship. She says that seeing Dad leave Mum when I was little made me desperate to hang on to our relationship at all costs. Mary says that subconsciously I probably knew that you weren't being faithful to me all along, but that I was willing to put up with it to keep you, because I didn't want you to leave me, the way Dad left Mum. I didn't want my inner child to be abandoned all over again. According to her, this issue is the elephant in the room and I need to discuss it with Mum, tell her how upset I feel about Dad leaving and stop pretending that simply ignoring it will make the pain go away. I didn't tell Mary that mentioning the words 'marital separation' in Mum's presence is out of the question. Dad's been gone for years and she still likes to pretend that he'll be back once he snaps out of it and comes to his senses.

Mary says there must have been signs of your infidelity everywhere but that I chose to ignore them. I tried telling her I didn't have a clue that you were cheating on me until I came home early that day and caught you and another woman in our bed, but I'm not sure she believed me because when I said that she just scribbled in her jotter and nodded a lot, as if she wasn't at all convinced. I never found out what her name was. Your lover, I mean. I never found out *anything* about her – you left too fast to talk about it. But I do know that she's not your new wife, because her face is imprinted on my memory and she looks nothing like the new Mrs Adler. And that makes me feel even worse, because if you'd left me for the love of your life I might be able to understand it.

That reminds me: I think Johnny the plumber might have split up with his latest conquest. I first suspected when he started playing his heavy metal CDs all night. I like a bit of AC/DC as much as the next girl, but having it thumping through the wall at 1 a.m. is not my idea of fun. So, the other night, after hours of trying to sleep with my head jammed under two pillows, I stumbled into the hallway and banged on his door to tell him to quieten down. When he answered he looked really haggard and pale. It was quite strange, because he just agreed to turn it off and he didn't even invite me in for a nightcap. You know how he is – usually when he dumps someone he's back to pestering anything with a pulse to sleep with him within hours, but this time seems different. Then, when I met him in the lift today, he didn't even leer at me like he usually does. And he wasn't wearing that awful aftershave either – you know, the one that can make it difficult to breathe if you get within six feet of him. When I asked him if everything was OK he just shrugged his shoulders and looked at me blankly. I recognized the look instantly – I could be wrong, but I think he's had his heart broken for the very first time. I feel a bit sorry for him, but I am relieved as well. Listening to all his porno moves was really wearing me out. I'd take AC/DC over that any day of the week.

I almost forgot: Derek's friend Homer has started repainting the flat. He's nothing like I expected him to be. I thought he might actually look like Homer from *The Simpsons* – you know, a fat slob swilling a Duff beer. But he doesn't have a beer belly or brush-over hair; he has a ponytail – a really long one that almost reaches to his waist. When I showed him round he said that Honey Dew would be the perfect yellow to transform the flat – he has it on his own walls and he says it's a really uplifting colour, especially in the morning when dawn breaks and the sun streams in. I didn't like to tell him that I never pull up the blinds in the morning, so there's no chance of sun streaming in anywhere, but once he showed me the colour card and I was sure I could stomach it, I gave him the go-ahead to start. Mary says it's healthy to take a risk. And at least I won't have to listen to Anna banging on about beige being the most boring colour in the world any more. It's bad enough that she keeps lecturing me about my love life, without having her lecture me about wall colours too. Anyway, I've been looking at the colour card he gave me in lots of different lights and I've decided that Honey Dew *is* quite a nice shade of yellow, all things considered. It's bright and modern-looking, and let's face it, I could do with being dragged into the future. You always used to say I was so old-fashioned and behind the times. Maybe it's time I got a bit trendier, even if it's only in the comfort of my own home.

Eve

Are You on Trend or Behind the Times?

Take our quiz and find out!

Your make-up bag is:
a) Filled with only the latest products. You have a clear-out every other week.
b) Bursting with years' old foundations and eye shadows. You're sure that if you keep it all long enough it's bound to come back into fashion.
c) You don't wear make-up. You wouldn't know how to apply it.

You hairstyle is:
a) Cutting edge – you got a fringe the day after Kate Moss showcased hers.
b) Practical – you usually wear it pulled back into a ponytail for work.
c) Unchanged since your school days.

Your wardrobe is:
a) Full of this season's designer labels. You wouldn't be caught dead wearing last year's look.

b) Full of tat from years ago. You're confident gypsy
   skirts will make a massive comeback soon.
c) Full of black. You never wear anything else.

Results

Mostly As: You are bang on trend, but maybe you need to relax a bit. Fashion should be fun, not a chore!

Mostly Bs: Your intentions are good, but you need to work a little harder to be fashion forward. Update your look and you'll get a whole new lease of life!

Mostly Cs: You need a complete makeover. Go straight to our fashion pages for some great tips!

Molly

'I'm sooo excited!' Samantha squeals. 'I can't *wait* to meet David Rendell!'

We're in the foyer of the Sheldon Hotel and Samantha is jumping up and down in her seat and clapping her hands together. If she had her hair in plaits she'd pass for an eight-year old.

I am trying very hard not to be sick. In fact I'm so nervous about seeing David again that trying not to throw up is all I can think about right now. It's not helping that the lobby carpet is possibly the most nauseating I've ever seen. The mixture of mustard and neon-green pure wool swirls is making me feel even worse. Or perhaps it's the red zigzag binding round the edges – yes, that could be it.

'I can certainly see why you went out with him, Molly,' Samantha goes on, caressing the photo of David that sits on the inside cover flap of his book. 'Is he as gorgeous in real life as he looks?'

I glance at the photo of David. It's nice enough, but it doesn't really do him justice. The photographer hasn't quite managed to capture the special twinkle in his eye that I used to love. I've seen much better shots of him. Like the one I took a few months after we first started dating. We'd just made our way through the sand dunes and onto the beach, arm in arm. David hated having his photo taken, but somehow that day I'd managed to persuade him and he finally gave in to me with a laugh and posed beside the water. In the shot he's half turned towards the camera, his gentle lopsided smile playing round his lips, his floppy fringe hanging low in his eyes. It's always been my favourite photo of him. For a very long time after we broke up I carried it carefully folded in my purse. I used to take it out and look at it every night before I went to sleep.

'He really is a ride, isn't he?' Samantha is still talking. 'You're mad to have split up with him!'

Then she seems to remember that I am a newlywed and that maybe talking about ex-boyfriends isn't such a good idea.

'Not that Charlie isn't a ride, mind, he certainly is – he's gorgeous too,' she says with feeling, changing direction. 'You know how to pick 'em, that's for sure!'

She's still bouncing up and down on the velvet upholstered Queen Anne chair. Her voice is an irritating buzzing noise in my ear – one I desperately want to swat away.

No wonder Minty rarely lets her out of the office. I thought she might be a welcome distraction today, but now I'm not so sure. If she doesn't stop talking soon I might have to kill her.

This is all going wrong and David isn't even here yet. For a start, I never should have trusted Samantha to order the cab. I should have known she'd be so enthusiastic that we'd arrive far too early. *And* she talked to the taxi driver all the way here. The poor guy was quite cheerful when we got in, but she beat him down so much with pointless chatter about traffic and weather and reality TV that he looked positively haunted by the time he dropped us off at the hotel entrance. He gave me a tight little smile as I was paying him, one that said 'I feel your pain', and then he sped off far too fast and almost knocked down a little old lady trying to cross Bridge Street. Now we're here and nothing is going as I thought it would.

I'd had it all planned. I'd arrive a little late – not too much, just enough to be cool. Then I'd sweep into the lobby looking radiant and composed and glance around distractedly, as if I couldn't really remember what I was doing here. As if I hadn't spent endless hours obsessing about the moment I'd come face to face with David again. I'd spot him, nod slightly in recognition, smile lazily and wind my way over to him slowly and confidently, moving my hips sensuously from side to side while maintaining eye contact. Samantha would be panting behind me, carrying my bag and looking like my PA.

I had it all worked out beautifully in my mind. I knew the only tricky bit was the lazy smile – that sounds much easier to pull off than it really is. It's very hard to do properly and not end up looking like you've been possessed or have some kind of weird lip twitch. I knew I'd be good at the swaying-hip thing though – the many times I'd practised my walk up the aisle would pay off there.

But the whole scenario hinged on being in control and making a grand entrance in my own good time, not getting there miles early and sitting fretting in the lobby, feeling powerless and trying not to retch on the vile carpet. If I wasn't feeling so ropey I'd kill Samantha with my bare hands.

I dig my compact mirror out of my bag to check how bad I look in this light. Of course, because I'm meeting David and want to be at my glowing best, I look absolutely terrible. My face is a road map of fine lines and wrinkles, and the bags under my eyes could carry enough luggage for a month's holiday. And it might just be the light in the lobby, but my skin has a definite tinge of grey about it.

Why can't I look good, just this once? Not supermodel good, obviously – I'm not delusional. I'd settle for looking like time has stood still since David and I last met, or, even better, that time has moved backwards and now I look like a dewy eighteen-year-old, not a haggard thirty-three-year-old who could use a small facelift.

I move my head from side to side to get a better view of how bad things really are. I piled on the foundation this morning to try to look presentable, but now it's settled into every crease and crevice in my face. It's meant to give a flawless finish – it's *meant* to buff away fine lines and conceal age spots. It's doing none of this. I don't look buff and youthful. I look like a drag queen on a bad day.

There's no way David won't notice the wrinkles. Or the grey skin. Not unless he's developed sight problems. Or cataracts. They can make your vision really cloudy. If he had a few early-onset cataracts, he wouldn't notice a thing. Not that I want to wish cataracts on him, of course – that would be awful – it's just that a bit of impaired vision would be handy right now. Or temporary blindness. Maybe he'll look into the sun on his way over and burn his retina or cornea or whatever it is – that could work. I look out the window. It's drizzling. The chances of him getting accidentally blinded are pretty slim.

'I know exactly what I'm going to ask him.' Samantha is still talking. 'I have it all prepared.'

I try to concentrate. If I engage in some sort of conversation with her it could help me, stop my stomach from rolling around like we're on the ferry to Wales in a gale-force wind and I'm clutching a white paper sick bag like it's my closest friend.

'Sorry?' I force myself to look at her, even though her clear skin and plump cheeks make me feel depressed. I used to have skin like that once. Maybe I should scrap the facelift idea and think about getting collagen injections. Or cheek implants. It probably wouldn't hurt that much. Or some Botox. Al swears by Botox. He hasn't frowned in years and says he's never felt better. Even if his face does sometimes look a little frozen. Maybe that's the price you have to pay. I wonder if we'd get a reduction if we went in together, like two for the price of one?

'What I'm going to ask him.' Samantha patiently repeats herself. 'I've done some research.'

She pulls a sheaf of papers from her bag. She has a blue elastic band tied round the pages, and there are Post-it notes peeping out here and there. I can see that there are lots of handwritten scribbles on the Post its. And question marks. I'm staring at the pages, horrified. Why does she have all this stuff with her?

'You see,' she leans forward to confide in me, 'I've read some of his earlier novels and I noticed quite a few inconsistencies in his plot lines, so I'm going to quiz him about them.'

What on earth is she talking about? Has she gone completely mad?

'What do you mean?' I ask.

'Well, because of my relationship with Steve, I've developed a real insight into the criminal mind. For example, when the murderer in David's *Night, Night Killer* goes on that killing spree, it's definitely his mother's cold attitude towards him that's to blame. But that's not really spelled out in the text – do you know what I mean?'

She shuffles her papers.

Oh God, Samantha has lost it. Exchanging letters with a death-row prisoner has unhinged her completely.

'Listen to me, Samantha.' I have to take her in hand, otherwise David will bolt, we won't get our exclusive and Minty will string us both from the nearest ceiling for fun.

'You are *not* to ask him anything. Seriously, I mean it. You are to take notes. That's all.'

Samantha's face falls.

'But I thought you wanted me to help?'

She looks devastated. I don't have the heart to crush her – and anyway, Minty will probably take care of that later. I'll back-pedal. Just a little. Not so much so that she thinks she can say anything, but just enough so that she doesn't lose all her confidence.

'I *do*,' I say soothingly. 'You *are* being a help already. It's just . . .' I search for something to say. Something that will stop her from sabotaging the entire meeting. Something to stop her talking at all.

'David is sociophobic.'

I have no idea how this has popped into my head.

Her jaw drops.

'Yes . . .' I'm warming to the idea. 'He can't bear being in public. It scares him. He comes out in the most awful rash. All over his body. And . . . he twitches. Really badly. Like he's having a fit.'

'Oh my God. That's terrible.' Samantha's hand flies to her mouth.

'Yes, I know. It's tragic,' I say. 'It affects lots of authors. Writing is such a solitary occupation, they can turn a little . . .' I twist my finger beside my head to let her know what I mean.

'Nuts?' she whispers.

'Exactly,' I say. 'It's horrible.'

'Was he like this when you were, you know, together?'

I pause. If I want to make it sound plausible, I might have to pretend. Otherwise, God knows what she'll say to him.

'Yes,' I say, feeling bad. 'That's why, you know . . .'

162

'That's why you broke up? Oh, that's awful.' Samantha's eyes are filling with tears. She leans across the table and grasps my hand. 'I'm so sorry.'

I'm starting to feel guilty – she's really falling for this. But it's for her own good. There's no way I can let her quiz David about his writing – I have to concentrate on completing the interview and then getting out of here as fast as possible, that's the only way I'll be able to get through it.

Samantha has left her seat and is leaning across the coffee table to hug me. She really needs to work on her boundaries, but maybe now is not the time to bring that up. As she moves to comfort me, her bag tips over and everything falls to the ground. Top of the heap is a massive pair of designer sunglasses, with diamanté encrusting on the sides. Another idea comes to me. If I was wearing a pair of oversized sunglasses maybe David wouldn't notice my haggard face as much. These are so huge they'd cover most of my face.

'Um, can I borrow the sunglasses?' I ask. 'David doesn't like to make eye contact with people – it's part of the condition. It freaks him out when people look him straight in the eye. If I'm wearing these he mightn't feel so uncomfortable.'

'Of course!' she hisses, thrusting them at me. 'Quick, put them on – he's coming.'

My stomach lurches – this is it. He's here. I just have time to shove on the glasses before he's standing in front of me.

'Hi,' he says. His voice is exactly how I remember it. Low and gravelly.

I see his face and all at once I can't speak. But I don't have to, because Samantha leaps to her feet.

'David, I am *so* thrilled to meet you – I'm *such* a fan!' She grabs his hand and pumps it energetically and then immediately leaps away from him. 'Oh gosh, I'm sorry. You probably don't like people touching you, what with your condition and all . . .'

She looks at the floor. I know what she's doing – she's trying not to make eye contact with him because of his sociophobia.

'Touching me? No, that's fine.' David looks confused.

'Oh, that's good. I just thought . . .' Then she remembers that I have told her not to talk and she falls silent.

He's standing before me. Oh my God, he looks amazing. I have to say something. My mouth is completely dry. *I have to say something.*

I struggle to my feet and the glasses slide down my nose.

'Hi, David,' I croak, pushing them back on. 'Nice to, um, see you.'

'Molly.' He nods at me. But he doesn't shake my hand. He doesn't kiss me on the cheek. He doesn't hug me warmly. He hates me – it's written all over his face. And why wouldn't he? I destroyed him.

'Would you, um, like a cup of tea?' I say, praying the glasses won't move again. If they do he'll see how awful I look and I desperately don't want that to happen. Not when he looks so gorgeous.

'Sure,' he nods, and it might be my imagination, but I think he smiles at me. I feel my insides go wobbly.

'OK. Let me take care of it,' I say.

That'll give me time to regain my composure. To give myself a stern talking-to. To try to remember that, even though my husband is missing, I am a married woman and therefore not allowed to have these sorts of feelings for ex-boyfriends. But before I can move, Samantha leaps in front of me.

'Let me!' she volunteers. 'I'll sort that out. Tea for every-one!'

'No, that's OK – I'll go.' I glare at her.

No, no, no, my insides are screaming. Don't be left alone with him. Not good, *not good* to be alone with him.

'Don't be silly.' She slaps me away. 'I'll do it – that's what I'm here for after all, to help!' Then she winks conspiratorially at me. 'Why don't you two … you know, catch up.' Then she's gone.

I will kill her. I will. I will.

I try frantically to think of something to say. Small talk? Should I ask him what he thinks of the awful weather? Traffic? Global warming? Reality TV?

No, stick to the task at hand. Get straight to work – that's safest.

'So …' I rummage in my bag and fish out my jotter and my Dictaphone to play for time. 'I have some interview questions lined up.'

That was good – that sounded very professional. I just have to keep that up and I'll be fine.

'OK.'

He's smiling again. Not as guarded this time – a bit warmer. Which is nice. Very nice. There's that tiny dimple at the side of his mouth. I'd sort of forgotten that. God, that's cute. And I think I can smell the musky scent of his cologne. I close my eyes behind my glasses and breathe it in. That cologne. It's my favourite.

'Molly?'

'Yes?' I gulp. Oh no, he's going to say something. Something deep. I can tell by the way he's looking at me. What if he asks me to explain why I broke up with him? What if he tells me I broke his heart?

'Can I ask you something?'

'Of course.' What if he leans across the table and kisses me? I gulp again. Where did that thought come from? Why on earth would he want to kiss me? Would I want him to?

I'm blinking stupidly at him. Luckily he can't see because of the massive glasses. Thank God I thought to put them on.

'Why are you wearing those glasses?'

'Sorry?'

'The glasses. You're sitting in a hotel lobby wearing sunglasses.'

'Ah, the glasses.'

I've got to think of a good excuse quickly. I can't mention my haggard face, obviously. Perhaps I could say they're a fashion statement. Or that I've become famous since we last met and I need them to fool the paps. My mind is racing.

'Em, I'm photosensitive,' I stutter.

'Photosensitive?' He raises his eyebrows. His gorgeous, bushy eyebrows.

'Yes.' I firmly push the glasses back onto the bridge of my nose – they're so heavy I'm terrified that they'll slip again. 'My eyes are very sensitive to the light – they get red. And bloodshot. And watery. It's horrible.'

'That sounds painful.'

He believes me. I'm so relieved.

'Very painful. I have drops. Special drops. I have to put them in every day . . .'

'That must be annoying.'

'Yes, it is.'

Where the hell is Samantha? Has she gone to China to get the tea?

'You weren't photosensitive before.' He's still staring at me. His eyelashes are so long. I suddenly remember the way they used to droop onto his cheeks when he fell asleep.

'Sorry?' I really wish he'd stop looking at me like that.

'When we were together. You weren't photosensitive then.'

166

'Yes, well, it's something that can develop. Out of the blue.'

'So you just woke up one day and it had happened?'

He leans back in his chair and smiles at me again. There's that tiny chip on his front tooth. I always loved that chip.

'Yes. Exactly.' I look at my jotter. I can't look at him any more.

'And it affects you even when it's raining outside? When it's not even sunny?'

'Yes.'

I have to change the subject. I clear my throat and try to concentrate. I have to start, move on, get out of here, not sit here staring at his mouth. Even if it is mesmerizing.

'So, we'd better start the interview, I suppose – thank you for agreeing to it.'

He shrugs. 'My publicist thinks it will help promote the book. Though I'm not sure how much I trust her judgement.'

He's not smiling any more.

My heart contracts. He's only doing this to promote the book. Not to meet me again. Of course – that makes perfect sense, why would I even think otherwise?

'Right. Well, the theme for this issue is true love.'

'So I hear.' He's still staring at me. I wish he'd stop it, I really do.

'My, um, first question for you is: have you ever been in love?'

I try to hold my pen but my hand is shaking. I click on my Dictaphone quickly. Thank goodness I remembered to bring it so I can record the interview. There's no way I can write like this.

He pauses.

'Yes. Once.' His voice is low, almost a whisper.

I raise my eyes to look at him.

'Have *you*? Ever been in love, that is?' he asks. His face is grim.

I try to say something but I can't. I swallow.

'But how stupid of me to ask you that. Of *course* you know all about love. I hear you got married.'

He's looking pointedly at my ring finger.

'Um, sort of,' I whisper.

'Sort of?' His mouth twists.

I'm going to tell him. I'm going to tell him that everything's a fat mess. That Charlie is gone, that I'm starting to think that my big white wedding was a sham, *that I can't stop thinking about him.* But I can't because he hates me. It's written all over his face. He despises me. I can't say anything.

'Well, congratulations. I hope you'll be very happy together.'

I swallow again. 'Thank you.'

If only he knew the truth. I look at the next question in my jotter and cringe. I have to ask it or Minty will eat me for breakfast.

'Do you believe in soulmates?' I croak.

I already know the answer to this question. I know the answer because he told me often enough that we were soulmates — that we were meant to be together, that the universe had decided that we were a perfect match and that our first meeting in that nightclub was destiny. I used to tease him and say that if destiny had a hand in it, could we not have met somewhere more glamorous, like Paris maybe. My eyes water thinking about it.

His eyes, meanwhile, are like flint.

'Absolutely not.'

'What?' The force of his words hits me like a physical blow.

'The idea that there is one person in the world who's meant for you and you alone is ridiculous. An idiotic notion that the greeting card companies want us to believe. Anyone who believes that is very foolish.'

He's almost snarling. I can feel his hatred for me bounce across the coffee table, and I blush.

Before I can say anything in reply, Samantha is back.

'Here we go!!!' She slams a full tray onto the low table. 'I'm sorry I was soooo long – service in here is really slow! Now, I got coffee and tea so we can have a choice – wasn't that a good idea? And – bonus – there's free biscuits!!!' She beams happily at us both.

'Actually, I have to go.' David stands up abruptly.

'Really?' Samantha's eyes widen. 'Are you finished already?'

'Oh yes, we're finished,' he says, staring pointedly at me. 'We finished a long time ago.'

Samantha glances at me, but I don't say anything. I can't.

'OK, well, we'll contact you to organize a photo shoot to accompany the piece. You could make our cover – wouldn't that be exciting!' Samantha is doing her best to fill the awkward silence and I feel so grateful to her I want to cry.

'I'm sure that will be thrilling.' David's voice is flat. I keep my eyes on the table. 'Call my publicist, she'll arrange it.'

Then, with a tight smile, he strides away, and behind my massive designer sunglasses I feel a tear slide slowly down my cheek.

Julie's Blog

9.01 a.m.

Mr X is working from home again this morning. Tried to wake him up but he just grunted at me, said he had some reports to complete and that he'd see me later. For a split second I felt like suffocating him with my goose-down duvet before I left – the one he'd been hogging again all night. I was nearly tipped over the edge when I discovered he'd cleared my cupboards of all my favourite breakfast cereals. He insists on cooking porridge from scratch for breakfast – which would be OK, but he's already burnt the bottom of my best saucepan. And he's so fastidious about recycling. I know it's all very admirable and good for the environment, but I really don't need to see a ten-point plan of the ways I can improve my carbon footprint tacked to my fridge door first thing. I need a coffee. A very strong coffee. Thank God the janitor sorted the machine out.

9.04 a.m.

UC One has just asked me if she thinks we should throw Mr X a 'little party' for his birthday tomorrow. She wants to 'get some cream cakes' and 'have a singalong'. I had no idea that tomorrow was his birthday, but UC One never forgets the special dates in everyone's lives thanks to her handy desk diary. She is going to conduct an ad hoc straw poll among all other UCs to determine support for the idea before going ahead.

UC One back at desk to confirm that she has taken a straw poll and other UCs think it would be 'fun' to buy cream cakes and spring a birthday surprise on Mr X. I considered telling her the whole thing was a horrendous idea – even worse than the time she organized karaoke in the canteen for the Be Happy At Work Day, but I felt a bit sorry for her so I didn't. I mean, I've already scored the Dick Lit gig and will get lots of glory for that. I should probably let her organize this as a sort of little consolation prize. So I lied and said it all sounded like a nice idea. Then I pretended to be absorbed in writing press releases so she would go away and leave me alone.

10.03 a.m.

Have just received terse email from UC One informing me that all the other UCs have voted me in charge of collecting money to buy the birthday cakes. I can tell UC One is furious she's not in control of the entire charade. She says she will bring the Official Money-Collecting Purse (the one she bought especially for the task and keeps in her 'bits and bobs' drawer) to my desk shortly. Once I have collected all monies, I must return it to her 'promptly' so she can purchase the cakes 'in good time'. Strongly suspect voting was rigged by all other UCs purposely to annoy her – they know she loves to organize everything.

10.08 a.m.

Just received flurry of emails from all other UCs saying that if I'm officially in charge of collecting the money then I may as well be in charge of *buying* the cakes too. UC One looks devastated.

10.11 a.m.

UC Two says that doughnuts and eclairs should be excluded from cake quota due to her wheat allergies. She suggests substituting with rice cakes.

10.16 a.m.

Rest of UCs have suggested that UC Two shoves her rice cakes where the sun don't shine.

10.17 a.m.

Email from UC One to all UCs suggesting that substituting plain rice cakes with chocolate-covered rice cakes could be 'a nice compromise'. She finished her email with three smiley faces and four exclamation marks.

10.22 a.m.

Flurry of emails declaring that everyone should not have to suffer because some people have ridiculous-sounding allergies that probably don't exist. Eclairs and doughnuts back on menu. UC One is looking defeated.

10.37 a.m.

UC One is wondering when I will commence money collection for Mr X's birthday cakes. She fears if I leave it any longer I may collect 'insufficient funds' and be forced to buy 'substandard patisseries'.

10.41 a.m.

Just received email from UC One to 'follow up on our conversation'. She has kindly reminded me that for office birthday celebrations she feels it unwise to 'leave anything to chance', so she usually pre-orders the cakes, 'to ensure that they are of the highest possible quality'. She included the phone number of her favourite baker, along with his website address and directions to his premises. She concluded the email with two smiley faces and three exclamation marks.

11.04 a.m.

Have spent last twenty minutes pleading with co-workers to part with cash for birthday cakes for Mr X. More than one of them suggested he 'pay for his own bloody cakes'. Could sense UC One observing me from her desk, pretending to work but obviously itching to step in and take over.

11.22 a.m.

UC One has sent email to say that if I had a cheerier demeanour I would probably wheedle more money from people. She has included two sample jokes she thinks may help. She also included four smiley faces and five exclamation marks.

12.01 p.m.

Mr X is still not at his desk. Where the hell is he?

12.03 p.m.

UC One has announced that she plans to erect a Happy Birthday banner for Mr X in the kitchenette. She needs her Official Money-Collecting Purse back to collect the extra funds.

12.09 p.m.

There's been a scuffle between UC One and UC Two over the birthday banner for Mr X. UC Two is taking a stand and loudly refusing to hand over any more cash for 'this overblown celebration'. Other UCs are grumbling among themselves and looking restless.

12.48 p.m.

Mr X is still not in. He's probably devising another recycling schedule to drive me mad, and I'm stuck here with a bunch of losers trying to organize birthday cakes for him. Right, that's it, I've had enough. I'm going out tonight.

12.51 p.m.

Email to N and R:

Wanna go clubbing tonight? Cocktails first – my treat!

God, I need a night out.

1.00 p.m.

Bloody photocopier is jammed. Making strange whirring noises like it's going to explode. Does nothing work round here any more? First the coffee machine, now the photocopier – I've a good mind to call the union. If we had a union.

1.01 p.m.

Email to janitor:

Urgent. Photocopier jammed. Needs fixing ASAP.

1.04 p.m.

Email from janitor:

Say 'please'.

Oh, for God's sake.

1.05 p.m.

Email to janitor:

Please.

1.06 p.m.

Email from janitor:

> Will be there ASAP. Have to URGENTLY sort out the sugar
> dispenser in the coffee machine first. People are very fussy about
> their coffee, you know.

1.32 p.m.

Very cute guy tinkering with the photocopier – who's he?
Where's the janitor?

1.39 p.m.

Just heard UC One introducing the cute guy who's tinkering
with the photocopier to UC Two. He is the new janitor …
the new janitor! Apparently he started last week! I haven't been
emailing the old janitor, the one with the skin problems
and the chronic dandruff that used to make me gag, I've
been emailing this new guy … the one with the incredible
shoulders and taut, firm butt!

1.42 p.m.

The new janitor is smirking at me. Crap – he knows I'm the
bitch who was emailing him. Will have to pretend I can't see
him. Will just hide behind these files.

1.51 p.m.

New janitor just left – but before he did, he shouted over
to me that if I want the photocopier to keep working then
people will have to stop messing with the electrics … whatever that means. Pretended I couldn't hear him, but I could
see him laughing as he walked away.

1.54 p.m.
Email from Mr X:

You can mess with my electrics any time.

When did he get back?

1.57 p.m.
Email to Mr X:

Very funny.

1.58 p.m.
Email from Mr X:

Do you know it's my birthday tomorrow?

2.00 p.m.
Email to Mr X:

I might have heard about that.

2.02 p.m.
Email from Mr X:

I'd like to do something special to mark it.

2.03 p.m.
Email to Mr X:

You would?

2.07 p.m.
Email from Mr X:

Yes, I would. I'm taking you out tonight. And I don't care who
sees us.

Oh God. He wants to go public. I'm not sure I'm ready for
this. And what about my girls' night out – it's all arranged

now. But it *is* his birthday tomorrow and he obviously wants to make a gesture – I can't say no, that would probably really upset him. And I guess it *is* sort of exciting. People are going to know about us! We're going to become official. But what if I become a social pariah? What if no one speaks to me ever again? People will think I'm the other woman – which I am, sort of. They might shun me in the street. And the office. God, what will all the UCs say when they find out? Some of them even went to his wedding! I distinctly remember a whip-round for his wedding present – not that I contributed a bean to that.

I think we need to keep it quiet for a bit longer. No one suspects anything right now – what's wrong with keeping it that way? Oh God, I can see him staring at me. I need to reply. Maybe I'll play along for the time being, just until I can think things through properly.

2.09 p.m.
Email to Mr X:
Sounds great.

Will just have to tell N and R that I'll make it up to them – I'm sure they'll understand.

2.11 p.m.
Email to N and R:
Hi gals, sorry but something has come up – I can't make tonight after all. See you both soon.

That's fine – vague but fine. I'm sure they'll be OK with that.

Just got email from *Her*. The interview with Dick Lit went well and now they want to organize a photo shoot as well. Crap – forgot to email Dick Lit and ask him how it went. Will do that quickly.

2.27 p.m.
Email to Mr Dick Lit:

Hi there, how did the interview go with *Her*? Sorry I couldn't go along with you, but I'm just so snowed under here. Anyway, you're such a pro I knew you wouldn't need me! I'm working really hard to persuade *Her* to do some pictures – I think it would definitely add some oomph to the piece, and I bet you photograph really well! They won't commit just yet, but I'm using all the tricks in my book, so fingers crossed!

There. No harm letting him think I'm busting a gut trying to get him publicity. Then when I announce that *Her* want to do a photo shoot he'll be really grateful and think I'm wonderful. A bit sneaky, but I have to maintain the upper hand – it's vital to keep authors on their toes. If they start taking you for granted then things can get very ugly very quickly.

2.48 p.m.
Email from R:

What do you mean you have to cancel tonight? I was really looking forward to it – I even got my hair done at lunchtime. What are you playing at, Julie?

2.51 p.m.
Email from N:

Julie, has this got something to do with Mr X? I'm beginning to wonder if he's worth it.

Wasn't expecting them both to be so annoyed. I'll have to make it up to them soon, but if Mr X wants to tell the world we're together I can't exactly turn him down. He's already left his wife for me, after all – I owe him. But I can't help thinking I would prefer to go out with N and R instead and have a night of pure fun, not worrying about Mr X, his wife or any other drama. When did my life get so complicated?

Open Forum

From Devil Woman: Wow! He's going to tell the world he loves her! Wonder what restaurant they're going to – I'd love to be a fly on that wall!!

From Broken Hearted: This is a very dangerous game you're playing, Julie. You'll end up destroyed, take it from me. I've been there and I have the therapy bills to prove it.

From Hot Stuff: Her friends are starting to lose patience, that's for sure.

From Broken Hearted: She'll have no friends left by the end of this, mark my words.

From Sexy Girl: That janitor sounds GORGEOUS! Tell us more about him, Julie!!

From Hot Stuff: Mr X must love her though. If he wants to go public, isn't that proof?

From Broken Hearted: I can guarantee that the only one he loves is himself. Let's see where he takes her. I bet it'll be some dive in the middle of nowhere – some place there's no chance they'll meet anyone they know.

From Devil Woman: What's he playing at then? Why did he even move in with her?

From Broken Hearted: Who knows how the mind of a man like this works? If I knew that I never would have got involved with my married man to begin with.

From The Plumber: Love is for suckers.

From Broken Hearted: I agree. Are you new, Plumber? I don't remember you.

From The Plumber: Yeah. I'm new. Have a lot of time on my hands and stumbled across this blog.

From Broken Hearted: Well, welcome online.

From Graphic Scenes: Has there been any hot sex yet?

Eve

Dear Charlie,

Anna has given me the details of my next blind date. His name is Butch and he's a prison officer. I have no idea how Anna knows a prison officer called Butch, and I'm afraid to ask. I told her I didn't think we'd be a good match seeing as I can't even watch *Prison Break* without breaking into a cold sweat. But she insisted that Butch was much more my type than Cyril the uptight accountant – she says he's kind, sensitive *and* artistic. I always thought that prison officers would be far too busy locking murderers into their cells at night to have time for the arts, but apparently Butch works in a nice prison for blue-collar criminals – ones who have conned the government out of tax and the like – not violent gangsters. He even runs a flower-arranging class for the inmates on Tuesday nights.

Mary the therapist says I should be optimistically cautious about this new opportunity – whatever that means. I am starting to think that Mary uses buzzwords just for the sake of it. And sometimes I feel I'm not getting my money's worth of good advice. I'm sure she rushed me out of my last session. She said it was because I've made such good progress recently, but I saw her packed weekend case peeping out from behind her chair. She was obviously getting away to her country house for the weekend. The country house that I'm probably single-handedly paying for.

Anyway, I haven't made up my mind what to do about Butch. I told Anna I'll do it, but I may have to come up with

181

an elaborate excuse when the time comes. The humiliating encounter with Cyril is still so fresh in my mind. Plus, if Mum ever found out that I was dating a prison officer she'd have a breakdown. She's still fretting that Mike and Stacey Holby, the religion teacher, have got together on the cultural exchange in Texas. She says Mike sounded very strange on the phone when she spoke to him last – like he was being held against his will. I told her that was ridiculous and that Mike was well able to handle himself, but she says she's not so sure and that heatwaves can do strange things to people. She's already ordered him an industrial-strength air-conditioning fan online to help him keep a cool head. She says those hand-held fans are useless and how could he be held accountable for his actions if he was relying on one of those in killer Texan heat.

In other news, Homer is a really fast worker. He's almost finished the undercoat on every wall already. I was worried he'd distract me from my writing by demanding fresh mugs of builder's tea every five minutes or prancing about with half his bum hanging out of his trousers like the labourers you see on building sites, but in fact he was so quiet I almost forgot he was in the flat at all. We barely spoke until the mid-afternoon, when I felt so guilty for not making him tea even once that I insisted he take a break. Turns out he only drinks herbal teas; orange pekoe is his favourite. He'd even brought his own tea bags with him, and he persuaded me to try one. It was really strange, but as we sat at the kitchen table I somehow ended up telling him all about Butch – that prison officer. He's a very good listener. Once I'd told him the entire story he said that maybe I should go on the blind date, that people can have unexpected hidden depths and that you should never judge a book by its cover. In spite of Butch's name, occupation and appearance (Anna showed me a picture of him on her mobile phone and it wasn't pretty), he might be extremely sensitive and caring. I'm not too sure about that though. The tattoo on Butch's knuckles certainly says otherwise – it spells HATE in big Celtic print.

After Homer left I took the rubbish out and bumped into Johnny the plumber. He was just standing by the bins staring vacantly into space. I'm getting a bit worried about him: he still looks dreadful and he didn't even try to make one wisecrack about my cleavage or my bum or anything. I was really shocked by his appearance. He was wearing an unironed shirt and had days-old stubble – and not the kind he sometimes cultivates to try to look more like Enrique Iglesias. It's the first time I've ever seen him looking like he hadn't just showered. Even when he's working he usually looks pristine – those specially made canvas overalls with the brass studs on the lapels are really smart. And I could have sworn he'd been crying: his eyes were all bloodshot and red-rimmed. He looked so downhearted that I asked him if he'd like to come in for a chat, and he did. Turns out I was right: he *is* suffering from a broken heart. His girl-friend left him for another man – a chippie called Tiny Tim who has the smallest willy in the business. I asked him how he knew (about the tiny willy, that is), and he said it was common knowledge on the building sites. Poor Johnny just can't understand how a woman could leave a man of his sexual prowess and expertise for someone like Tiny Tim, who everyone knows hasn't had a woman in over three years. At least that's what I think he said. He was sobbing so hard at that stage it was really tricky to make out anything. I told him that life can be very unexpected and that I should know – I'd been through a lot of heartbreak myself. He seemed comforted by that, and he perked up a bit when I told him how devastated I'd been when *you* left *me*. I even told him the real reason we broke up, but I didn't say anything about being devastated all over again when I found out that you'd got married – there was no point sending him over the edge. Instead, I suggested that he spruce himself up, go out on the pull and find himself a one-night stand. But he just sighed and said he wasn't ready to put himself out there all over again. He said he didn't really care that all the other lads were slagging him about Tiny Tim, he didn't care that his ex had humiliated him by leaving him for a man with the smallest willy in the industry, he just wanted her back. He said he's never felt like this about a girl before, that it wasn't just the sex he missed since she was gone: he missed everything about her, even the way she used his razor on her legs and never cleaned the bath out. It was a revelation. Johnny the plumber isn't just a sex-mad Lothario, he has real feelings, despite what I always thought about him. In my head he was a tough nut, but really he's super-sensitive, just like me. It really made me think about what Homer had said. Maybe I do judge a book by its cover; maybe I should give Butch a chance. You never know, we could be soulmates. I could even end up with a LOVE tattoo on my knuckles to match his HATE one, although I hear having a tattoo is incredibly painful. Maybe I could use a washable ink stencil instead.

Eve

Are You a Tough Nut or Super-sensitive?

Do you take life's knocks on the chin or do you cry at the drop of a hat? Take our test and find out!

You find out that your friends have organized a weekend away – and you haven't been invited. Do you:
a) Lock yourself in your room and cry all weekend. How could they betray you like that?
b) Give them the benefit of the doubt. There must be a reasonable explanation, all you have to do is ask them what it is.
c) Plot your revenge. No one disrespects you like that and gets away with it.

Your boyfriend confesses that he thinks your new jeans may not be all that flattering. Do you:
a) Lock yourself in the bathroom and refuse to come out for hours. You'll never forgive him for insulting you.
b) Thank him – you appreciate his honesty. Now you can return the jeans and get a refund.
c) Tell him he's put on a few pounds and start calling him fatty. That'll teach him to be so free with his opinions in the future.

Your favourite movies are:
a) Romcoms: you love feel-good films that make you laugh, cry and forget all about the real world.
b) Documentaries or indie flicks: you like to keep informed of current events.
c) Thrillers and horror flicks, the gorier the better.

The last time you cried was:
a) This morning – when you couldn't find your hairbrush.
b) Last year – when you didn't get the work promotion that you worked so hard for.
c) You can't remember: crying is for losers.

Results

Mostly As: You're a big softie. Perhaps you'd find it easier to cope with the world if you toughened up a little.

Mostly Bs: You have a pragmatic approach to life, but you're not afraid to let yourself go every so often – nice work!

Mostly Cs: You're a tough chick who never lets her barriers down. You need to develop your softer side – it's not a sign of weakness.

Molly

'Are you sure you don't mind helping me with this?' Lee says, beaming her megawatt, melt-chocolate-in-an-instant smile at us. 'It's not exactly what you signed up for!'

Samantha and I are in a city-centre bookshop with Lee Merkel – publicist for chick-lit queen Carla Ryan – as part of our 'Day in the Life' feature for the magazine.

'Of course not!' Samantha chirps, enthusiastically hauling some more of Carla's books from boxes and dusting them down.

I grimace. She'd be just about bearable if she wasn't so cheerful all the time.

'We're happy to help,' I say, trying not to show my teeth too much when I smile. I really have to look into getting them whitened. Lee's teeth almost glow they are so perfectly snowy, and being in her company is making me very conscious of how badly stained mine have become from too much coffee and red wine.

Maybe if I had teeth like Lee's then Charlie wouldn't have left me. The thought pops into my head unannounced. Maybe if I flossed every day and used whitening toothpaste he'd still be at home and we'd still be happy. Maybe it's not just my teeth that are the problem. Maybe I have halitosis as well. Maybe my breath reeks and no one has ever told me.

I try to remember if people have been gagging in my company, or avoiding me altogether. Then I discreetly cover my mouth with my hand, give a little cough and sniff. I can't smell anything, but that means nothing. People with bad breath never know it. Not until someone plucks up the courage to tell them, that is.

We're here for a Carla Ryan readers' event. She's due to read an extract from her new book and then sign copies for the legions of fans who are already queuing up outside the shop doors to meet their heroine in the flesh. Carla hasn't done an event like this in a few years, so the excitement is fever pitch. Technically, like Lee says, Samantha and I don't have to help: we just have to take notes for the magazine feature on how fabulous Carla is and how fame and wealth haven't changed her one iota, etc., etc. But Lee is on her own and, by lending a hand, I'm hoping we'll earn *Her* lots of brownie points and she'll give us exclusive access to more of her writers. She's got the best author list in town. All we have to do is unpack books and stack them neatly beside a desk where Carla will sit to sign them. It's quite therapeutic. And the added bonus is that it's keeping me busy. Which means I can't think about Charlie and the fact that, even though it's almost his birthday, he still hasn't contacted me. I have no idea who he's with or how he's going to mark the day and that really unsettles me. But helping Lee means I don't have time to dwell on it. It also means I can't think about David, that awful interview or the fact that he now seems to hate me with every ounce of feeling in his body. Working hard like this means my mind is fully occupied. Well, most of the time. Except for when I'm worrying about my yellowing teeth, receding gums and halitosis.

'What's Carla's new book about?' Samantha asks Lee, holding Carla's new bonkbuster, *Second Chance at Love*, aloft.

'Oh, you know, the usual – lots of drama and steamy sex. The same old formula.'

Lee winces as she hauls more books from boxes. There

are masses of Carla's fans waiting outside to meet her and get their hands on a signed copy, and we have to make sure there are enough novels here for all of them.

I turn the book over and read the blurb:

Riley Hunt and Morgan Marshall were lovers until fate tore them apart and separated them for ever. Broken-hearted, Riley vows never to love again. But then dangerous Michael Cox comes into her life. Can Riley finally find happiness and forget Morgan?

'Do you like Carla?' I ask, examining the cover and wondering why all women's novels look exactly the same. There was definitely something in Lee's tone that makes me wonder if she's a Carla fan.

'Sure, of course I do,' she says carefully. 'I mean, she's a best-seller; Embassy Publishing makes a fortune from her sales. But, strictly off the record of course, sometimes I think her storylines are a little far-fetched. I mean, all the happy-ever-after stuff – who believes in that any more? I just don't get why women fall for all that romantic schmaltz. It's so unrealistic.'

Lee sounds exactly like Penny in the *Her* office.

'Well, her fans love her,' I say with a smile.

'Yeah, her readers love her, that's for sure. I guess maybe deep down we're all suckers for romance. Women certainly lap up her stories. If we could get her to agree to a ghost-writer we'd really be in the money. They gobble up the books faster than she can write them.'

'I don't know much about her,' Samantha says, piling some books on the floor beside the signing desk. 'She's very mysterious, isn't she?'

'Yeah, that's all part of her persona. She likes to retain an air of mystery about herself.' Lee rolls her eyes. 'High maintenance is her middle name. She doesn't usually do interviews – you guys are lucky she agreed to this. Ever since that ex-PA of hers dished the dirt to the tabloids a few years ago, she's been paranoid about the press.'

'I know,' I say, patting myself silently on the back, 'Charlie says she almost never does media.'

The words are out of my mouth before I realize it. What made me say that? What made me bring up my missing husband? I want to kick myself. I hope Lee doesn't ask about him.

'Who's Charlie?' Lee says, right on cue.

'Charlie is Molly's gorgeous husband.' Samantha nudges me playfully. 'Molly's a newlywed, which just goes to prove that romance *is* alive and kicking, right?'

'That's right,' I say, willing the ground to open up and swallow me whole.

'And does your husband know Carla?' Lee asks.

'Um, I think he met her once. He works in the industry,' I mumble, hoping I can change the subject fast. I don't want anyone quizzing me about Charlie right now.

'Hang on . . . you don't mean Charlie Adler, do you?' Lee asks. 'I *heard* he got married recently.'

'That's him,' I say, trying my best to smile brightly.

'Wow . . . well, congratulations.'

I think I see a strange expression flicker briefly across Lee's face, but I'm not sure why.

What if she's heard that Charlie has left me? What if she knows all about it? They're both publicists for the book trade, it's not beyond the realm of possibility. What if the entire industry knows about us? I would die. I can feel my cheeks starting to burn.

'So what did Charlie think of her?' Samantha asks. 'Carla Ryan?'

Lee and Samantha both look expectantly at me.

'I can't really remember,' I say vaguely, thinking I'll crown Samantha with Carla's new book if she mentions Charlie's name again. I'm sure my embarrassment is written all over my face. 'I think he said she was very guarded – didn't give away too much about herself.'

'Yeah, that sounds about right,' Lee says. 'Still, it's all part of the mystique, I suppose. And with her looks, keeping her face out of the press suits us perfectly. Not that she knows that, of course.'

Samantha nearly falls over a stack of books to hear what Lee says next.

'What do you mean?' she asks.

'Well' Lee looks over her shoulder and whispers, even though there's only the three of us here – 'I probably shouldn't say this, but haven't you ever noticed that there's never a photo of her on the jacket covers of her books?'

'You're right!' Samantha says, flipping the book round in her hands and searching it for an author photo.

'There's a simple reason for that.' Lee leans in. 'She's not exactly a stunner.'

'Really?' Samantha says. 'I never thought about that before. I always presumed she was a glamorous sex kitten, just like the heroines in her books.'

'Far from it. She may write about exquisitely beautiful women, but she's actually very plain. That's why we're happy to play along with her obsession about privacy. As far as she knows we're respecting her boundaries, but the truth is that this strategy works for us. Over-exposure of her face could spoil the public's demand for her novels. It could really damage sales.'

I always knew that young, good-looking authors were promoted more by publishers, but now that Lee has admitted it

I realize how depressing it all is. Carla may be the queen of chick lit but she'll never be a cover girl. It's really very unfair.

'Poor Carla,' Samantha says, her face troubled.

'Yeah. The public wants to think she's a sexpot who writes in a negligee,' Lee goes on. 'Really she's a middle-aged woman with a lip that needs some serious waxing.'

'And if her fans knew that, they wouldn't buy into the whole sexy image?' Samantha asks.

'That's right,' Lee admits. 'This industry is just smoke and mirrors. So far, the fact that she's wanted to keep her private life private has worked well for us. But now she's decided she wants more publicity.'

'Is that why she's agreed to do this feature with *Her*?' I ask.

'Yes. It's also why she wants to do this readers' event today. Her arch-rival Noreen Brady beat her on sales last year. Carla has realized it's because Noreen gets far more press coverage, and she's gunning for her. Off the record of course.' Lee sighs.

I think about Noreen Brady. She's another female author writing in the same genre, except Noreen is a platinum blonde with ample assets that she likes to show off – which doesn't do her profile any harm, that's for sure. No wonder Carla has decided to up the ante on the publicity stakes. A brewing catfight between two of the top chick-lit writers in the country sounds intriguing – that would be a major scoop. Maybe I could persuade Lee to tell me more. Minty would love this sort of angle for the magazine article.

'Are you sure you can carry those boxes, Molly?' Lee asks.

'No problem.' I heave another box across the room and start emptying the books onto the table.

'That's great. I'm sorry there's so many, but there are already hundreds of fans here.' She sighs heavily again.

'Are you OK?' I ask, hauling some books over to the desk, where I start to arrange them artistically in stacks on the floor.

'Sure. It's just that these readers' events can get a bit tiresome after a while. Still, at least we know loads of people will turn up. I've been to ones where no one comes at all.'

'Really?' I'm horrified. 'How awful.'

'Oh yeah, it's the pits. It can really crush a writer's confidence.'

I try to imagine what it would feel like to have no one turn up to hear you read from your new book. It must be soul destroying. Sitting at a desk, twiddling your thumbs and watching people pass by would be so humiliating.

'So, what time is Carla going to arrive?' I say.

'Any minute, so we'd better get cracking.' Lee smiles at me and I vow to do a really great job for her. I whiz around making sure there's a variety of pens for Carla to use, and filling the jug on the table with iced water in case she flags a bit. I'm wondering if I should get a few snacks to perk her up in case she's hungry when she gets here – an energy bar maybe, or some nuts. But before I can decide what to do, Samantha squeals.

'She's coming!'

Seconds later a tiny woman with a large pashmina wrapped tightly round her sweeps into the room. Lee was right. She's no oil painting. She has fleshy bags under her eyes and a definite hint of a moustache across her lip. There's even more hair sprouting from a large mole on her left cheek. She's also wearing a strange-looking head turban made of multicoloured polyester material with a large brooch pinned to the front. It's the strangest thing ... although it could come in handy if you were having a bad hair day. Maybe I should ask her where I could get one.

'Carla, darling,' Lee coos, air-kissing her, 'you look *gorgeous*.'

Lee is lying through her teeth. There is no way on earth that this woman could be described as gorgeous. I'm not sure she could be described as remotely attractive, even in the best light. She is plain, with a capital P.

'Hi, Lee,' Carla says, patting her very weird turban. 'God, now I remember how much I hate this shit. Why did I ever agree to do it?'

'Don't worry,' Lee says soothingly. 'It'll only take a little while, I promise.'

I gulp. This is a huge lie. The queue of women (and at least one man) waiting to listen to Carla read and then have their books autographed is now snaking from the shop door down the street. She's going to be here for *hours*.

'And you know how much readers love their signed copies.' Lee is still talking. 'It's great for sales.'

Carla curls her lip. 'Readers! Always wanting more, more, more. They never leave me alone – writing to me, emailing me, wanting to meet me.' She's ranting. 'I should have stayed at home!'

'Carla, this is Molly.'

Lee takes me by the arm and shoves me in front of Carla, obviously as a distraction. 'She's from *Her* magazine. She's been helping me set up here. I think you'll be thrilled with how it all looks.'

'Hi there.' I grin nervously. 'It's lovely to meet you.'

'*Her*, did you say?' Carla eyes me from head to toe and then offers me her hand to shake.

'That's right – *Her* magazine,' I confirm. 'We're absolutely thrilled you've agreed to let us be here today.'

I'm gushing, I know I'm gushing. But I think the situation

calls for a little brown-nosing: Lee did say she was high maintenance.

'Hmm . . .' Carla narrows her eyes. 'So long as you don't misrepresent what I'm about. I know you media types. You'll dig anywhere for a story, preferably an untrue one.'

I can see Lee out of the corner of my eye. She's wringing her hands anxiously.

This isn't good. If Carla thinks we're not going to give her a glowing write-up she might pull out of the feature altogether, and that would be a disaster.

'Have you read my books?' she asks now, her eyes boring into mine.

'Of course!' I lie. 'I'm a *huge* fan.'

'Really?' Carla arches an eyebrow at me. 'How nice. Which was your favourite?'

'My favourite?' I bluff.

I suddenly wish Samantha would say something. Why has she chosen this particular moment to be dumbstruck? She's standing beside me, staring silently at Carla's turban, her mouth slightly open.

'Yes. Your favourite book. Of mine.'

Carla's smiling tightly at me, her turban thing swaying gently from side to side as she does.

Oh dear God. What am I going to say? I have no idea what any of her books are called, except for the latest one.

'Let me think . . .' I'm playing for time, pretending that I'm considering her entire back catalogue of work before I pick the winner. 'There are so many great ones to choose from.'

I look at Lee, willing her to understand that I'm bluffing and that she needs to step in and save the day. But Lee just smiles encouragingly. Now I'm going to look like a complete idiot in front of her as well. She'll never let me tag along with her again if I insult one of her top authors.

'I would have to say' – I look at the posters of Carla's new novel pinned all over the walls and decide that it's my only option – '*Second Chance at Love*. It's just great.'

'Oh, you've read it already?' Carla frowns. 'That was quick. Which character did you like best?'

I'm starting to sweat. At least Lee has dragged Samantha away to tell the store manager that we're ready to start, so she's not going to witness me make a complete fool of myself.

'Um, the male character was fascinating,' I say. 'Would you like a drink of water? Maybe a fruit bar?'

But there's no distracting her.

'Do you mean Michael?' Carla frowns at me.

'Yes, *Michael*.' I'm so thrilled to have a name to play with that I pounce on it with glee. 'He was *fabulous*.'

'A violent alcoholic was *fabulous*?' Carla's eyes narrow.

'Well, yes.' How the hell did I get myself into this? 'But he had redeemable qualities, don't you think?'

She's quiet for a moment, obviously processing this information. Then she leans towards me. This is it. She's going to tell me to get out, that the feature is off, that she never wants to see me again, that she's calling Minty to tell her to fire me. I hold my breath.

'You know what? You're the first person I've spoken to who really *gets* Michael. I mean, yes, he's violent, but only because his own father was violent towards him. You've seen the inner Michael, the Michael I'm hoping my readers will be able to empathize with.' She smiles at me again and I exhale.

'Well … that's great!' I do a little thumbs-up sign to let her know how delighted I am.

'What about Morgan?'

'Morgan?'

'Yes, Morgan. What did you think of him?'

'Morgan was amazing. He was so' – I search for what I think would be a good word to describe a Carla Ryan hero – 'manly.'

Carla smiles. 'That's the perfect word for him. Manly. Did you really believe that he and Riley were meant to be together?'

'Absolutely!' I say, getting into the spirit of things. 'It's obvious that they're soulmates!'

'You're right. They're destined to be together, no matter what.' She nods approvingly at me. 'Have *you* met your soulmate?'

The room is suddenly still.

'Yes, yes, I have,' I say quietly, and I know I mean it.

'Yes, I thought so. I can tell these things about people.'

She smiles at me again and I start to think that maybe she's not that plain after all. There's something about her face that is suddenly quite beautiful, if you ignore the moustache.

'Would you like something to nibble on before you start?' I say, trying to change the subject. 'I can pop to the shop and get you something.'

I'm hoping she'll say yes and I can escape, because now I desperately want to. Talking about soulmates has made me feel very uncomfortable.

'That's very sweet.' She smiles again and the hair on her upper lip winks at me. 'But I'm not that hungry. I had a treat in bed earlier and I have to say . . . it was very satisfying. Do you know what I mean?'

She raises one eyebrow at me and I realize she's not saying that she had a ciabatta roll and a fruit smoothie under the covers.

I smile nervously back. I hope she's not going to start confiding details of her sex life. That would be deeply embarrassing.

But before I get a chance to reply, I hear a sort of chanting noise.

'What's that?' I say, mostly to myself.

'The fans,' Lee says. She's back again, Samantha by her side.

Carla raises her eyes to heaven. 'They like to sing songs that I've mentioned in the book. It's just another reason why I don't usually do this stuff.'

It's true: there is the unmistakable sound of dozens of women singing 'Love on the Rocks' by Neil Diamond.

'God, those women should get a life,' Carla sighs.

Then she adjusts the turban thing, stalks to the signing table, picks up a pen, pastes a fixed smile on to her face and nods at Lee to open the door.

Four hours later I'm on the way home, exhausted. I've been jostled, bribed and propositioned by so many women desperate to meet their idol that I'm completely wiped out. I even had to break up a scuffle when one woman accused another of trying to skip the queue. And there was almost full-scale war when one fan managed to have two photos taken with Carla.

Carla had kept her steely smile intact for the camera, but her eyes had glittered dangerously as the flash popped.

'Only one photo per fan,' Lee hissed at me. 'She'll freak if that happens again. Will you tell everyone else?'

I looked at the fans, all swaying in time to 'Love on the Rocks', which they were still singing. They looked like a well-behaved bunch: I was sure they'd understand that Carla had only so much time to speak to each of them.

I clapped my hands to get their attention and, when that didn't work, I jumped up and down and waved my arms in the air. Unfortunately, one fan thought I was merely getting into the spirit of things.

'A Mexican wave, let's do a Mexican wave!' she yelled, and before I knew what was happening, a hundred chick-lit fans were waving their arms up and down and stamping their feet.

'No, no!!' I yelled. 'I have to tell you: only one photo per person.'

But no one heard me: they were all too busy dancing wildly and chanting Carla's name. So, I did the only thing I could think of. I wolf-whistled. I've always been a good wolf-whistler; it's one of my party pieces. Al reckons I could pierce an eardrum if I really wanted to.

'Listen,' I said, once I'd got their attention. 'Carla can't wait to meet each and every one of you' – that was a lie, but they didn't need to know that – 'however, you can only have one photo taken with her, OK? Please don't ask for more as refusal might offend.'

I threw that little quip in for good measure. There's nothing like a bit of banter to defuse an awkward situation.

'Listen, chicken,' a middle-aged woman in a Carla look-alike turban at the top of the queue almost spat at me, 'I've been waiting *hours* to meet Carla. I've bought all her books *and* her audio tapes. If I want two photos then I'm getting two photos.'

'I'm sorry,' I said as passively as I could, 'but it's policy. Carla is really pressed for time so there's only one photo per person.'

'Listen, chicken,' she roared, 'I'm getting as many bleedin' photos as I want – do you HEAR me?'

'Hey, calm down!' the one male fan in the line said. 'That's no way to behave.'

I smiled nervously at him, taking in the HATE tattoo on his knuckles. Maybe he'd rescue me if things got really ugly.

'Get lost, fat boy!' the savage fan snarled. 'You can't tell me what to do.'

Right then, Samantha appeared, her face thunderous.

'Listen, CHICKEN!' she bellowed, shoving her nose close to the fan's face. 'There is one photo per customer. Take it or leave it.'

The crowd gasped. If this didn't work, there was going to be a stampede.

'OK, OK.' The savage fan shrugged her shoulders. 'If you're going to be funny about it. It's only a friggin' photograph.'

Then she broke into another verse of 'Love on the Rocks', everyone started the Mexican wave again and the entire episode was forgotten, just like that.

'These chick-litters need taking in hand. Too much romance can affect the mind,' Samantha said, rubbing her hands together like a nightclub bouncer who'd just chucked a troublemaker out on the street. 'It's mob mentality. That's how it works on the inside as well – Steve explained it all to me, the pet. When things get out of hand you have to know how to handle yourself or you're mincemeat.'

I nodded mutely at her, suddenly glad she was writing to a death-row prisoner. She certainly knew how to take care of things when the going got tough.

Now I'm almost home and all I want to do is run a steaming bath and fall into bed. I can already imagine what the hot water is going to feel like against my aching limbs. I know sleep will come easily tonight.

I struggle through the front door and dump my things on the floor, not caring that half the contents of my tote spill across the tiles, including the powder compact from my make-up bag. And then I spot it.

There's a white envelope sitting on the doormat, with my name printed neatly across the front in black ink. I recognize the handwriting immediately. There's no mistaking it. It's Charlie's. My runaway husband has written me another letter.

Julie's Blog

Am furious. Turns out that Mr X's idea of taking me out to dinner and going public involved driving for over an hour to a restaurant in the middle of nowhere. At the beginning I was quite pleased. I wasn't sure I even wanted everyone to know about us yet, so I was glad to be going somewhere a bit out of the way. But then it occurred to me: if Mr X was taking me to eat miles away from anywhere, what did that mean? And suddenly it came to me. It meant he was lying. He didn't *really* want anyone to know about us, he had just said that because he thought that was what I wanted to hear. I started to get madder and madder. As far as he knew I wanted to go public – I hadn't told him any different. So I asked him if he was trying to hide me away. He said of course not – he had just heard that this particular Thai restaurant did the best green curry ever and he was desperate to taste it. I didn't believe him for a second, and I told him so. In fact I called him a big fat liar. He said that was a highly insulting accusation and we had a huge row. He yelled he'd already left his wife for me and what did I expect, it wasn't going to be all roses in the garden – going to a Thai in the middle of nowhere had to be better than eating crappy takeout in my minuscule flat. Then I shouted back that I hadn't *asked* him to leave his wife – which is true – and that maybe he should have thought to consult me before he landed on my doorstep because I'd had plenty of room in my *minuscule* flat before he moved in. Then *he* said I was ungrateful and manipulative and this was the worst birthday he'd ever had; *I* said he was arrogant and selfish and that technically it wasn't even his birthday yet; and we drove all the way back home without eating anything and he stormed off. Now I have no idea where he is, and quite frankly I don't care.

11.01 p.m.
He's not back yet and he hasn't even texted to say where he is, which is so childish it makes me want to scream.

11.34 p.m.
Still no sign of him. Have a good mind to go out clubbing, just to annoy him, because if he thinks I'm going to sit here and wait for him like some ... some obedient WIFE, then he is badly mistaken.

11.56 p.m.
That's it. I'm off. He can sleep on the path for all I care.

Open Forum

From Broken Hearted: See? I told you so. Heartache.

From The Plumber: Hey, Broken Hearted – you're up late. Wow, I wasn't expecting that little development!

From Broken Hearted: Hi, Plumber. So you read all the previous entries then?

From The Plumber: Yeah, like I said before, I have time on my hands. I thought things were going quite well between them though?

From Broken Hearted: Things aren't always what they seem. How come you're up so late?

From The Plumber: Just listening to some AC/DC. It always makes me feel better.

From Broken Hearted: I love AC/DC!! Why do you need to feel better though? Did something happen?

From The Plumber: Yeah, my girlfriend dumped me for some loser, that's why I have so much time on my hands these days.

From Broken Hearted: I feel your pain. Love sucks.

From The Plumber: Ain't that the truth.

From Broken Hearted: Hey, are you a real plumber?

From The Plumber: Yeah, I am. Why?

From Broken Hearted: I have this leak in my bathroom. Do you think you could help?

From The Plumber: Sure, no problem. Here's my phone number – give me a call.

Eve

Dear Charlie,

I went on my blind date with Butch the prison officer
tonight. I thought about everything Homer had said and
I realized he was right: people aren't necessarily defined by
their looks. For example, I'd thought that just because
Homer himself was a painter and decorator he'd be loud
and vulgar, but he's not like that at all. In fact he's a very
peaceful sort of person to have around. He likes to listen to
classical music on his iPod while he's painting. Sometimes
I can even hear him humming softly along to Vivaldi from
my office as I work; it's a very comforting sound. I think he
may be the most courteous person I've ever met — he's
almost old-fashioned, he's got such good manners. I'm sure
he gave a little bow yesterday when I walked by him to get to
the bathroom. We've taken to meeting in the kitchen every
day at three for a hot drink. We just drift in there around
that time and chat. He's even converted me to his herbal
teas. Yesterday he brought some chamomile bags with him
— I'd told him I wasn't a great sleeper and he said they might
help. I tried a cup just before bedtime, and you know what,
he was right — I'm sure it did. He even gave me good advice
about what to wear to meet Butch. He said he'd noticed
that the blue top I'd worn a few days before had really
brought out the colour of my eyes and that even if Butch
was a hardened prison officer he wouldn't be able to resist
me. I couldn't be sure, but I think he was a little embarrassed after he said that; he went a bit pink and then he

rushed back to his painting before he'd even half finished his drink. See? A total gentleman.

Anyway, Butch and I agreed to meet in an organic juice bar in town. I thought it was a slightly strange choice for a prison officer, but I didn't argue, not even when he texted to say he'd wear a pink carnation in his buttonhole so I would know who he was. I didn't like to tell him that this probably wouldn't be necessary, that I was sure he'd be the only person in an organic juice bar with a HATE tattoo on his knuckles.

I got there bang on time. I didn't want to take any chances after the last disaster, and I was afraid that a prison officer might be even more of a stickler for time than an accountant. Who knew what he might do if I was late? He might escort me off the premises in handcuffs or threaten to throw me in solitary confinement.

I saw him the second I walked in: he was perched on a stool at the counter, a massive pink carnation in his lapel, his HATE tattoo clearly visible. He was reading a thriller called *Night, Night Killer*, one of those David Rendell ones, and slowly sipping on a wheatgrass shot. He looked even scarier in person than he had on Anna's mobile phone: his head had been newly shaved and his muscles were practically popping out from underneath his skintight T-shirt. I almost turned round and walked back out again, but then I remembered what Homer had said about not judging a book by its cover so I took a deep breath and made my way over to him. As I got closer I could see that he wasn't nearly half as scary close up as he had been from a distance. When he saw me he started to smile widely, and then sprang from his chair to say hello. My spirits lifted – he was friendly at least. But it was right at the moment when he stood up that it happened: his book fell to the floor and the jacket slipped off to reveal what was really underneath. There, in gold swirly lettering, was Carla Ryan's new novel, *Second Chance at Love*. He hadn't been reading David Rendell's thriller at all; he'd been reading the queen of chick lit's new romance. For a minute I didn't know what to say. Why would a prison officer called Butch be reading a Carla Ryan book? There was something seriously wrong with this scenario. He tried to cover up by saying that his sister had swapped them as a joke, but halfway through his explanation he suddenly stopped, took a deep breath and said he had something important to tell me before we went any further. I braced myself. After Cyril the accountant telling me he couldn't go on a date with a person who wasn't punctual, I didn't know what to expect. Then Butch told me the truth. He's a huge Carla Ryan fan. Such a huge Carla Ryan fan that he queued for nearly four hours to get a signed copy of her new book at a readers' event. He'd even had his photo taken with her: he took it out of his wallet to show me; he'd had it laminated especially. Apparently his prison experience nearly came in handy when he thought he was going to have to break up a fight while he was there. Some of the fans wanted more than one photo with Carla and that caused ructions. He says the really fanatical chick-litters can get quite aggressive if you cross them. Butch even wrote to Carla last year. The personal reply she sent him is his most prized possession. He's had *that* laminated too. It's pinned to his bedroom wall at home.

It felt a bit strange to be talking to a man about romance novels, but then I decided not to judge, just like Homer had said. After all, I was having quite a nice evening in spite of myself. The organic wheatgrass wasn't too vile if you held your breath while you drank it, and it was fascinating listening to Butch describe his work in jail. He really does teach a flower-arranging class to inmates on a Tuesday night. They're even holding a floral exhibition in the jail's dining hall in a few weeks. All in all, it was turning out to be quite a pleasant date. In fact, it was going so well that Butch suggested prolonging it by visiting a trendy bar I'd never heard of for a real drink. I hadn't been to a bar for years and didn't really want to go, but by then I was almost gagging on the wheatgrass and I kept hearing Mary the therapist's voice telling me to 'try new things, try new things'. So I decided to grab the bull by the horns and embrace the experience. After all, Butch had spent a fortune on wheatgrass shots for me – I owed him something.

There was a huge queue outside the door when we got there, and I have to admit I was secretly relieved when it looked like we weren't going to get in. But then Butch bumped into his friend Al. Turns out that Al knows everyone who's anyone and he was on the list, so we just swanned straight past the hordes lining up outside. We were ushered into the VIP lounge where there were velvet couches and even a dance area. The music was pumping, the crowd was buzzing and I felt like a real VIP – it was brilliant. But we'd just got a drink when Butch and Al hit the floor and started bumping and grinding against each other to 'Lady Marmalade' in a way that I thought was unusual for two straight men. And then, before I knew what was happening, they were French-kissing under the strobe lights. I was really shocked. I mean, I knew things had moved on since I'd last been to a trendy city-centre bar, but surely it was strange for two straight men to snog? And they weren't the only ones. Loads of other men were at it too. In fact, the club seemed to be filled with men. As far as I could see, there were only three other women there, and they were drunkenly licking salt off some guy's chest before slamming tequilas and then falling about laughing hysterically. It slowly began to dawn on me. I was in a gay bar. Butch the prison officer was gay. Why he had even agreed to go on a date with me in the first place was beyond me – I was the wrong sex for a start. He'd told me the truth about his Carla Ryan infatuation, but he'd still kept the biggest secret to himself. It would have been almost funny if it hadn't been so tragic. I didn't bother confronting Butch, there was no point, he was still locked in Al's arms, so I left them to it, crept out without saying goodbye and flagged down a taxi to go home. I wanted to crawl under a rock ... which of course is why I managed to hail the chattiest cabbie in history, who wanted to tell me all about the joys of a perfect marriage and how he was taking his wife to Marbella for their ten-year anniversary. By the time I stuck my key in the lock I was thoroughly depressed and vowing never to go out again.

Then, when I swung open the door, I heard a rustling sound. Someone was there. I was being broken into. You know the way experts say that when you're faced with a do-or-die situation you experience fight or flight? Well, for some reason, I was consumed with rage. How dare some hooligan break into my home, into my sanctuary, and violate it? There was no way I was going to run. I was so mad that I decided there and then I wasn't going to let him get away with it. I don't know what possessed me: usually I wouldn't say boo to a goose. I peeped round the living-room door and there he was, kneeling in front of the TV, obviously trying to figure out if it was worth anything (it's not: it's the same one we had when we were together, the temperamental one that turns off whenever something comes on that it doesn't like). Before I knew what I was doing, I had grabbed the massive vase from the hall – you know, the mosaic one that you always hated – and cracked it across the back of his skull. It was only as he was falling to the floor, tiny pieces of mosaic tile crumpling round him, that I spotted the ponytail. It was Homer. I was so worried I'd killed him that I threw the bucket of sugar soap he was using to wash the walls over his head to try to revive him. He came to very quickly, but by then I was sobbing uncontrollably. I couldn't believe that I had attacked such a nice man. And he was so lovely about it all. He said it could have happened to anyone and that it was his own fault for not telling me that he was going to stay on and finish the skirting boards. And then he pulled me into his arms and gave me a big bear hug and I lay against his torso convulsing in tears until suddenly I felt really calm and peaceful, as if everything was going to be OK. His flannel shirt was soft against my face and I could feel his chest rise and fall, his hands pat my back and his kind voice in my ear tell me it was going to be all right. And then, just as I was starting to feel a whole lot better, he pulled away abruptly, said he was very sorry but he had to go, and sprinted out the door before I could say another word. I couldn't believe it. I had suddenly turned from Miss Mousy to Miss Feisty ... and in the process I had managed to scare away a great painter and decorator. From the look on his face, I don't think he'll be rushing back any time soon.

Eve

Are you Miss Mousy or Miss Feisty?

Are you shy and retiring or can you hold your own? Take our quiz and find out!

On a windy day, your dress blows up and reveals your knickers to a busy street. Do you:
a) Take cover in the nearest shop. You'll never get over the humiliation.
b) Smile and wink at gawping onlookers and ask if they'd like an encore.
c) Feel slightly embarrassed but also glad you're wearing your nicest undies.

You have to give an important presentation to the board. Do you:
a) Feel terrified and fret non-stop for days beforehand.
b) Not give it a second thought. You'll blind them with your charm and a low-cut top.
c) Prepare as much as possible and project a positive and professional attitude.

Your man is late for a dinner date. Do you:
a) Wait outside the restaurant. It would be mortifying if people thought you'd been stood up.
b) Wait at the bar and flirt outrageously with the waiter. That'll teach him to be punctual next time.
c) Go straight to the table and order a starter while you wait – you're starving!

Results

Mostly As: Don't be so timid, sister. Not everyone is looking at you. Work on your confidence and give yourself a chance to shine!

Mostly Bs: It's good to be sure of yourself, but your confidence can come across as far too cocky. Tone it down, girl.

Mostly Cs: Your self-assurance is inspiring. Take a bow, girlfriend!

Molly

Dear Molly,
It's almost my birthday and I miss you. I want to come home. Please
call me to arrange.
Love,
Charlie

P.S. I couldn't help but notice that there were plastic bottles in the
recycling, so I transferred them to the general waste bin where they
belong.

I put the letter down. I've already read it dozens of times.
I've scrutinized every single word to try to decipher how I
feel now that Charlie has finally contacted me. I should be
ecstatic. I should be over the moon that my husband has
come to his senses and wants to return home. But I don't
feel ecstatic. I don't feel anything. I am completely numb.

I close my eyes and try to see Charlie standing before me.
Maybe if I can do that I'll be able to feel something. Maybe
then I'll be overjoyed that my life is going back to how
I knew it and everything will be normal again. I clench my
eyes shut and try to concentrate. But it's not Charlie's face
that appears from the darkness, it's not his face I see: it's
David's. Those huge brown eyes, floppy fringe and chipped
tooth pop into my head before I can even think.

I snap my eyes open. I can't be thinking about David
now. I have to concentrate on Charlie. My husband. But it's
hard when, for some bizarre reason, I can't remember what

he looks like. I know it must be my mind playing tricks on me, but I can't see his face. I can't remember the exact shade of his eyes. I can't visualize how he walks or any of his mannerisms. I must know them all, but for the life of me I can't recall even one. And that is freaking me out.

Leaping up, I grab our wedding album from the shelf and shake the photos free so I can examine them. Dozens of pictures of Charlie and me looking happy and in love fall into my lap. I pick up one photo of us whirling giddily round the dance floor. Charlie's face is wreathed in a huge smile and he's gazing at me like I'm the only woman in the world for him. We look so graceful, as if we actually know what we're doing. As if we're perfect dance partners, the wind at our feet and the crowds cheering us on. I can remember that moment vividly now – I can almost feel Charlie's arms firm against my back as he twirls me round, moving confidently and with ease, like he's done it a million times before. At the time, I knew that he was loving every minute of it and I was trying hard to, even though a voice of doom kept hissing in my ear that I was sure to trip and end up flat on my face with my designer wedding dress round my ears. But from the photograph you can't tell this – we looked the part. Practising our waltzing with Al had really paid off.

That had all been Charlie's idea. He wanted everything to go without a hitch on the big day. It was the one thing he and Al had actually agreed about. So when Al volunteered to teach us to dance like pros, Charlie jumped at the chance. I wasn't so convinced. I would have preferred not to make such a big deal of the first-dance thing, and I told Al so when we met alone for coffee, without Charlie.

'You have all the grace of an elephant, Molly,' Al had said. 'Someone has to make sure you don't make a complete and utter fool of yourself.'

'But can't I just do what I always do?' I'd asked.

'What? You mean shuffle around a bit and look at the floor?' Al looked horrified at the thought. 'The eyes of everyone in that room will be on you, Molly. If you don't practise you'll be a laughing stock. Do you want to be a laughing stock?'

'Um, no,' I'd mumbled, feeling defensive.

Surely my dancing wasn't that bad? I mean, I wasn't going to offend people, was I? Wouldn't they be too busy admiring my beautiful dress to notice anything else anyway?

But deep down inside I knew that, even though Al was being overly dramatic as usual, he had a point. We were having a big wedding and loads of people would be looking at me. I had to get it right. Like Al kept drumming into me, this wedding was a production and we couldn't afford for any of it to be sloppy. People would expect us to twirl gracefully round the floor after the meal. We couldn't disappoint them. But I was still reluctant. I hadn't factored this into my endless list of things to do for the wedding and it was going to eat into more of my precious time. I had enough to do trying to deal with the musicians, florists and everything else. My head was spinning with all the balls I was trying to juggle at once. Learning to do the perfect waltz was way down on my list of priorities.

'Do you *really* think we need to?' I'd asked, hoping for some sort of reprieve.

'Of *course* you need to!' Al had insisted. 'This moment will live *for ever* on DVD. FOR EVER. If you make a mess of it, you'll never forget it, EVER. And neither will anyone else, believe me. People are still talking about Gary and Lucy's wedding – for all the wrong reasons.'

He'd looked at me meaningfully.

Gary and Lucy's wedding had been legendary. Gary had

got really drunk on the champagne he'd been pouring down his neck since before the ceremony to calm his nerves, and during their first dance Lucy had had to practically drag him round the floor in a vice-like grip. Then he'd turned green and thrown up all over her one-off Swarovski-crystal-encrusted wedding dress. He'd had to be helped up to their bridal suite while Lucy sobbed hysterically in the ladies toilets and then got even drunker than Gary and made a pass at the DJ. The thought of something similar happening to us made my blood run cold.

So I finally agreed that Al would teach Charlie and me some moves – moves guaranteed to have people wondering if we had Latin blood. Which is how, every Tuesday night for six weeks before the wedding, Charlie and I practised our first dance in Alastair's living room.

The first session was the worst. Even Charlie seemed a bit surprised by my two left feet. He had this really bemused expression on his face, as if he couldn't believe that anyone could be such a bad dancer. He hadn't a clue that I couldn't really dance at all. But then I am very good at hiding it. When other people are bopping on the dance floor at night-clubs, I kind of sway about so you don't really notice that I'm not actually moving my feet. Because it's when I have to move my feet that the trouble starts.

It began at a youth-club disco years ago, where I was shaking my stuff and thinking I was looking hot until I saw the boy of my dreams sniggering with his friends and I instinctively knew my Tiffany moves were the reason why. I'd been shaking my hair and spinning wildly to 'I Think We're Alone Now', sure I was dazzling him, when all the time he'd been laughing his head off at me. Then there was the night I got tipsy at my cousin's wedding and Tanya convinced me to try a few Abba moves on the floor. I ended up being carted out of the wedding on a stretcher, with a suspected broken foot, then taken by ambulance to the ER, Tanya flirting with the medics all the way. It turned out I'd only sprained my ankle, but the doctor said it could have been much worse and I'd had a very lucky escape. Extended family members still bring it up every time I have the misfortune to bump into them. Apparently someone taped the entire thing and they're still hoping it'll get on *Blunders on Camera*.

There was also the time work had a *Saturday Night Fever* disco for charity and I was roped into doing a John Travolta-style dance with everyone else. I tried just to do the pointing bit and keep my feet still, and I even thought I'd pulled it off until I saw the video on the company website a week later. I was still getting emails about it for months afterwards.

So to say that I was nervous about the dancing is an understatement.

Charlie, on the other hand, was a real dark horse. While I had been hiding my shameful secret from him, it turns out that he had a secret of his own: he was a natural mover. He had grace, he had rhythm, he even had good dance hair. Hair that moved gently as he swayed – unlike mine, which had a tendency to become uncontrollably frizzy if I was whirled around too much. Even Alastair was impressed with his poise.

'Most straight men are useless on the dance floor,' he whispered to me as we were taking a break, 'but I have to admit, Charlie is almost good.'

Coming from Al, this was a huge compliment. His standards are very high. He once won a ballroom-dancing competition, and he still takes his pink salsa suit out to stroke it every week.

I was completely mortified as I shuffled round the living

room, bumping into Charlie and stamping all over his toes. I was never going to get the hang of it; it was completely pointless. But by lesson three, things had become a bit easier. I let Charlie take the lead and I relaxed into him, allowing him to guide me round. It was almost fun. I say 'almost' because I never let myself go entirely, just in case I started doing some *Saturday Night Fever* moves by mistake and made a holy show of myself all over again.

Looking at the photos now, I try to remember the good times we had practising for that first waltz. I try to feel that special spark between us. We look really happy in almost every shot; there must have been something special between us. We look like the picture-perfect bride and groom. But I know we can't have been – not really – not if everything fell apart so soon after we exchanged vows.

I pick up the letter again. It's there in black and white. Charlie misses me. He wants to come home. But he hasn't explained why he left in the first place. He hasn't apologized. He hasn't said why he never answered any of my calls. He hasn't begged for my forgiveness. I should be angry about that, I know. I should be furious that he walked out and now he wants to come back and pretend that nothing happened. That everything is fine. But I'm not angry. I'm far too calm. Maybe I'm in complete denial about everything. Maybe I should see a doctor. Or a shrink. Or maybe I should . . . have a drink. Just to focus my mind. Not to get so steaming drunk that I can blot everything out – that would be really immature. Just a small drink to help me loosen up and decide what to do.

I'm not usually one to drink by myself. Unless I'm cooking – then I might have a little glass, just to set the mood, but that's allowed. In fact, it's almost expected. You chop and stir-fry things, you take a little sip of Pinot Noir. You stir-fry some more, you nibble on some crackers and cheese, just while the whole gourmet sensation you're making is coming together. Then you have a second glass. It's not as if I'm in the habit of drinking entire bottles of wine on my own on a regular basis. OK, so there was that time I drank a bottle and a half and Charlie found me snoring on the sofa when he came home from work, red wine drooling from my mouth and the stir-fry a soggy mess in the pan, but that was just the once. Maybe twice. But usually I wouldn't dream of drinking alone. Drinking on your own is the first step towards serious alcoholism, and I'm not going down that road.

An hour and a half later I feel a lot brighter. It's amazing how the power of positive thinking can really change your frame of mind. OK, I may be a bit drunk. Just a teeny bit. I'm not staggering around the room or anything. Then again, that may be because I'm lying on the sofa. In a foetal position. But – and this is the really critical bit – the room isn't moving when I close my eyes. So I am not officially drunk, just a bit tiddly, and that's totally fine.

I close my eyes just to check, and the room spins quite a lot. Maybe I'm a bit drunker than I thought. I try to remember how you're supposed to work out if you've had too much alcohol. Count backwards as fast as you can? No, that's the way to find out if you're going senile early. Walking in a straight line – that's the one. If I can walk in a straight line, I'm fine. I open one eye and look at the floor. Even trying to peel myself off the sofa seems like a huge effort. Trying to figure out if I can walk properly will probably send me over the edge.

Then it strikes me. I know why I'm feeling so woozy: it's because I haven't eaten anything. That's what's making me so light-headed. Everyone knows you have to line your stomach or you're asking for trouble, and I haven't eaten much today – I was too busy at the Carla Ryan event. That's bad. They'd never do that in a nice civilized European country like France or Italy. I should've had a few olives, maybe some baguette, just to soak up all the wine. Of course, that would require my having olives or baguette on the premises, and the chances of that are slim to none. But normally I wouldn't dream of drinking without at least a full pack of crisps to keep me company. And salsa dip. God, I'm hungry. Maybe I have a bag of stale crisps somewhere. I'm thinking about where they could be when the phone rings.

Instantly forgetting that I'm too drunk to stand, I leap off the sofa and stumble across the room to where my phone is vibrating and tinkling simultaneously on the window ledge. It's Charlie, I just know it. He's calling to explain everything. He's already asked me if he can come back. Now he wants to beg for my forgiveness – he just forgot to write that part in the note. He's going to explain it all to me, I'm going to remember how much I adore him and this nightmare is going to finish once and for all. The relief is enormous. I won't be forced into making any life-changing decisions. I won't have to think about whether the love between us was ever real, because this was all a horrible misunderstanding that we'll both laugh about when we're old and grey. At our golden wedding anniversary bash, surrounded by our hundreds of friends, family and well-wishers from all over the world, we'll tell our grandchildren how Grandpa once played a trick on Granny by pretending to run out on her after a few weeks of marriage. He was such a joker, he kept it up for ages, but when he came back – oh, how we laughed. We laughed so hard we couldn't stop. Then I'll take out my false teeth and ask one of the grandkids to dip them into the punch the caterers have made, just to show what a great sense of humour I still have. It'll be so funny.

I grab the phone, but the number isn't one I recognize. It's not Charlie. Unless … unless he's calling me from a public phone booth or a hotel somewhere. Unlikely, as he had a bit of a phobia about using public phones, but it's not impossible. I snap it open, my fingers fumbling clumsily. This is as good a time as any to talk to him. Drinking has given me Dutch courage, so I may as well make good use of it.

'Hello?' I say breathlessly.

'Is that Molly?' a woman's voice asks.

'Yes.' It's not Charlie, not unless he's had a sex change. I have no idea who it is.

'Hi, Molly. I'm sorry to bother you at this late hour. This is Rita Hyde Hamilton.'

My mind is blank.

'Your wedding coordinator?'

Now I remember. Rita works at the hotel where we had our wedding reception. She's the lovely, super-organized person who helped us choose table settings and talked us through our menu choices. She was so helpful when we were making all the arrangements, and really patient when I couldn't decide on the colour of the petals we wanted to scatter on the tables, and which gourmet chocolates to leave as gifts for the guests. It's only a shame she was nowhere to be found on the day itself, when the soup was cold and the band turned up so late.

'Hi, Rita,' I say, trying to sound sober and as if I'm pleased to hear from her. She was always so kind, but the truth is I have no idea why she's calling me.

'Like I say, I'm sorry to call so late and interrupt you two lovebirds,' she jokes, 'but I just wanted to remind you that we're expecting a cheque to settle your outstanding bill here at the hotel. If you could forward something to me in the post, I'd be really grateful. Those pesky accountants are breathing down my neck.'

'Of course.' I curse silently. 'No problem.'

This is really embarrassing. I was supposed to send her a cheque straight after we got back from honeymoon, but with everything that happened I forgot all about it.

'Great!' she says briskly, obviously embarrassed to have to remind me to pay for my own wedding. 'So, how is married life anyway? You two are blissfully happy, no doubt!'

'Of course!' I say, the lie tripping off my tongue. 'Things have never been better!'

'I bet!' she giggles. 'All you newlyweds are the same, mooning over each other – you make me sick!'

I laugh gaily along with her to show I get the joke before I make my excuses and hang up. If only she knew the truth. We're not happy newlyweds mooning over each other; we're a disaster zone. We barely made it through our honeymoon before Charlie scarpered into the night – or morning – I still don't know when he left. I have no clue where he went or why, and have spent days trying to contact him while he ignores me completely. Now, just when my ex-boyfriend has turned up out of the blue and managed to completely confuse me, Charlie wants to come back, just like that. Like nothing ever happened. I slump back into the sofa and reach for the wine bottle. I feel like having another drink. I know it's probably not a great idea, but maybe finishing off the second bottle of red might do the trick and help me forget about the mess that is my life. Because suddenly that's all I want to do: forget.

Julie's Blog

9.01 a.m.

Feel sick. And hungover. Why did I drink so many cocktails last night? It seemed like such a good idea at the time, but now my head feels like it's going to explode. I'll kill UC One if she mentions Mr X's birthday one more time. She's already draped a Happy Birthday banner in the kitchenette to surprise him. She's also bought blue balloons and plastic bugles, and has reminded us that a little birthday singalong might be 'pleasant'. She's even remembered to bring her harmonica to add to the 'party atmosphere'. Thank God I remembered to pick up the cream cakes on the way in or she would have killed me.

9.12 a.m.

Flurry of emails from UCs about birthday celebrations for Mr X. UC Two has pointed out that the birthday banner is crooked. UC Three says she will eat the cakes but will under no circumstances blow a bugle. UC Four says he has consulted the HR manual and no one is legally obliged to partake in social activities that lie beyond the remit of their job specification: press-ganging people into social events is passive bullying and he will be staging a silent protest at his desk if anyone cares to join him. UC Five says he is happy to partake in the celebration, but only if he can have the jam doughnut and not the custard slice.

9.16 a.m.

UC One is so upset that people are not partaking enthusi-astically that she has locked herself in the kitchenette with the banner, bugles and balloons. Can hear her sobbing from here.

9.18 a.m.

Email from Mr X to all UCs:

> It's my dreaded birthday today, so I'd like to take you all for drinks after work this evening – my treat.

9.20 a.m.

Huh, well, he can choke on his birthday drinks for all I care. I wouldn't go if he came begging on his hands and knees.

9.26 a.m.

Flurry of emails from all UCs, who are more than happy to partake in planned birthday celebration now that Mr X is treating them to drinks after work.

UC Two went to inform UC One that everyone is in great form again, so the birthday cakes are back on. UC One has reluctantly agreed to unlock the kitchenette door.

9.29 a.m.

Email from Mr X:

> I'm sorry about last night. Things got far too heated, so I went to a friend's to cool off. Are you coming for drinks tonight? If I get a cake I'll let you blow out my candle . . .

Huh, *now* he wants to talk dirty to me. Last night when he stormed off he didn't want to know me. I won't reply, even if it is his stupid birthday. He doesn't deserve it. And the

really good thing is because he stayed with a friend he has
no idea that I wasn't home until 4 a.m.!

9.35 a.m.
Email from Mr X:
> Aren't you talking to me? The least you could do is wish me a
> happy birthday. You're hurting my feelings.

The bloody nerve. Right, will give him a piece of my mind.

9.37 a.m.
Email to Mr X:
> Happy birthday then.

9.38 a.m.
Email from Mr X:
> I meant in person.

9.40 a.m.
Email to Mr X:
> I'm incredibly busy. Can't chat, sorry.

That'll teach him that I won't come running every time he
snaps his fingers.

10.01 a.m.
Email from N:
> What a great night! It was hilarious when you licked the salt off
> that guy's chest before you slammed your tequila. I can't believe
> I joined in! Wasn't that gay bar brilliant? I haven't laughed so
> much in ages!!

Oh God. Can't remember that.

10.03 a.m.
Email from R:
> How's your head? Mine's awful! I can't believe we had so many
> tequilas on top of all that wine!

Oh God, I'm going to be sick.

10.24 a.m.
Just back from Ladies. Burst through the door, knowing
I was going to throw up, and there, fixing the hand dryer
that never works, was the new janitor. I just had time to
skid into a cubicle and slam the door behind me before
I retched my guts into the toilet bowl. How humiliating.

10.25 a.m.
Email from janitor:
> Are you OK?

10.27 a.m.
Email to janitor:
> I'm fine.

10.29 a.m.
Email from janitor:
> You didn't sound fine – you sounded violently ill.

10.31 a.m.
Email to janitor:
> I'm fine. Please leave me alone.

God, I'm mortified.

10.32 a.m.

Right. Have to get through the rest of today. Will just grit my teeth and get on with it. Anyway, feel a bit better now and I don't think anyone noticed what happened. I would have got away with it completely if the janitor hadn't been in the toilets. He seems to be everywhere I look these days.

10.41 a.m.

Made very important call to *Her* about photo shoot for Mr Dick Lit at top of my voice so everyone would know how in demand he is. Pretended I was talking to *Elle* of course.

10.52 a.m.

Just called Mr Dick Lit to say that I had set up top photo shoot with *Her*. Hinted that it had taken many, many calls and brown-nosing to secure it for him. He didn't sound very grateful. Bloody writers.

12.02 p.m.

UC One wants to know if I am emailing all interested parties to inform them when exactly birthday cakes will be served.

12.06 p.m.

UC One says that shouting at everyone to get into the kitchenette will not do, as this will alert Mr X to the surprise. She is taking matters into her own hands.

12.10 p.m.

UC One has sent long-winded email informing all UCs to be in kitchenette at 12.30 sharp. Tussles over cakes will not be tolerated: it is strictly one cake per person. Anyone who attempts to start a food fight will be ejected.

12.13 p.m.

UC One wants to know why the cakes are not in the fridge. Have just remembered that cakes are under my desk – shoved them there this morning in a hungover daze.

12.14 p.m.

Cakes smell a bit off. May have been a mistake to get all those fresh cream slices.

12.20 p.m.

Was forced to admit to UC One that cakes may be inedible. She said if we all got salmonella poisoning it would have been my fault. Luckily, she thought ahead and took the precaution of making some of her famous chocolate and orange muffins.

2.00 p.m.

Birthday cakes ordeal finally over. Went OK, except UC One told Mr X I had forgotten to put cakes in fridge and had almost killed everyone. Mr X said, 'Tut, tut' and then winked at me when no one was looking. Am warming to him a bit.

2.05 p.m.

UC One has sent official email saying she has appointed herself the Head of the Social Affairs Committee. She presumes there are no objections seeing as she saved today's little celebration.

2.09 p.m.

All other UCs are up in arms. UC Three says she would prefer a good dose of gastric flu to entrusting all social gatherings to UC One's care.

2.12 p.m.

Email from Mr X:

> You still have some cream on your lip. Do you need a hand wiping
> it off?

2.15 p.m.

Email to Mr X:

> I think that would be highly inappropriate, don't you?

No harm being snooty with him for a while longer. He
can't expect me to forgive him that easily. As far as he knows
I sat up all night waiting for him to come home. He has no
idea I was downing shots and licking salt off strangers' chests
in a gay bar.

2.18 p.m.

Email from Mr X:

> Just trying to be helpful.

2.20 p.m.

Email to Mr X:

> Well, perhaps I don't need your help.

I hope he feels really bad — it serves him right.

2.24 p.m.

Off to shop. Am suddenly ravenously hungry and a BLT
and full-fat Coke will hit the spot. Will swish past Mr X's
desk as if I haven't a care in the world.

3.05 p.m.

Oh God, oh God. Have just accidentally shagged Mr X in
the stationery cupboard. Met him on the stairs on way back

from lunch. Tried to be snooty and aloof, which was a bit tricky because I had a massive stain on my shirt where the ketchup had dripped out when I'd wolfed down the BLT. But then Mr X growled that I was driving him wild with lust, and before I knew it we were snogging passionately. Very, very bad. But felt very, very good. Thank God I was wearing decent underwear.

3.09 p.m.
Just thought: Mr X and I just had making-up sex. No wonder it was so good. Sex after an argument is always the best kind. Perhaps I should engineer a few more arguments soon – not that I want to argue with Mr X, but that was the best bonk we've had since he moved in.

3.11 p.m.
Just discovered Post-it note stuck to seat of my skirt – hope no one else noticed.

3.15 p.m.
Emailed N to tell her what happened. Have to confide in someone or will burst. Didn't mention that Mr X had left his wife or that he was now officially living with me though – best not to get into that yet. Also begged her not to tell R, who will probably get all judgemental and preachy.

3.18 p.m.
Email from N:
    Tell me more!! Was it AMAZING?

3.33 p.m.
Was in middle of email describing hottest sex of life to N when UC One stopped at desk and presented me with a

manifesto telling me why she should be Head of the Social Affairs Committee. Had to pretend to be interested in the fact that she has many innovative and inspiring ideas for team-building while trying to minimize email about sex with Mr X. Luckily UC One was so busy droning on about her leadership qualities that she didn't notice.

3.38 p.m.
Email from Mr X:

> I love the way you frown when you're concentrating.

3.40 p.m.
Email to Mr X:

> I'm frowning because I'm trying not to make any mistakes typing this press release. I am a diligent, conscientious employee.

3.42 p.m.
Email from Mr X:

> I didn't mean the frown you make when you're typing . . .

This is so much fun! Forgot that his saucy banter could have this effect on me – we definitely need to fight more often.

3.44 p.m.
Oh my God. I knew something felt strange – I forgot to put my underwear back on after the shagathon with Mr X. Which means it's still somewhere in the stationery cupboard.

3.50 p.m.
Just met the new janitor outside the stationery cupboard, holding my thong and looking puzzled. Snatched it from his hands and sprinted off before he could say a word.

Open Forum

From Devil Woman: OMG!!!!!!!!!! Love it!!!!!!!!

From Broken Hearted: Oh no ... Julie, I thought you were starting to see the light. I can't believe you've made such a serious mistake.

From The Plumber: Hi, Broken Hearted. I agree with you.

From Devil Woman: Oh, come on. This is great. At least it's exciting!

From Angel: How do you think his wife would feel if she found out about this sordid affair? Adultery is disgusting.

From Devil Woman: Why do you keep reading this blog if you find it all so disgusting? I think you're secretly getting your kinky kicks from all this, Angel ...

From Sexy Girl: I agree! It's the quiet ones you have to watch out for!

From Angel: I would never have an affair with a married man. I am above that sort of behaviour.

From Devil Woman: Why don't you get off your high horse and stop being so uptight? No wonder no one will publish your book!

From Angel: That was totally uncalled for, Devil Woman. Then again you probably think chick lit is highbrow.

From Hot Stuff: Hi guys! Did you hear that Carla Ryan's new book is out? I got a signed copy at a readers' event! I had to queue for ages, but it was worth it! I love her!!! Long live the queen of chick lit!

From Angel: Spare me.

From Devil Woman: Tut, tut, Angel. Jealousy will get you nowhere!

From Angel: The woman can't write. Why would I be jealous of her?

From Graphic Scenes: Wow, hot sex – at last!

From Angel: Pervert.

Eve

Dear Charlie,

It's been a few days since I almost accidentally killed Homer and my sleeping patterns are all over the place. I feel so guilty for attacking him with the vase that I've been having horrible nightmares and then waking up in the middle of the night, my heart hammering, frantic that he'll never forgive me.

Last night I tried the visualization trick that Mary the therapist taught me to use before I drop off. She promised it would guarantee nice, peaceful dreams and banish the nightmares for good. All you have to do is concentrate on what you want to dream about for five minutes before you close your eyes. It actually worked: I had an amazing dream about George Clooney and his limited-edition custom-made motorbike, just like I'd imagined. We were on his Harley, racing along the Amalfi coast at a hundred miles an hour, the wind in our hair, the sun on our skin. I was clinging to his muscular back for dear life and he was looking back over his shoulder at me, grinning that dazzling Hollywood smile that makes any woman in her right mind go weak at the knees. You might be wondering what George Clooney could possibly see in me, but in the dream I wasn't painfully skinny and too tall, my teeth weren't crooked and my hair wasn't limp. I was curvy and petite, with a perfect smile and wild gypsy curls. I even had a gorgeous golden tan and not that blotchy red heat rash that I usually get as soon as the temperature goes above fifteen degrees. Do you remember how I had to take those antihistamine tablets every time we went abroad? Of course you don't: I used to take them secretly because I didn't want to bother you with my itching skin. I knew the fact that I had to wear long-sleeved, high-necked tops when everyone else was in string bikinis irritated you, especially when you used to bronze so beautifully at the first ray of sun. I can still remember the golden glow of your skin in the evening light, just after you'd showered and applied that expensive body lotion you used to love so much.

But in my dream I was nothing like the hive-ridden, pasty-faced person I am in real life. I was *fabulous*, and George was absolutely besotted with me. Then, just when things were getting really interesting, the dream got weird. George morphed into Homer and suddenly it was *his* motorbike we were on, it was *his* muscular back I was clinging to so tightly and it was *him* who was dazzling me with his gorgeous smile. When I finally jerked awake, woken by the ringing telephone, I was sweaty and confused and wondering what it all meant.

It was Anna on the phone. She was calling to apologize for sending me on the blind date with Butch. She claims she had no idea he was leading a secret double life and that if she'd known then she would have come along herself for a good night out in that gay bar and helped him come out of the closet properly. She needs cheering up, that's for sure. She's very down at the moment because she and Derek are having even more problems. He just can't seem to kick this women's knickers thing, and Anna says if she finds one more stretched pair of her best frillies in her undies drawer she'll swing for him. It's one thing to want to wear your wife's knickers under your overalls, it's another ruining her best La Perla pair by squeezing your hefty bum into them.

Anna says the only thing keeping her mind off things is concentrating on helping me find new love. She's already got another man in mind for me, and this time she reckons he could be the perfect match. He's called Larry and he's a vet, which means he's wealthy and loves animals and, according to her, he's very handsome to boot. I really wanted to tell her that she needn't bother setting me up again – I'm not sure I can face another disastrous blind date – but she sounded so excited about it all that I hadn't the heart to say no. And, if I'm honest, the dates have kept me so occupied recently that I've barely had time to think about you or your new wife. I might even be able to forget about how heartbroken I am if Mum didn't keep reminding me. If she produces your wedding photo from her handbag one more time I might have to swing for someone myself.

She popped round today, laden down with goodie bags she'd scored at another charity luncheon. I knew Mary wouldn't have been pleased – according to her, this is another area of my life that I need to take ownership of. She says that I can't control the way my mother behaves, I can only control how I react to her behaviour – which makes perfect sense, but isn't all that useful. According to Mary, I am a grown woman and must set boundaries and limits – so if Mum wants to call over, she can't just barge in unannounced, she must ring in advance to arrange a mutually convenient time. I tried to tell Mary that this would never work – Mum drops by whenever she wants and doesn't take no for an answer; that's why she's such a force on all those charity committees – but Mary said that for people to respect me, I must learn to respect myself. That's all well and good, but I can't bring myself to upset Mum any more just now. She's still feeling fragile after hearing that another woman has managed to snare you when I couldn't.

And she's also very wound up about Mike and Stacey, so I didn't want to upset her by talking about boundaries. Besides, I wanted to get my hands on some of the charity luncheon loot she had with her – those ladies who lunch really go to town on the freebies. There were lotions and potions and perfumes and lots of fab treats peeping out of the bags she was carrying, and I was itching to get at them. Mum has drawers full of luxury pampering products at home, she doesn't need any more. She couldn't possibly have time to use even half of them. It was an obligation, my duty even, to take a few of them off her hands. I managed to slide a couple of prime samples out without her noticing while she was nattering on about Mike and Stacey and how worried she was about 'the situation'.

Apparently, Mike left a message on her answerphone to say he has a very big announcement to make, and she's terrified it means that he's proposed to Stacey or something equally as disastrous. I tried to calm her down by saying maybe the school team had won a basketball game and that's why he sounded so excited, but she wouldn't listen to me. She just kept going on and on about Mike wasting his life on a girl who wasn't good enough for him and never would be. She hardly even noticed how good the flat is looking. Turns out Mary was right: bright colours really can be mood adjusters. The yellow Homer chose is so cheerful that it's hard to feel anything but upbeat when I'm surrounded by it on almost every wall. I really think I'm starting to feel a tiny bit happier, even if I'm not sleeping very well at the moment.

If only Homer wasn't acting so strangely. He's been practically monosyllabic since I skulled him with the mosaic vase, and I can only assume he's furious with me, even though he was so nice straight after it happened. I can't blame him, I suppose. If someone assaulted me with a blunt object I might be wary of them too. He won't look me in the eye any more, and he even worked through our usual herbal tea break today. Worst of all, he didn't hum to the classics on his iPod once. I really missed that. Even Tom has taken against me. He glares at me every time I try to talk to him, as if to say what a complete idiot he thinks I am, and he won't leave Homer's side. I passed them both in the hall on the way to the bathroom and Tom was winding his way seductively round Homer's legs while Homer tickled him under the chin. They both stopped when they saw me, and looked the other way. I was so mortified I hid in my office for the rest of the day. I'm convinced Homer was painting far faster than usual as well. He's probably frantic to get out of here and away from me once and for all.

Maybe I should just concentrate on my date with the vet to get my mind off things. Perhaps Anna is right, perhaps he *is* just my type ... if I have a type, that is.

Eve

What Does Your Taste in Men Say About You?

The type of guy you're attracted to can speak volumes. Do our quiz to reveal all!

You like a guy to look:
a) Well groomed – hand-made tailored suits are a must.
b) Macho. There's nothing nicer than a well-oiled muscle and a bulging bicep.

c) Intellectual. Extra points are given for wearing glasses.

What kind of hobbies does your man enjoy?
a) He doesn't have time for hobbies: he's too busy checking his investment portfolio.
b) Fitness: he's in training to defend his Iron Man competition title.
c) Reading: he's a real bookworm.

What is your man's most endearing quality?
a) His ability to tot up a bill without a calculator.
b) His ability to crush a can with his fist.
c) His ability to quote entire passages from great works of literature.

In bed, your man likes you to:
a) Be quick. He keeps up with the Japanese markets so he's only ever free for ten minutes at a time.
b) Be wild. He loves a good wrestle between the sheets.
c) Be talkative. Reciting poetry really gets him hot.

Results

Mostly As: You want the good things in life, but remember: there's more to a relationship than material possessions. Sometimes 'having it all' can make you feel empty inside.

Mostly Bs: You like your brawn and that's OK, but don't forget that for long-term happiness your man needs to have some brain too!

Mostly Cs: An intelligent man can be a real turn-on, but just make sure you inject some fun into your relationship too. Love doesn't have to be a serious work of art!

Molly

I wake up on the sofa, my face stuck to the leather seat, my temples pounding. I lift my head a fraction to get my bearings and a searing pain shoots from my forehead to the tips of my toes. What's going on? I feel like I'm dying – it's like an articulated truck has reversed over me again and again, just for fun. My throat is like sandpaper, my eyes are almost completely glued together and my cheek is crusty with drool. Maybe I'm getting the flu. Or something even worse. Like pneumonia. Or a brain tumour. It certainly feels as if my head is going to explode. Then the fog clears for a second and I remember the wine. I drank wine. Lots and lots of wine. Again. Since I got that letter from Charlie a few days ago I've been drinking far too much almost every night. But this morning is the worst I've felt. And I'm on the sofa, which means that I must have fallen asleep here. I never even made it to bed.

I inch my face away from the sofa, wincing, as another wave of unbelievable pain stabs my skull and my stomach heaves.

There's no way I can go to work today, not in this state. I can barely move, let alone make myself presentable and Minty-ready. I'll have to call in sick. Which means I'll have to explain to Penny why I can't come in today. The thought fills me with dread and another wave of nausea washes over me. Officially, Penny is the advertising manager, but she prides herself on taking care of HR 'on the side'. Minty gave her the HR gig because she felt that Penny wasn't being stretched enough by calling people up and threatening them with grievous bodily harm if they didn't pay for advertising that had run in the magazine. She needed an extra challenge to get her teeth into. And Penny took to HR like a duck to water. She relishes executing the ridiculous company policy that if you're sick you can't just email an excuse, or leave a message and get the answerphone to do your dirty work for you. No, at *Her* you have to call Penny directly on her special HR line and explain why you can't possibly drag yourself into the office and put in a good ten hours at your desk. Minty came up with the idea in order to discourage misuse of sick leave. Minty doesn't believe in sick days – she doesn't believe in being sick full stop – but that's because, although she only weighs about five pounds, she has the constitution of an ox and never gets so much as a sniffle. I personally like to believe that germs can't live in such a hostile environment.

I'll have to come up with a really good excuse or Penny will know I'm lying. It can't be anything too obvious. I can't tell her I have the flu – she'll never fall for that. Maybe I could say I've contracted a flesh-eating parasite from a mosquito bite on honeymoon. Or how about some sort of superbug that even antibiotics can't cure? My head is pulsating with the worst hangover I've had in years and I can't think straight, but it's crucial that I concentrate and come up with something credible. It's already past nine. I have to call within the next five minutes or Penny will know for sure that I'm pulling a sickie and then she'll never let me forget it.

I could say I had an accident. Nothing life-threatening or really serious, just a personal injury that would put me out of action for a while. Something plausible and not so outlandish that she'll suspect anything is amiss. Eventually it comes to me. I'll say I've hurt my shoulder. You can't be expected to do any sort of work when you've injured your shoulder and you're in agony. That'll have to do.

I pick up my phone to make the call before I lose my bottle.

'Penny speaking.' She's already adopted her stern HR tone.

'Hi, Penny,' I croak, my head pounding. At least I don't have to use my 'pretend-sick voice'. I sound genuinely dreadful.

Penny says nothing.

'You're never going to believe what happened to me.'

'You're right,' Penny says brusquely. 'I probably won't believe it.'

I ignore that and concentrate on sounding honest.

'I hurt my shoulder. I can't move it. I'm in complete agony. I tripped and fell down the stairs. I'm lucky I didn't break my neck.' I prattle on and on and on, adding lots of details, hoping I sound authentic.

'Poor you.'

Sarcasm drips down the line. Penny can tell I'm lying, it's obvious. I know I'm a terrible liar and the stone-cold silence on the end of the line means that she knows that too.

Maybe I'm laying it on too thick. Maybe I shouldn't have hinted that if I go back to work too early I could end up in a head-to-toe cast for months. I've tried to imply that I've been almost crippled, but she doesn't sound all that sympathetic. In fact, she sounds like she couldn't care less. It's not like I'm the type to call in sick frequently. OK, so I may have taken a day here and there in the run-up to the wedding, but that's only to be expected. How else are you supposed to organize an extravagant ceremony for two hundred after working hours? It's just not possible.

'So, you *slipped* down the stairs, did you?' Penny sounds like she's taking notes. 'And that was . . .?'

'Em, last night?' I stutter, praying she believes me.

'Okaaayyyy.'

There's lots of rustling in the background. She's definitely flicking through official stuff – probably the company file dedicated to employees like me, the one that's got 'Big Fat Liar' scrawled in red letters on the front.

'And you'll be back . . .?'

'Tomorrow?' I offer.

There's another silence, while she writes all this down.

'Um, are you still there?' I ask timidly.

'Yes. I am,' she says coldly. 'I will need a doctor's note – ASAP, of course. For the file.'

'Sure,' I say brightly, feeling even sicker, 'that's no problem.'

I hang up, wondering if I can persuade my doctor to falsify a sick note. Perhaps if I lay on the mental anguish aspect of the situation thick enough, he'll take pity on me. That shouldn't be too hard. I have every reason to be in serious mental anguish, so it's not like I'll have to make up that part. But at least the call is over. Now I can use the rest of the day to figure out what to do about Charlie's letter. The time has come for a decision. I can't put it off any longer.

I know the ball is in my court. He made it clear in his note that he wants to come home and it's up to me to decide what to do. Do I take him back and try to carry on as we were before he left so suddenly? Or do I change the locks and refuse to see him? If he explained why he left in the first place, would I understand? Or do I even want to know what his reasons were? It's all so confusing, but the choice about what to do next is mine and there's no getting away from it – I can't run away and hide. *Not like I did when Mum and Dad died.* This thought bounces into my aching skull without warning, and deep down I know it's true. When it all got too much to bear, I ran. I didn't call it that at the time, but that's what it amounted to.

I decided to leave about a month after the accident. I wasn't eating or sleeping or even talking much by then. Instead I spent most of the time replaying everything over and over again in my head. The more I thought about it, the more convinced I was that it had been my fault. No one came right out and accused me of causing their deaths, but I knew deep down what everyone must be thinking. *I* had invited them for lunch. If I hadn't, they would still be alive. It was simple. I would have done anything to have turned back the clock, but that was impossible so I shut myself away and hid from the world. I couldn't face anyone – I couldn't even face myself. So when a cousin who'd moved to San Francisco invited me to stay for as long as I wanted, I knew it was exactly what I needed to do. I had to get away, as far away from everything as soon as I could. I knew it would be much easier for everyone if I left. Including David. *Especially* David.

I think back to how he reacted when I told him I wanted to leave Dublin. He'd misunderstood at the beginning.

'Good idea!' he'd said, when I told him my plan. 'Where will we go? How about Italy? Or Greece? Greece could be nice. I could do some research for my next book while you relax – it'd be fun.'

He tried to take my hand in his, but I pulled away.

'No,' I said, 'you don't understand. I don't want you to come. I want to go on my own.'

In a split second, his smiling face fell and those brown eyes were suddenly full of confusion.

'On your own?'

He pushed his messy fringe off his forehead, something he used to do when he got anxious.

'Yes, I need some time alone. I want to think.' I couldn't look him in the eye – it was too hard.

'OK,' he said at last. 'Of course, I can understand that. You've been through so much. How long are you thinking? A week? Two?'

His face crumpled when I told him I didn't know when I'd be back. That I didn't want him to wait for me. That I realized that I didn't love him after all, that we weren't meant for each other and that Mum and Dad's deaths had made me see that life was too short to waste it with someone who wasn't right for you.

I didn't mean any of it of course. I loved him so fiercely it hurt. I knew that I'd never love anyone else the way I loved him. And that was the point. Because I knew I couldn't go through this pain again if anything ever happened to him. Losing Mum and Dad was unbearable – if I lost David I wouldn't be able to go on. That's why I had to leave him now. The more time I spent with David, the more I loved him. Letting him go now would spare me even more heartache in the future. It made perfect sense. And besides, he deserved better: I was a mess, and even though he was being kind and supportive, he must have been sick of me. I didn't tell him all this though – better to let him think that I was leaving because I didn't love him any more. Better that he hated me. I hated myself. And so I went to San Francisco and tried to forget all about what had happened. I worked part-time in an Irish bar downtown and concentrated on partying too hard. Before I knew it, a year had gone by and Tanya and Al were begging me to come home. I suspected that, if I didn't, then I probably never would, so I nervously packed a bag and flew to Dublin, telling myself I would stay for a week, maybe two. When I got back I found that the pain of losing Mum and Dad had faded, just a little, so that it was almost bearable to be there again. And it was so lovely to see Tanya and Al that two weeks quickly turned to three. Then I fell into the job at *Her* and the idea of going back to San Francisco became more remote. But I still didn't contact David. I never called him to explain that I had lied about my feelings for him. I let him go on believing I didn't love him, that I had never loved him. No wonder he looked at me with such disdain at the Sheldon Hotel. There was no disguising how he felt. It's obvious he hates me for what I did to him.

But there's no point thinking about David right now. Right now I have to concentrate on Charlie, and to do that I need to clear my head. It's so fuzzy from the alcohol that it's impossible to think straight. I know the only thing that will work is getting some fresh air. A brisk walk will help me focus on what I should do. My stomach heaves at the thought of getting off the sofa, but before I can change my mind I grit my teeth, pull on the nearest pair of boots and leave.

Within two minutes of hitting the pavement, I'm regretting it. My boots dig viciously into my feet with every step I take. Not putting on my trainers was a big mistake. The boots were a bargain buy in the sales, but they were always too tight for me. By the time I admitted this to myself and brought them back to the shop, the sales assistant wouldn't let me return them. Not even when I explained to her that I was afraid they would cut off circulation to my calves, and that I could be struck with a serious thrombosis at any second. I've been trying to convince myself that they fit ever since. Now my toes are numb and my heels are screaming in agony. They're probably bleeding – I'm afraid to look.

My head throbbing with pain, I blink in the bright sun-shine and try to decide whether to keep going or turn right round and run/hobble in my too-tight boots back home. The sunlight is too bright, the path is too lumpy and, worst of all, there are *people*. People who look like they haven't got a care in the world. People who are smiling, chatting on their mobile phones, carrying on as if life is perfectly normal. They don't have runaway husbands writing to them, wanting to come back. They don't have ex-boyfriends appearing out of nowhere and confusing them. They have quiet, peaceful lives – I can tell by their faces. Like the woman walking towards me, talking to someone on her phone.

'OK then,' she says, casual as you like. 'I'll see you at the movies at eight.'

She passes me and I resist the urge to glare at her. It's obvious she has no worries or traumas. She's probably going to a movie tonight with the love of her life. They'll sit in the back row, holding hands and sharing a bumper bucket of popcorn, completely oblivious to the hell that other people are going through.

Next up is a man, walking a dog. A golden Labrador. I've always wanted a golden Labrador. They're so cute and lovable and licky. I wanted one so badly that I'd even given it a name in my head: Lellie. I used to love fantasizing about taking bracing walks across the hills with Lellie, throwing sticks for her to fetch. OK, so I'm not a big fan of walks, or the outdoors, but still, I could have changed. Lellie would have helped me appreciate nature more – I could have grown to love wet grass and mucky leaves. And it would have been a great excuse to get the sheepskin shearling coat I've always wanted. Charlie never liked dogs. He said they shed too much, and that getting one would mean watching the leather sofa get scratched to shreds. But David *loved* dogs – he always wanted a golden Labrador too. He was a real doggie person.

I'm standing on the path, watching the beautiful dog do a quick wee against a telephone pole, when it happens. A couple amble towards me. A very happy-looking couple holding hands and grinning stupidly at each other. I can *feel* their happiness bouncing off them and slamming into me. They are in that bubble of love which nothing and no one can penetrate. The man looks just like David: tall, scruffy, with shaggy hair. In this light, with my head fuzzy from a hangover, he could pass for him.

In the distance I hear a voice, a really bitter croaky voice, say, 'Make the most of it while you can – it won't last.'

I look round to see who's talking, but there's no one there.

Then I notice that the couple are staring at me, in the way that people usually stare at mad Aunt Nora when she does something inappropriate, like shouting at the traffic warden or sticking out her tongue at the lollipop lady. They have the same expression that I've seen on people's faces when she takes one of her funny turns: kind of annoyed, but a little bit afraid as well.

'Do we know you?' the man is saying, frowning at me, then wrapping his arm round his girlfriend's shoulder and pulling her even closer – as if that was physically possible. Up close, I can see he doesn't look at all like David really. He's much smaller and he has kind of a mean mouth.

'Sorry,' I mumble.

I suddenly realize that *I* was the one who said that. There's no bitter old crone hanging round street corners berating young loved-up couples – there's only me. I am the mad old crone. I am losing the plot. I'm now talking to complete strangers in the street. Not just talking to them even, but telling them not to count on love because it will come back to bite them in the end. I'm going insane: it's official.

The couple walk quickly away, the girl looking over her shoulder as if she half expects me to take a running jump at her and wrestle her to the ground. I can't believe what I've just done. Maybe I need help – a one-on-one with a psychiatrist. Or perhaps something more concentrated – like an intensive residential course somewhere. It mightn't be too bad, not if there were steam rooms and massages on site.

I quickly start half-jogging, half-hobbling back home. I have to get back inside before I say or do anything even worse. It's not safe for me to be out here; who knows what else I might do? I look around and realize I've come further than I thought. I definitely can't walk back because my feet are throbbing with pain, so before I have time to think about it I'm waving down a passing taxi, stumbling into the back seat and giving directions to my flat.

'Tough day?' The taxi man catches my eye in the rearview mirror as I lean back into the seat and try to breathe. He can obviously tell from my expression that things are not rosy in my garden.

'You could say that.' I smile wryly at him. It's not his fault my life is so awful; there's no point being rude. And anyway, I like taxi drivers – they're always so interesting. They all have brilliant stories to tell about people throwing up in the back of their cabs or having humdingers of arguments. If I wasn't feeling so awful I'd get him to tell me some.

'Well, cheer up, love. It might never happen.' He winks back at me.

I smile weakly at him but I don't answer. It already *has* happened, I want to tell him. I'm in a living nightmare and I have no idea how it all came to this.

'Anything nice planned for the weekend?'

The cab driver isn't giving up. He really wants to make small talk.

'Not really,' I offer, hoping this will be enough to placate him. 'Do you?'

I hope he doesn't. I don't want to hear about it if he's doing anything even remotely nice.

'Yeah, I'm taking the wife to Marbella. It's our ten-year anniversary.'

He's beaming at me. In fact, I'm not sure if I'm imagining it, but I think he's puffing out his chest with pride, just a little.

'That's nice,' I say, horrified. He's going to tell me all about his perfect marriage, I just know it. I wonder if I can get out here, before I have to hear all about how happy they are together, how they love each other more now than they ever did, how they're probably going to renew their wedding vows in sunny Spain. But the traffic is streaming by so I'm trapped in the back seat. I couldn't get out even if I wanted to.

'Yeah, we can't wait. You married?' He glances at me in the rear-view mirror again.

'Um, yes,' I say, feeling more uncomfortable. Technically, I'm still a newlywed, even if I don't feel remotely like one. I twist my wedding band on my finger. It feels hot against my flesh, like it shouldn't really be there.

'That's nice.' The taxi driver nods approvingly. 'How long you been hitched?'

'Not long,' I say, desperately trying to think of something to change the subject. I'll ask him about football – that's a good one. Now, which league is which? Is the premier league different to the championship league, or are they the same thing? Or maybe premier league is rugby? For the life of me, I simply can't remember. I've never been any good at pretending to like sport, and now my mind is utterly blank. I can't even remember the name of a team.

Before I can head the taxi driver off with a weather comment, he's in again.

'Yeah, I wouldn't do without my missis. She's an angel on earth.'

He sniffs. From where I'm sitting it looks like his eyes are actually welling up with tears. This is all I need.

'Oh,' I squeak. I don't know what else to say.

'Yeah, we've been through thick and thin together, so we have. She's my best friend, do you know what I mean? There's no one else in the world I'd rather spend my days with.'

We're stopped in traffic and this gives him the opportunity to blow his nose loudly into a handkerchief he's just produced from up his sleeve. This would be the perfect chance for me to give him the fare and escape, but I can't because what he's just said has rocked me to the core.

'Yeah, I know what you mean,' I say weakly, my head spinning. And I do. Because that's the way things were between David and me. We were best friends as well as lovers. He was the one person in the world I wanted to spend every day with, the one I wanted to share every experience with.

'Yeah, there has to be that something special between you – that magic – for it to last.' The taxi driver snuffles now, overcome with emotion. 'We're so lucky, aren't we? Not everyone finds their soulmate.'

He gives me a watery smile and I nod my head, misery washing over me because I have a horrible feeling that Charlie and I never felt that way about each other. I'm not sure we had that magic between us, that special something that keeps people together for ever. *That special something that David and I had.*

'Is this your place, love?' the taxi driver asks, interrupting my thoughts.

He pulls up to the kerb outside my flat, the car shuddering to a halt.

As I look at my front door, my heart sinks. I don't want to go back inside and face Charlie's letter or what it means. I don't want to have to figure out what to do next. I want to tell the taxi driver to keep driving as fast as he can away from here, to keep going and never stop, because deep down inside I'm starting to think that getting married to Charlie might have been the biggest mistake of my life.

Julie's Blog

9.01 a.m.
Very bad night. Got so frustrated trying to get Mr X to stop snoring that I finally gave up and slept on the sofa. This has got to stop. It's been going on for days now. I don't think I can take much more.

9.02 a.m.
Maybe I could get him some nasal strips – that might help.

9.03 a.m.
Or I could ask him to have one of those operations – the ones where they cut out the frog thingy in your throat so you don't snore any more.

9.06 a.m.
Or I could ask him to move out and get his own place, then I could have some peace and quiet and complete control of the TV remote again ... Oh, where did that come from? I don't mean that. At least I don't think I do. It's just that I was really hoping things would be good between us again after the wild stationery-cupboard sex, but they're not, and I can't help feeling that it's because, deep down, we have absolutely nothing in common except a passionate lust for each other ... and even that's waning. I couldn't help but notice in the harsh bathroom light this morning that Mr X is getting a small bald patch. And, even worse, wiry hair is growing in his ears.

9.08 a.m.

It must be the sleep deprivation. It's making me really grumpy. I'll be fine once I get a good night's rest.

9.09 a.m.

But if he tries to tell me just one more time that I haven't lived until I've tried organic porridge, I'll kill him, I really will.

9.18 a.m.

Just saw the new janitor. He cocked his eyebrow at me as if to say, 'I know all about you leaving your knickers in the stationery cupboard, you harlot.' God, he's gorgeous. I bet he's a great dancer. And I bet he doesn't think that watching a documentary about global warming is a fun way to spend a night. He looks like he could move. In more ways than one. Not that I'm thinking about that, because I'm completely committed to Mr X, but sometimes I wish things could go back to the way they were – when it was just lots of secret shagging and no strings attached. And no boring documentaries.

10.55 a.m.

Email from N:

> You know that new James Law movie, *Back to the Wild: Even Wilder*? Guess who just snagged us invites to the wrap party!!!!! You have to come!! He is such a riiiide!!!!!!!

Damn, damn, damn. Really want to meet James Law – he's been all over the papers since he split with his ex, Angelica – but Mr X has already said he's going to make us a special meal tonight. Have a horrible feeling it will be something with raw vegetables in it again. Maybe I could do both.

Will email N to get further details: time, location, dress code, probability of actually meeting James.

Email from N:
> Blazin' Saddles bar, 6 p.m. You'll definitely meet him – we have special passes to the VIP area!!!!!!

Have to cancel Mr X now. This could be my one and only chance to meet James Law, the king of the 21st-century Western. I'm sure he'll understand.

Will just send him a carefully coded email to break the news.

11.07 a.m.
Email to Mr X:
> Really have to stay late tonight. I've been working so hard on the campaign for Mr Dick Lit that I've loads of other stuff to catch up on. Don't want any of my other clients suffering! Can we do dinner tomorrow night instead?

No point telling him the truth – that would only make him feel bad. Can't believe I have an exclusive invite to meet James Law tonight, *in the flesh*. If UC One knew she'd die – ha!

11.10 a.m.
Mr X back at desk. He's just opened my email.

11.11 a.m.
He doesn't look happy. He's frowning – and not in a cute, crinkly nose way, in a really angry way. He's also bashing files about. There could be a chance he hasn't taken this

well. Unless he's annoyed about something completely different. He *has* been behaving a bit strangely since his birthday – really grumpy and touchy.

11.14 a.m.
Email from Mr X:
  OK.

Right. So he *is* annoyed about tonight. Well, that's totally selfish of him. As far as he's concerned I'm staying behind to work, so what's his problem? It's not like he knows I'm going to meet James Law at a wrap party. And even if he did know, he shouldn't mind. He should be happy for me. I *love* James Law, and tonight could be the only chance I ever get to meet him. It's very selfish of Mr X to make me feel bad. I don't make him feel bad for moving in with me, even though he didn't ask me first.

11.17 a.m.
Maybe I *should* make him feel bad about arriving on my doorstep without any prior consultation with me. Maybe then he wouldn't make such a fuss about nothing. Well, he's not exactly making a fuss I suppose – he hasn't said much. But that's not the point. The point is, even if he doesn't know it, he's making me feel guilty for wanting a fun social life. And that's not right. Just because he thinks sitting indoors cooking leeks and taping National Geographic is fun, doesn't mean I do. Perhaps I should tell him how I feel – that I can't stand the way he carefully wipes his organic mushrooms with recycled kitchen paper before he sautés them in ethically sourced extra-virgin olive oil, or that even the thought of sharing another intimate meal with him in my flat makes me want to scream.

11.19 a.m.

But I can't tell him any of that. He left his wife for me. He's already proven how much he loves me, I can't let him down. Even if I am starting to feel a little ... suffocated. Not trapped exactly. But close.

11.21 a.m.

God, he looks really morose. The guilt is killing me. I'd better email him back.

11.22 a.m.

Email to Mr X:

> I can still do tomorrow night. We could go out?

11.25 a.m.

No reply from Mr X. Still looking very sulky and banging files about. Will just have to let him get over it.

11.31 a.m.

Just got email from UC One. As self-appointed Head of the Social Affairs Committee, she has planned an action-packed activity weekend for all employees. She says it will be an excellent opportunity for bonding while partaking in orienteering, kayaking and hill-walking. Cannot think of anything worse. Nothing to worry about though – am sure Mr X will veto it as a ridiculous idea. Will send him a joky email to make friends. He'll *have* to reply to that.

11.34 a.m.

Email to Mr X:

> Where does she get her ideas from: the stupid store?! That trip sounds like hell in the Highlands!

11.36 a.m.
Mr X has sent email to everyone to say UC One's corporate-bonding weekend is an inspired idea and we must all go. What's he playing at? He can't possibly think it's a good idea for employees to decamp to a remote location and pretend to like each other.

11.55 a.m.
Mr X still ignoring me.

11.56 a.m.
Maybe I shouldn't go tonight. Am sure I could meet James Law another time.

11.58 a.m.
Email from Mr X:
> Urgent. Need publicity update for Dick Lit campaign ASAP.

Hurrah! He's sending me coded messages again – that's a start.

12.00 p.m.
Email to Mr X:
> Of course. We can 'discuss' it later.

12.02 p.m.
Email from Mr X:
> I would prefer a written report on my desk first thing in the morning.

12.04 p.m.
Email to Mr X:
Yes sir, Mr Boss sir.

At least he's got his sense of humour back.

12.06 p.m.
Email from Mr X:
I'm not joking. First thing in the morning. I told you: I can show no favouritism.

Oh my God, he's not joking! He's taking revenge because I'm going to meet James Law tonight! He's almost ... threatening me! Am *furious*. Now I'll have to write a detailed PR report before I leave work. If I miss meeting James Law, I'll never forgive him. Never.

2.15 p.m.
Email from Mr X to all employees:
Further to my last email, I want to stress that *all* employees will be expected to attend the upcoming activity weekend – lame excuses will not be accepted. Unless a family member dies, you will be there.

Am trying to think of a family member I haven't killed off yet.

2.18 p.m.
Email from janitor:
Hey there. You going on this weekend away?

He obviously sent that to me by mistake. Why would he care if I was going or not? Will just ignore his email.

2.26 p.m.

Email from janitor:

Hey there. I said, are you going on this weekend away?

Oh my God. That email *was* for me. Why does he want to know if I'm going? What's it to him?

2.29 p.m.

Email to janitor:

I might.

2.31 p.m.

Email from janitor:

I think you should. We could get to know each other properly. We could 'bond'.

Is he flirting with me or am I imagining it?

2.33 p.m.

Email to janitor:

Are you flirting with me?

2.35 p.m.

Email from janitor:

That depends. Have you ditched Grandad yet?

Oh my God. He knows about me and Mr X. He's put two and two together. I have to deny it.

2.37 p.m.

Email to janitor:

I don't know what you mean.

2.39 p.m.

Email from janitor:

Sure you do. Don't worry, your secret is safe with me. Come on the trip. It'll be fun. I promise.

Open Forum

From Devil Woman: I *knew* it! She likes the janitor!

From Hot Stuff: And he likes her! God, he sounds gorgeous ... and is it just me, or is anyone else going off Mr X a bit?

From Angel: I thought you said Mr X and Julie were like Cathy and Heathcliff?

From Hot Stuff: Yeah, but didn't one of them die in the end? I have to watch that again, I'm sure I have it on DVD somewhere.

From Sexy Girl: Well, I am totally going off Mr X. Can you believe Julie might have to miss meeting James Law? I'd never forgive anyone if they did that to me. I LOVE him.

From Devil Woman: You know what ... now we know where the wrap party is going to be, we should go!!!

From Hot Stuff: OMG! Do you mean it? I would DIE if I got to meet James Law.

From Sexy Girl: Devil Woman, you are inspired!! It'll be a blast. Hey, is Broken Hearted online? A good night out would really cheer her up.

From Broken Hearted: Hi there. Sorry, I can't make it. I have something else on.

From Devil Woman: What about the Plumber then, does he want to go?

From The Plumber: Sorry, I have plans too . . .

From Devil Woman: You two are SO rumbled.

From Broken Hearted: What do you mean?

From Hot Stuff: Are you guys dating??? OMG, that is soooo romantic! Julie's blog has brought two people together!!!

From Devil Woman: We'll have a drink for you guys tonight – toast the happy couple! Hey, Angel, don't suppose you'd like to come?

From Angel: Maybe. If it's not too rowdy.

From Devil Woman: I bet you secretly love James Law. Go on, admit it.

From Angel: I do not. But it might be interesting – in an anthropological way.

From Sexy Girl: Loosen up, Angel. We are hitting Blazin'
Saddles hard!!!

From Devil Woman: Yeeeee hawwww!!!!!!!

Eve

Dear Charlie,

Things are finally looking up! I went on my date with Larry the vet and it turns out that Anna was right about him. He was absolutely gorgeous – six foot tall with a body to die for, amazing green eyes and blond hair. He could have stepped right off the pages of a Carla Ryan novel – I know that because I've finally started reading *Second Chance at Love* and it's not half bad. I'm thinking I may even email Butch the prison officer to tell him I've become a chick-lit fan too. And not only was Larry gorgeous but he was charming as well – funny and witty and warm. I was absolutely dazzled by him. We hit it off straight away, laughing and chatting at everything and nothing – just like we'd known each other for ages. We were halfway through our first drink in the country pub where we met, the conversation was flowing and I was beginning to think that maybe my luck was really changing, when the pager Larry was wearing on his very cute hip started buzzing. Turns out he was on call and a farmer whose cow had just gone into labour wanted him to check that everything was going OK. I tried to hide the fact that I was disappointed he had to leave so soon – after all, we'd been getting on so well – but then he suggested that maybe I could come! He said that it wouldn't take long and then we could get back to our drink. For once in my life I decided to go with the flow, so we piled into his Land Rover and sped to the farm, where an elderly farmer was waiting at the gate looking very anxious. Larry asked me if I wanted to come and see, but I opted to wait in the jeep. I'd seen *All Creatures Great and Small* dozens of times – I knew that a cow giving birth was not going to be a pretty sight. Sitting by myself, watching the glum sheep baying at me from the field opposite, was a far better option. But about half an hour later, Larry came galloping from the barn, dripping in cow slime and yelling that he needed my help. He was going to have to turn the calf to ensure a safe delivery. I knew what was coming next: he wanted me to stick my hand up that cow's bum, just like James Herriot used to do in a cow emergency. But no, he only wanted me to talk to the poor distressed cow and keep her calm while the farmer took an urgent phone call about some corporate camping trip. Apparently he rents out some of his land to firms for those ridiculous bonding weekends that you used to go on sometimes.

So there I was, talking to Daisy the cow (I'm not sure she was called Daisy, but I thought that using a real name had to be better than just saying 'Good cow, good cow' over and over again) and telling her that everything would be all right, that once she saw her baby calf she'd forget all the pain and suffering she was going through. I wasn't too sure if that was completely true of course, but Daisy didn't need to know that.

I said I was sorry there were no epidurals for cows and that maybe next time she might consider a nice C-section – she could be the cow that was too posh to push. Just when I thought I was running out of positive things to say, and she was starting to look like she wanted to strangle me, Larry gave a cheer: the baby calf was here. Then he threw his arms around me and gave me a massive kiss and said I was the best helper he'd ever had; the farmer came back and said if he didn't know better he would have thought we were an old married couple; I wiped off the slime and after-birth Larry had gotten on my best Jigsaw cardigan when he hugged me; and we all trooped inside. And under the pine trestle table, just as the farmer poured me a nice cup of hot sweet tea, Larry felt for my hand and squeezed my fingers tight. And I only had to think for a second or two before I squeezed back.

I didn't tell Anna how well everything had gone, I didn't want to raise her hopes, but I think she guessed because yesterday she dragged me on a shopping trip and insisted I get some new bright clothes to go with my new bright flat. I resisted at first – you know I'm not much of a spender, it's been years since I bought myself anything new and even longer since I took a holiday – but it was so much fun that I gave in eventually. I wouldn't like to say how much I spent, but Anna kept telling me I'm worth it and for once I didn't argue with her.

Eve

Are You a Saver or a Spender?

Take our quiz and find out!

You see a pair of fabulous shoes that you really want but can't afford. Do you:
  a) Buy them immediately on your credit card. You only live once!
  b) Buy them if you have the spare cash. You're trying to cut back on credit card use.
  c) Walk away. If they're still there in the sales you might reconsider.

All your friends are going on an extravagant two-week holiday abroad, but you know it's far too expensive. Do you:

a) Book the trip without a second thought. You wouldn't want your friends to think you were tight.

b) Agree to go for a few nights instead of the full two weeks. That's a reasonable compromise.

c) Tell your friends to send you a postcard. You'll go next time – when you can afford it.

At the end of every month you are usually:

a) Stony broke and already in debt to friends and family.

b) Surviving but counting the minutes to pay day when you can have a life again.

c) Still comfortable – and you've saved almost half your salary.

Results

Mostly As: Hey, Miss Spendthrift – ever heard of a phrase called credit crunch? It's time to tighten that belt a little!

Mostly Bs: Your intentions are good, Little Miss Should Know Better. But you need to follow through with the good deeds – that dream home won't buy itself, you know!

Mostly Cs: You are a fiscal dream, Little Miss Money Bags. But try to treat yourself and your friends every now and again – you don't want to turn into Little Miss Scrooge.

Molly

'Oh my God!' Al screeches down the line, and my eardrum vibrates. 'Are you OK?'

I've just told Al that I fell down the stairs and hurt my shoulder. I've left no detail out because I know that, on the other side of the partition, Penny is listening and possibly taking notes for her top-secret HR file. Since I came back in, she's been waiting for me to forget to pretend that I've got an injured arm, I just know it. She even threw one of her precious KitKat bars across the partition earlier on purpose to see if I'd try to catch it with my bad hand.

'I'm fine,' I say bravely. 'I'm in a lot of pain, of course, but I'm soldiering on.' I throw that in for good measure.

'You didn't ... you didn't do it on purpose, did you?' Al asks. 'You know, because of Charlie and ... everything?'

I can hear veiled excitement in Al's voice. He loves nothing more than a bit of drama. He'd never admit it, but he'd probably be secretly thrilled if I was suicidal.

'Of course not,' I say.

'So you're feeling OK? About Charlie ...?'

The last thing I want to do is talk about Charlie. I haven't told Al or Tanya that he's written to me asking to come back, or that I'm starting to think our marriage has been a terrible mistake, and I'm not going to – not until I figure out exactly what to do.

'Yes, I am,' I reply, trying to sound upbeat and confident.

What I really want to say is 'Kill me, kill me now. Something quick and painless and immediate. Push me under a bus – you could make it look like an accident.' I read about that in the paper only last week. Some poor woman who had just got back from her holiday in Orlando looked the wrong way and stepped right under a 46A. The police reckoned she forgot she was back in Ireland and that traffic drives on the left here. It was really tragic – she was still wearing the Mickey Mouse T-shirt she bought in Disneyland.

'Do you want me to come over tonight?'

I can't see Al today. If he sees me then he'll wheedle everything out of me and I don't want to tell him, not just yet.

'I'm fine, really,' I say. 'I'm just going to lie low after work. I'll call you tomorrow, OK?'

'Don't make me come over there and kick your door down,' he says in mock seriousness.

'Al, you weigh about seven stone, you couldn't kick a cat flap in.' In spite of myself, I start to laugh.

'Yeah, you're probably right,' he says, sighing. 'OK then, I'll get a hot gym bunny to come over and help me. I do love a man in a leotard. I saw this *really* cute guy at the gym yesterday – I think he might have a thing for me.'

'What about your prison officer?' I ask. 'Butch, wasn't it? I thought things were getting hot and heavy between you two?'

'You're right – they were. But then I found out that we had nothing in common. I mean, I can't have a relationship with a man who reads Carla Ryan novels!'

I laugh out loud.

'Now, you're sure you don't need me?'

'I'm sure, I promise.'

I hang up and try to get back to work, remembering to wince with fake pain every so often for effect. Having a shoulder injury was an inspired idea. And who knew I could be so inventive? It took me no time at all to wrap a bandage from my neck to my wrist with some first aid supplies I had in the bathroom. Then all I had to do was stick my arm in a makeshift sling, and I looked like the genuine article. The only tricky part was the train ride into work. I decided that it was critical to practise being disabled before I had to fake it in the office, so I forced myself to use only one hand to balance both a book and a coffee at the same time. It was going quite well until I spilled some of the coffee on the woman sitting opposite me and I thought she was going to break my other arm for real. At least I got a seat though, that part was great. Usually I have to stand on the train, but being temporarily disabled meant I could sit and just concentrate on looking brave for the whole journey. And work has been a breeze so far. I'm even thinking I might prolong the shoulder thing for a while. Samantha has been so nice to me all morning that it's almost worth it. It's not even that hard to remember to act like I'm in agony. In fact, I've got so good at the little charade that I've almost convinced myself that I *have* hurt my shoulder. I'm even whimpering with pain when no one is looking at me.

'Are you sure you should have come back quite so soon?' Samantha says now, looking at me with concern as I make a pained expression for the umpteenth time.

'I'm OK.' I smile, flinching a little. 'I don't know if I'm up to photocopying though.'

I look feebly over at the stack of press releases from publicists waiting to be copied so Minty can look through them. Photocopying is my least favourite job. Somehow that damned machine always seems to jam whenever I go anywhere near it.

'No, of course not.' She tuts in sympathy. 'You poor thing, that could do you even more damage. I'll do them.'

'Eh?' Penny pops her head over the partition. 'You never do anything for me!'

'Penny, that's really insensitive of you,' Samantha says, frowning at her. 'Molly here is in serious pain. She probably should still be at home taking things easy.'

I smile angelically. This is great. I do feel a bit guilty that Samantha has fallen so completely for my story, but then again she likes to look after people – it makes her feel good.

'Will I get you some chocolate?' she goes on. 'You might need perking up – you look a bit pale.'

'Ah no, I'm OK,' I say, 'I'm not really hungry.'

I suck in my cheeks to emphasize my cheekbones. The more haggard and skeletal I can look, the better. I'm not lying about the hunger: my appetite is still a bit off. Funny though, I'm starting to think I might be able to manage a packet of crisps. Cheese and onion ones would be lovely. And maybe some chocolate – just a square or two. I might get her to run to the shop for me later.

'Well, you need to mind yourself after such a nasty tumble,' she says, patting my good arm. 'I know someone who took a terrible fall and got such a fright they didn't eat for three weeks.'

'What a load of horseshit,' Penny sneers. 'They were probably trying to make a false insurance claim. People can be very dishonest.'

I feel my cheeks burn. I know that's a veiled message to me. Penny doesn't believe my story, that's obvious.

Samantha ignores her. 'Have you seen Minty yet?' she asks me.

'Not yet,' I gulp.

I'm dreading seeing Minty. If she finds out that I'm faking my arm injury I may as well throw myself down the stairs for real. I've been trying to keep a low profile and stay out of her sight all morning. Mostly because I'm afraid that she'll know immediately that there's nothing wrong with me, but also because, even though I've made good progress on the Carla Ryan piece and David's interview for the next issue, I still haven't started the feature on marriage yet and she's bound to want to see it soon.

I've arranged stacks of paperwork all over my desk to hide behind and keep out of her eye line. It's working quite well, but I know it's only a matter of time. When she eventually spots me she'll remember I'm supposed to have finished it days ago and then I'm going to be in big trouble. Capital B, capital T. I had a really close call in the Ladies earlier. I could hear her in the stall next to me – she has a very distinctive peeing noise, she likes to practise her Kegel exercises while she goes, so there's lots of stopping and starting of the flow. Once I knew it was her, I sat on the toilet seat with my feet jammed up on the wall so she wouldn't recognize my shoes, haul me out of the cubicle and demand the piece right there in front of the energy-efficient hand dryer. I wasn't taking any chances. Everyone knows that Minty likes to check under cubicle doors to make sure that people aren't taking too many toilet breaks. She firmly believes that if everyone practised their Kegels as much as she does, they'd only have to pee twice a day: once in the morning, once in the evening. She thinks weak bladder control is for sissies – she even tried to get it timetabled for discussion once. And of course there was that really embarrassing incident when a temp who'd just had her first baby sneezed during a briefing and Minty asked if she was going to have to get the chair re-upholstered. Sometimes I'm sitting opposite Minty in a meeting and I can tell she's doing internal squeezes, just from the concentrated expression on her pinched little face.

The thing is, I can't write that marriage piece. Every time I try, my mind goes completely and utterly blank – like it used to when I was doing school exams. I know the information must be in there somewhere, but I can't get it out onto the page. The problem is the hook. All I have to do is get a good hook and then the rest will flow. But getting the hook is proving impossible and I'm gripped by a terrible fear. I stare at the screen, willing the words to come.

'*The day I got married was the happiest day of my life,*' I type slowly, making sure to only use the fingers on my good hand, just in case anyone is watching. So far, so good.

But ... was it really the happiest day ever? I mean, I certainly *thought* I'd been happy at the time. I close my eyes and try to visualize my walk down the aisle. I can see myself floating along to the soft strains of classical music. I'm smiling and nodding serenely at people as I glide, just like Mother Teresa, but in a figure-hugging designer wedding dress. I'm going for the graceful, angelic look. With just a hint of understated Hollywood glamour. All the gliding practice that Alastair made me do is really paying off: the endless traipsing round the living room with an encyclopedia balanced on my head, my shoulders out and my bum in – it's working a treat. I may have done irreversible damage to my spine by carrying a ten-pound book around on my skull for weeks, but it's all worth it now. So what if I end up in a wheelchair by the time I'm thirty-five? I can hear people actually gasping with joy – unless someone is having a chronic asthma attack ... I can't be sure. But they all look like they're in awe, and that's the most important thing. I wonder if I shouldn't lift my hand and give them a little wave, like the Royals do, just to let them know I bestow my kindness upon them. Then again, that could be too much – it might alienate them. So I decide to nod a bit more instead, and then mix it up by bowing my head demurely now and again and lowering my eyes, like Princess Diana used to do in her heyday. I think it's the perfect blend. It says, 'I'm beautiful, but modest. Saintly, but humble.'

Tanya is in front of me in her one-of-a-kind satin appliqué bridesmaid gown. Her back is as ramrod straight as mine, but I think that's because her dress is now two sizes too small, on account of her putting on a bit of weight since the last fitting. She claims that she can't have gone up two dress sizes in as many months, and that the dress designer, Zandray, must have made a complete mess of the measurements, but I think she's fooling herself. Zandray is a legend in fashion circles, a creative genius who designs gowns for all sorts of celebrities, and he doesn't make mistakes – even if Tanya swears she smelt sweet sherry on his breath last time he got the tape measure out. Whatever the reason, she has to suck in her belly, which means she's walking very slowly in front of me. Strangely, it's working brilliantly: she looks like a lowly handmaid, preparing the path for her queen (that'd be me). I'm starting to think I should have given her a basket of petals to scatter about, just to add to the mood. Still, I can tell that she's in serious pain. Of course, that could be more to do with the complicated up-do that the hairdresser gave her at the last minute. Fixing hair extensions to her head to give the illusion of volume was an inspired idea, even if Tanya wasn't very happy and said she looked like a big-haired freak.

If I'm honest, I'm secretly pleased that she's put on a bit of weight, because at least now I'll look slim in the wedding photographs. It's terrible to admit this, I know, but I've spent years as the podgy sister, sulking beside her in Polaroids. Today is my time to shine, and if that means Tanya has to be humiliated a little, then so be it. From this angle, I can now understand why she was concerned about wearing satin though. It *is* a little unflattering on her bum, especially now you can see the massive seams of her suck-it-in corset digging into her buttocks through the fabric.

I shoot a glance to the side, just to check that everyone is paying attention and that all eyes are on me. They should be: I look amazing. Not just OK, or passable, but properly beautiful. The two hours with the make-up artist has sorted that out. I was devastated when Jenna wasn't able to come at the last minute – she is the best make-up artist around and she'd sworn blind she'd be able to do my face for the day – but apparently there was some emergency with a strung-out model and a temperamental designer on an underwear photo shoot across town and she had to send her assistant Cassandra instead.

I was dubious about Cassandra at first. She looked nothing like Jenna, who wears her hair knotted on top of her head in a chic, Parisian way. (When I try to knot my hair I always end up looking hard-faced and common, and not at all like I should be strolling along the Champs-Elysées with a poodle at my feet.) Cassandra was arty and had a very angry expression, although I think that may have been part of her 'look' – at least that's what I told myself in an attempt not to cry with fear. She was wearing a tie-dye T-shirt and had at least half a dozen earrings in her left ear and a tattoo saying *fuckwit* in Celtic script on her forearm. She made me very, very nervous, but I didn't have much choice about it all. It was her or nothing. There was no way on earth I could do the make-up myself. I always forget to rub the foundation in properly round my jawline, and my hands shake so much when I try to apply eyeliner that I usually have to give up. Still, it turned out well in the end. The only thing I'm not completely sure about is the bright blue colour she put on my eyelids. She insisted I needed something to highlight my piggy eyes, and that aqua blue would make them 'pop'.

'But shouldn't I go for a more traditional look?' I'd asked as I was sitting trapped in the make-up chair, a giant bib wrapped round me so I couldn't move. I really wasn't certain if the 1980s colours would suit my complexion – they hadn't the first time round. I could still remember being the laughing stock of the youth club disco when I turned up in my new Madonna look, neon bright make-up and all.

'Maybe beige would suit my complexion better? I was thinking we could do something softer ...' I trailed off, remembering the beautiful make-up Jenna had done in her practice run.

Cassandra had frowned at me, looking mortally wounded.

'Well, you can have beige if you want to be like every other bride in the country,' she'd eventually sniffed. 'But I thought you wanted something special, something a bit different. Aqua is a very directional colour. It was huge at the shows in London.'

I looked round, frantically trying to catch Tanya's attention to get her opinion, but she was pretending to be dead while the hairdresser attacked her with an industrial-sized hairdryer and what looked like a rat's tail.

'OK then,' I whimpered, and closed my eyes, hoping for the best. When I opened them again, my face had been transformed by eyeshadow and blusher and a bucketload of glitter.

'What's that for?' I asked, feeling panicky. Surely glitter was a bit OTT?

'The photos, of course,' she said, as if I was a brainless

fool who hadn't a clue how these things worked. 'You want to sparkle!'

Then she looked off into the middle distance, all dreamy and misty eyed. 'You look just like the models at the Dolce show this season. *Fierce.*'

Before I had time to think about whether 'fierce' was really the look I was aiming for, I was scrambling into my dress and I was on my way to the church.

Now though, as I glide up the aisle, I'm delighted I took her advice. I never should have doubted her – even if she kept growling at me as she sponged on the foundation. She obviously knew what she was doing, all the aqua and the glitter really seem to be dazzling people: I can see lots of them pointing at me as I glide by. Jaws are quite literally dropping. It feels brilliant. This must be what the super-models feel like every day of the week: sexy and powerful and the centre of attention. I suddenly wonder if I don't have an international career in modelling ahead of me. I'm really rather good at this strutting stuff, I could make a small fortune. If only there was a talent scout in the congregation, a big name in the fashion industry. Of course, he'd have to be searching for a particular look, like someone who's only five foot four, is on the curvy side and has piggy eyes. Then again, quirky is the new sexy, everyone knows that. I mean, there are supermodels raking in millions who you wouldn't look at twice in the street. Well, you might, but only to gawp at their twig legs or towering height or lollipop heads. And my body is looking the best it's ever been. Which usually wouldn't be saying much, but today I know it's looking pretty spectacular. For once, my curves aren't the wrong side of podgy: the seaweed wrap has sorted that out. I'm so glad I paid all that money to have it done; it was really worth it to get rid of all the bulges. Besides, being wrapped up in all those bandages wasn't too bad; once you got used to them and didn't breathe in the revolting fishy fumes it was almost bearable. I'm not sure how long the effects will last though, so, just to make sure, I'm wearing a bust-to-hip roll-on corset. Fat rolls can be sneaky. You never know when they might pop back out to say hello and try to grab some of the limelight. But right now my gorgeous dress is hugging every contour, my skin is gleaming (I've had so many pre-wedding facials most of the top layers of my epidermis have been stripped away) and my hair is perfect (no frizz, no kinks, just soft and bouncy and like a TV ad). This is my perfect moment, the moment when everyone will see that I'm glamorous and poised and elegant. I'm so happy. Maybe the happiest I've ever been.

I open my eyes and try to hold on to that feeling. If I can remember it properly then I should be able to translate it on to the page.

'*Being married is amazing.*'

That's not a bad hook. Maybe not punchy enough, but it could work. Then I hear a little voice inside me. 'What would you know about an amazing marriage? Your husband hightailed it out of here faster than you could say one-month anniversary, your sister and your best friend think he might be having an affair and you're starting to think the whole thing was one big mistake. You're not qualified to write about love or marriage or any kind of relationship. You're a relationship disaster zone.'

Sometimes I wish I didn't have such a strong inner voice. It's really hard to concentrate when it yaks at me all the time.

'*Marriage is a meeting of minds as well as bodies.*'

Well, that's a big fat lie. For one thing, Charlie's mind is a bit of a mystery to me: he reads *The Economist* and he hates

The X Factor. And we never really had the whole passionate thing. But I'm not going to think about that part, because that would just depress me even more and I've been feeling bad enough ever since that taxi driver made me realize what was missing in our relationship.

'*Marriage can have its ups and downs.*'

'*Marriage is for life.*'

Nothing sounds right. It's hopeless, I can't do it. I'm dead.

When Minty finds out that I haven't even started it, she'll go ballistic. She might even throw something at me. She chucked her precious quartz paperweight at someone once. Luckily it missed, but it hit a wall in her office with such force that it left an enormous crack. The crack was never repaired. Instead Minty drew a love heart round it, just to remind everyone what she's capable of.

But even if she doesn't throw something, she'll definitely shout at me. If yelling was an Olympic sport, Minty would get the gold medal. Even worse, she might start that whispering thing she does to scare people, when she talks so quietly that you have to nearly crawl across her desk to understand what she's saying. It's amazingly effective. When she does that, you know you may as well pack up your belongings and run.

Maybe I should tell her about Charlie. Maybe then she'd cut me some slack. I could send her an email and confide that I'm going through an emotionally difficult period and need some compassion in the workplace. But she'd probably forward the email to everyone and then they'd all know. Like that time when the IT guy told her he needed time off to see a shrink for his OCD. She sent that mail to everyone she knew – she thought it was hilarious that he couldn't leave the house without switching his lights on and off fifty-three times. The poor guy left soon after.

No, I can't tell her. If I tell her then everyone will know, and I just can't face people talking about me. It was bad enough when Mum and Dad died and every time I walked into the room people stopped talking. It would be worse if everyone knew that Charlie had given up on us so soon after we got married, even if he wants to come back now. And he's not even had the good grace to die; he's just abandoned me. An orphan *and* a deserted wife – that would be enough tragedy to keep the office going for weeks. And, worst of all, Minty would probably want me to write about it if she thought it'd make a good feature. She wanted Penny to write about being stood up at the altar after all.

'Molly, fab news!' Samantha chirps, placing a steaming cup of tea in front of me and interrupting my train of thought. 'You know I've been trying to set up that photo shoot with David Rendell? Well, he's finally agreed to it. Isn't that great?'

My stomach lurches. This is all I need. I don't want to see David again. I don't want to see him look at me the way he did during the interview, like he despises me, like he hates me with every fibre of his body.

'Aren't you pleased?' Samantha asks, looking disappointed that I'm not hopping across the desk to hug her. 'I thought you'd be delighted that I took the initiative and organized everything.'

I look at her sad face and I know I have to lie to save her feelings.

'Of course I'm delighted!' I give her a big smile. 'Great work, Samantha.'

She skips away and my heart falls. I'm going to see David

again, and this time it's going to be worse than before. This time will be much, much worse, because now I know what I threw away when I left him.

Julie's Blog

8.01 a.m.

The nightmare has become a reality. We are on a minibus on our way to the corporate-bonding campsite facility. We have been allowed to bring one pair of stout walking shoes (as if I possessed such a thing) and one change of clothes (including naff wet gear), but no make-up, alcohol or electronic equipment. Luckily, I managed to sneak this BlackBerry along so I can still blog. I also smuggled some body glitter, mascara and lipstick. No one gets to see me au naturel as long as I can help it. I'm sitting at the back of the bus, as far away from Mr X as I can. I'm concentrating on ignoring him as much as possible. The more I think about it, the more I realize that he really *is* suffocating me. I've given up almost everything for him – clubbing, takeout food, a good night's sleep – and what has he done for me? Not much, besides keeping me awake at night with his snoring and almost poisoning me with his cooking. And now he's winding me up at work – he's really piling on the pressure about Mr Dick Lit's campaign. He keeps on and on about the fictitious *Elle* feature. I'm almost convinced he wants me to fail. I'm glad I'm sitting back here, especially because the janitor is sitting directly behind me. I can almost feel his breath hot on my neck.

9.05 a.m.

UC One has just started a country and western singalong and is encouraging everyone to join in the chorus of some

Dixie Chicks song. I will have to pretend to fall into a coma soon if she doesn't stop. That's if I don't fall into a coma for real. The absolute boredom is already killing me.

9.07 a.m.
The janitor just passed me a tiny flask of contraband whiskey and whispered in my ear to take a sip. I could be wrong, but I think his tongue lingered next to my ear lobe at least two seconds longer than necessary. Starting to feel just a tiny bit better.

9.30 a.m.
We are here. Here being a farm in the middle of nowhere. A crusty old farmer welcomed us at the gate and directed us to our tents, which are plonked in a circle round the perimeter of a muddy field. We now have ten minutes to drop off our stuff and then meet at the designated spot to begin the activities. I wonder if I just hid out in my tent, would anyone notice I was missing?

9.39 a.m.
The janitor just stuck his head in my tent and said not to even think about hiding out and that he was going to bring the whiskey flask in case the going got tough. It was the first belly laugh I've had in ages. Mr X's tent is across the other side of the field. I could see him chatting to UC One as he emptied his rucksack. Am quite glad he's so far away – at least I might get a good night's sleep for a change.

10.48 a.m.
Just finished a trust-building exercise. We had to choose a partner, allow ourselves to fall backwards into their arms and trust they would catch us and not let us drop to the

ground. UC One grabbed Mr X immediately and then threw herself at him, winding her arms round his neck as she fell. The instructor had to explain to her that she was missing the point: she was supposed to turn her back to Mr X, close her eyes and fall slowly into his arms while he caught her. I could tell by the look on her face that she hadn't missed the point at all: she'd engineered the whole thing and was thoroughly enjoying slobbering all over him, pretending that she was terrified.

I paired up with UC Two. I hadn't realized quite how hefty she is. I really had to struggle to keep my balance when I was catching her. The janitor was paired off with UC Three. I had to force myself to stop staring at him as he caught her time and time again, his muscular arms curving easily round her sides without skipping a beat.

3.04 p.m.

Just back from the assault course. Had to clamber over obstacles, slither through tunnels and swing across dykes, all to prove that we can work well together as a team. It was completely pointless. Everyone knows that we'll never help each other again when we get back to the office: PR is all about one-upmanship. Highlight was watching UC One plunge into the water after she lost her grip on the rope. It was pretty funny, especially when Mr X had to wade in and come to her rescue.

11.03 p.m.

In tent. Thank God that day is over. UCs are all still singing stupid boy scout songs round the campfire. UC One has just passed round lighters and told everyone to hold them in the air for fun. She's lucky I didn't set fire to her thermal fleece bobble hat.

11.07 p.m.

The janitor just stuck his head in my tent and asked if I wanted to go and see a baby calf that was born a few days ago. Said I would, but only if he can give me some more of that contraband whiskey. Where's the harm? Going to see newborn baby animals is cute and perfectly innocent. It's not like anything's going to happen.

12.41 a.m.

Oh God. Just accidentally snogged the janitor in the cow shed. I didn't mean to, but he's so sexy and the calf was so cute and it just happened. And my God – it was AMAZING. It was all I could do not to throw him into the haystack and live out my farmhand fantasy. But now I'm crippled with fear. What if Mr X finds out? What if someone saw us? I'll have to sneak over to his tent and talk to him; try to explain before anyone else gets there first.

1.00 a.m.

Just back from Mr X's tent. I didn't get a chance to explain anything because when I pulled the tent flaps aside I saw he was in there with UC One. They tried to tell me they were just practising their trust exercises for tomorrow, but it was obvious what was going on. You don't have to be half-dressed to engage in corporate bonding. The truth is staring me in the face: Mr X is now cheating on *me*, the person he cheated on his wife with. Talk about ironic justice. The thing is, I'm not that upset. Well, I am a little. How could he do this to me when he told me he loved me? I know the answer to that, of course. It doesn't take a scientist to figure out that he never loved me at all.

I feel really ashamed of myself. I should never have got involved with him in the first place. I knew he was engaged when all this started, it was my fault as much as his. I keep thinking about his wife and how she must have felt when she discovered he had left her. I hope she knows what a love rat he is. If I'm honest, though, most of all I'm relieved, because if Mr X is with UC One that means he's not my problem any more ... I'm free!

Open Forum

From Devil Woman: That bastard. I can't believe he was cheating on her.

From Broken Hearted: I can. It's textbook.

From The Plumber: You were right, Broken Hearted. You are so insightful.

From Devil Woman: Oh, get a room you two!

From Hot Stuff: It sounds like she had a lucky escape.

From Angel: I feel a bit sorry for her actually.

From Devil Woman: Eh? I thought you always said she was going to rot in hell for having an affair with a married man?

From Angel: Well, yes, I did. But she sounds like she's sorry for what she did. Maybe I was a bit hard on her.

From Devil Woman: Angel, I don't think you're as militant as you make out.

From Hot Stuff: I think you're a big softie.

From Sexy Girl: It's not soft the way you can down cocktails! What were you like at that wrap party?

From Angel: Sorry about that. I hadn't drunk alcohol in a long time.

From Devil Woman: Well, you should get out more then!

From Angel: It wasn't as bad as I thought it would be, I have to admit.

From Devil Woman: Hey, Sexy Girl, where did you disappear to at the end of the night?

From Sexy Girl: If I told you I snogged James Law, would you believe me?

From Hot Stuff: OMG!!!! That is so ROMANTIC!!!!

Eve

Dear Charlie,

I've invited Larry the vet for dinner. I can't believe that I had the courage to do it, but when he called to ask me out again I heard myself suggesting that maybe he'd like to come round here for something to eat. I really don't know what possessed me, but Mary the therapist is very pleased. She says that I need to be open to love and welcome it into my life, and if that means cooking a traditional roast chicken dinner for eight then so be it. Yes, eight. You see, I've invited Anna and Derek to come along too. Anna says that Derek doesn't deserve a nice roast dinner after what he's put her and her underwear through, but I told her she'd have to put her animosity towards him to one side for this meal, just for me. She's sworn she won't throw anything at him, even if she thinks he's having another relapse, but I'm going to seat her as far away from the condiments as I can, just in case. I've seen her hurl a pepper pot before and it wasn't pretty.

Mary says inviting Larry to dinner is an important step for me because it means I may be ready to trust someone again, and that this could mark the start of a whole new chapter in my life. She says that if I believe I'm worthy of good things, then good things will happen to me, so I'm busy telling myself that I deserve to have an exquisite dinner party where nothing gets burnt, no one gets too drunk and, most of all, no one gets hit over the head with a pepper pot.

Johnny the plumber and his new girlfriend are coming

too. He met her on some Internet chat site and they hooked up properly when she got him to fix a leak in her bathroom. It sounds bizarre, but they look really happy. I found them snogging passionately beside the lift yesterday and couldn't help but ask them both along. They asked whether they could bring some AC/DC to help set the mood – they're *both* fans apparently – but I told them that I'd already got the music sorted because I'm planning to ask Homer for some of his classical stuff to play in the background. I'm really happy for Johnny. He hasn't looked as alive in ages.

I've asked Homer too. He's still been acting strangely since the whole vase episode, but he's just about finished the painting and I really want him to be there for the first dinner party I host in my new, improved yellow flat, especially as he was the one who chose the colour in the first place. He looked a bit unsure about the idea initially, but I told him I wouldn't crack anything over his head if he came along and then he smiled this funny, almost sad smile and said that was a pity. Then there was this awkward silence, and to break the ice I said he should bring his girlfriend along because I was inviting a hot date myself so it would mean even numbers. Anna says he's been dating some bimbo on and off. I can't imagine Homer with a bimbo – he's so intelligent and well mannered – but Anna says the bimbo is mad about him and rarely lets him out of her sight. Anyway, he went a bit red when I mentioned the hot date thing, and then he said OK, and I was so happy that I couldn't help but give him a quick hug and tell him I've really missed our little chats over herbal tea. He hugged me back briefly and I immediately remembered the night I whacked him over the head and he'd wrapped his arms around me and I had rested my head on his chest. Then he backed away and the moment was lost again.

Anna is really excited about the dinner. She keeps asking me if this is it – if Larry could be the One. She's even more eager to find out if I'm going to jump his bones, as she puts it. I told her that I didn't know if there was any chemistry between Larry and me – that he seemed like a really nice guy and that was good enough for the time being. But Anna said that was horseshit and if there was any chemistry I would know all about it – I'd feel it in my bones every time I looked at him or touched him. I felt a bit strange when she said that, but I tried not to linger on it too much. I don't want any distractions, I have enough to concentrate on trying to sort out a dinner party for eight. Even thinking about making the gravy has me breaking out in a cold sweat. Sex and passion are the last things on my mind.

Eve

Are You Red Hot or Ice Cold?

Is passion important to you? Do you need to spice up your love life or is the flame of lust still burning brightly between you and your man? Take our quiz and find out!

You think sex is:
 a) Overrated. You'd much prefer to watch a good
    soap opera.
 b) Underrated. Everyone should be doing it as much
    as possible.
 c) Gross. All that sweating and heavy breathing
    leaves you cold.

Your favourite position is:
a) Missionary. That way you can watch TV over his shoulder.
b) On top. It's much more intense that way.
c) Comatose. You usually pretend to be asleep.

You have sex:
a) Once a month – more when the Hollywood writers strike was on.
b) Every day – you still can't keep your hands off your man.
c) As little as possible, and never on Fridays – it really musses up your blow-dry.

Results

Mostly As: You need to add a little spice to your love life. Why not pretend your man is one of your favourite soap stars? Fantasizing can really heat things up in the bedroom.

Mostly Bs: You and your man still have it going on. Make sure you're not wearing him out, tiger!

Mostly Cs: Sex shouldn't be a chore. Let your hair down and loosen up a bit – you might just enjoy it!

Molly

'Oh my God. He wants to come back?! What are you going to do?' Tanya hisses down the phone.

I've briefly told Tanya about Charlie's letter. I've also told her that I'm surrounded by people at a photo shoot so I can't discuss it in graphic, Technicolor detail, no matter how much she wants me to. I should have waited to tell her when I could talk properly, I shouldn't have said a word about it, but she knew by my voice when I answered her call that something had happened, so I had to fess up. I've been avoiding her – which hasn't been hard to do because she's in New York on business – so she was already suspicious.

'I don't know,' I say carefully in a low voice. 'I have to think about it.'

If I'm honest, I've done nothing *but* think about this whole mess since I got Charlie's letter, but I still don't know exactly what I'm going to do. I've become more and more convinced that things were never really right between us, but I can't decide if we should try to salvage our relationship or not. All I know for sure is that time is running out. Charlie will be waiting to hear from me, and if I don't get in touch soon, odds are he will arrive on my doorstep himself and demand an answer.

'Have you thought about what we said? About . . . Charlie and another woman?'

I can hear her clearing her throat as she asks me that. I know that even mentioning it again is making her uncomfortable, but she feels she has to. She wants to protect me, just like when we were little and another child was nasty to me in the playground.

'Not really, I haven't had time, work has been crazy.'

This is a lie. I don't know for sure if there's anyone else involved, but I've started to think it's a strong possibility. The most worrying thing is that I'm not consumed by jealousy at the thought of Charlie in another woman's arms, and I know that can't be normal.

'Well, don't make any rash decisions. Think everything through fully.' Her voice is anxious.

'OK, I promise,' I say. 'Now, I'd better go – the shoot is about to start.'

'Who's it for, anyway?' she asks, and I toy with the idea of telling her that it's for David, that I'm doing a feature on him for *Her*, that today we've booked a studio to get some shots for the magazine, but I can't bring myself to say it. Tanya adored David. I know that secretly she'd be thrilled if she knew we'd met again. How can I tell her that he hates me now? That he despises the ground I walk on? She'd be horrified. And anyway, if I did tell her, I'd *never* get her off the phone.

'No one you know,' I lie. 'I'd better go, he's here.'

That last part is true. David has just walked into the studio. He hasn't spotted me yet because when Tanya called I half hid myself behind a pillar towards the back of the room to talk to her in semi-private. I snap my phone shut quickly before Tanya can ask me any more awkward questions and I hover there now, glad I have a minute to compose myself before I have to greet him. I sidle right behind the pillar and peek out to get a proper look. And when I do, I can't help but catch my breath. He looks great. His cheeks are flushed and he's panting slightly. He must have sprinted up the stairs. He never could take the lift; he always insisted on running up, two steps at a time, as fast as he could.

'Come on, Molly!' he'd yell when I grumbled that if God wanted us to take the stairs then he wouldn't have invented elevators. 'Don't be a lazybones!'

Then he'd grab me by the hand and haul me up as many flights as I could manage. I often pretended to have a stitch just so he'd throw me across his shoulders and carry me the rest of the way. He was so strong, he would fling me easily across his back, making me feel like I was a featherweight slip of a girl, instead of the sturdy thing I was in reality. He always made me feel protected and cared for. It was one of the things I loved most about him. I knew he would keep me safe, no matter what.

I look at him now as he shrugs off his coat and runs his hands through his hair, all the while frowning just a little. I can tell he's anxious. He hates having his photo taken, so he must be dreading this. I'm surprised he agreed to it at all. I have a sudden insane urge to run across the room, throw my arms around him and tell him that everything will be all right, that I'll make sure it's OK, that I'll make it easy for him. I've already removed the pineapple from the fruit basket because I know he's allergic to it. Looking at him now, it's all I can do not to hurl myself into his arms and swear to protect him from anything dangerous that will ever come his way, no matter what. But I can't, because I know if I do he'll look at me like I'm the most pathetic creature on the planet, just like he did in the hotel lobby during that terrible interview.

'What are you doing back there, silly?' It's Samantha. She's in her element. She chattered non-stop all the way over here. Strangely, it was quite comforting to listen to.

'Nothing,' I mutter, hoping she didn't catch me mooning over him.

'Here, take my glasses,' she says, smiling kindly and holding out the massive sunnies to me. 'You know, so you can chat to David without him freaking out.'

I pause for a split second before I put them on. As far as Samantha knows, David can't look anyone in the eye without having a nervous episode. And last time I met him, I told him I was photosensitive. If I don't wear them today, he'll know I was lying to him. I can't let that happen. I have to keep pretending so he doesn't find out the truth — that I was only wearing them so he couldn't see my haggard face.

'OK, we're going to make this as painless as possible,' the photographer shouts, interrupting my thoughts. 'David, you're a handsome bloke so it shouldn't be hard. What's the look we're going for?'

The photographer turns to find me. I'm meant to tell him the type of thing that would work well on our magazine pages. I should have done this long before David arrived. Now I have to speak in front of him. I feel my cheeks burn with shame as I shuffle out from behind the pillar.

'Ah, there she is!' the photographer calls sarcastically. 'The woman with all the answers.'

David glances up and I see a look of faint shock register on his face before he quickly hides it. He didn't expect me to be here today, that's obvious.

'So, what are you looking for?' the photographer asks again, cocking his head quizzically. He's impatient, I can tell. He probably has another job to get to and he wants this to be over as quickly as possible.

'Um . . .' I stumble over my words, trying to think of the right thing to say. Nothing comes. I know I must look like a disorganized idiot, but I just can't think of what I'm supposed to say. I've done these photo shoots a million times before, I know what I'm doing, so why has my tongue decided to stick to the roof of my mouth now?

The photographer stares at me. He has a reputation for being a hothead who doesn't suffer fools. I can almost see him twitching with annoyance. If I don't come up with something credible soon, he'll probably explode.

'Moody!' Samantha offers confidently from behind me when I still say nothing. 'Sexy-moody to be exact. That's what we're looking for.'

I smile gratefully at Samantha, who beams back.

The photographer jerks his head at us like he knows exactly what we mean.

'OK, sexy-moody. Gotcha. Shouldn't be a problem.'

I look at David. He's chatting amiably to the photographer's assistant, who's angling his body in the best position to catch the light. His half-smile pierces my heart and I struggle for composure.

'David, you can do sexy-moody, right?'

'I'll try,' he says quietly, staring steadfastly ahead.

'Great!' the photographer yells. 'Let's get started.'

The assistant does a last-minute adjustment to the studio lights and within seconds the photographer starts to snap, yelling directions to David as he goes.

'Good, that's great. Lift your chin. Not too high. Perfect!'

David looks into the lens, his expression unreadable.

The photographer stops snapping.

'I need more. I need you to look soulful. Think of something sad that happened to you and project it through your eyes.'

'Sad?' David asks.

'Yeah! Sad! You're devastated. You're heartbroken. The

love of your life has left you and you're in bits. I want you to feel it! I want you to show it to me!'

In slow motion, David turns and looks straight at me and I feel my hands start to shake. His eyes bore through me. My whole body is shaking now. I've seen him look at me that way before. He looked exactly the same when I told him I didn't love him any more. When I told him I wanted to leave and I didn't want him to come with me. The expression on his face now is just as it was then. It's bleak.

In a flash I'm right back to that moment when I turned my back on him and walked out of his life, and I know for sure now that he will never forgive me for it.

'That's it! *Perfect!*' I can hear the photographer snapping and yelling and before I know what I'm doing, I'm running out of the studio, wrenching the sunglasses from my face and throwing them to the floor as I sprint. Tears are streaming down my cheeks and I fight to catch my breath.

I can hear Samantha call my name but I keep going. I want to run for ever. I race down the stairs and out through the front door, gulping for air. If I can just get outside, I know I'll be able to breathe properly again. I force my way through the throngs of people on the footpath, blind with tears, only knowing that I have to get out of here and fast, not caring who's in my way. Then I collide head on with someone, someone who refuses to move. I dodge right and then left to try to pass, but still the person hulks in front of me, refusing to budge.

Through my tears I can see a vague outline of something multicoloured on this person's head. It looks like a turban.

'What the fuck is going on?' the person says, and I know who it is immediately. It's Carla Ryan, the queen of chick lit.

*

An hour later, Carla and I are sitting in a quiet booth in a wine bar, sipping our second glass of house red.

'So, what you're telling me is that your new husband upped and left you straight after your honeymoon?'

'Yes.' I nod. 'That's what I'm telling you.'

'And now he wants to come back?'

'Yes.' I nod again.

This whole situation is surreal. I'm pouring my heart out to a woman I have only met once before, but for some reason it feels like the most natural thing in the world.

'That's crazy. Who does he think he is, some sort of ridiculous chick-lit character?' Carla smirks across the table at me and I can't help but smile back.

Obviously she reads her own reviews: her books have often been accused of having far-fetched characters and plots – even her publicist thinks so.

'So, what are you going to do?' she asks, topping up my drink from the bottle we ordered.

I fiddle with my glass.

'I don't know.'

'It's quite simple really, if you think about it.'

'It is?' I'm confused. How can she possibly think that all this mess is simple?

'Of course. Do you love this wandering husband of yours?'

I think about this.

'I'm not sure,' I answer.

'You're not sure?' She cocks a straggly eyebrow at me. She could definitely do with a good plucking session. Maybe some Indian threading – that's meant to work wonders.

'I thought I did,' I say eventually. It doesn't sound very convincing, even to me.

'What does that mean?' Carla puts her two elbows on the

299

table and leans towards me, narrowly missing the bottle of wine.

'Well, he really wanted to marry me,' I offer weakly. 'That must have meant we were in love, right?'

'People get married for all sorts of reasons.'

I ignore that. That's a notion I definitely don't want to think about.

'He was so smitten,' I say. 'He chased me – you know, really pursued me – like in a romance novel.'

'And he persuaded you to marry him?'

'Yeah. I was so blown away by it all, I guess I didn't worry too much about how I really felt. I was just swept along . . .'

As I say it, I realize it's true. I was so overcome by all the romance and grand gestures that I didn't take the time to examine my own true feelings. My stomach flips at the thought.

'Is there another woman, do you think?' Carla asks.

'I don't know.' I think about what Tanya and Al said, that Charlie having an affair could be the perfect explanation for all this.

'If there was, how would you feel about that?'

I think about Charlie with someone else, kissing someone else, making love to someone else. If I really loved him I'd be devastated at the thought of him with another woman, surely? But I'm not and I know that can't be right.

Carla scratches her turban and twists it about, scowling as she does.

'Would you mind if I took this damn thing off?' she asks, and before I can answer she wrenches it from her head and a mane of glossy chestnut hair falls to her shoulders.

I gasp. She has beautiful hair. I can't imagine for a minute why she would hide it all under such a hideous polyester wrap.

'I like to keep something for myself.' She smiles slowly, seeing my expression. 'I know what people say about me – that I'm plain and past it. This is a side that no one gets to see but me, and that's the way I like to keep it. Well, no one but me and my lovers of course!' She laughs throatily. 'That bitch Noreen Brady might have a fight on her hands for the number one slot on the best-sellers list this year. She thinks she's all that with her brassy hair and her fake boobs, but I scrub up quite well, you know.'

I smile across the table at her. If only her publishers knew what she really looked like they might reconsider putting her photo on the jackets of her books.

'You told me when we first met that you had found your soulmate. Was it Charlie?'

'No,' I say eventually, and I know it's true.

'Well, if Charlie isn't your soulmate then who is?'

I twist my glass again but I don't answer her, I'm terrified to say it out loud. Because saying it out loud means I would have to admit it to myself, and I'm not ready to do that.

Carla stares at me and then smiles widely. 'Let me ask you this. If this *was* a Carla Ryan novel, if you *were* writing this story, what would be your happy ending?'

A scenario comes flooding into my mind but I push it away quickly. There's no point even thinking about it because this isn't some chick-lit novel where the happy ending appears miraculously out of nowhere. This is real life, and real life is far more complicated.

'I've been asked to write a feature on why I got married,' I say, changing the subject.

'OK, go on.'

'The thing is, I can't remember why I did. Do you think that's strange?'

'Like I say, people get married for all sorts of reasons,' she says. 'The heroine in my first novel married a man she didn't love for money.'

'I didn't marry Charlie for his money, I know that much.'

'Why do you think you did then?' she asks softly.

'Because I wanted to forget someone else.' The words are out of my mouth before I can stop them.

'Your true soulmate?'

'Yes.' A tear slides down my cheek. I can't believe I'm confiding in a complete stranger like this, but it feels like the right thing to do.

'Everyone makes mistakes, Molly,' Carla says, reaching across the table for my hand. 'It's never too late to start again.'

I say nothing, but I know it *is* too late for me. David hates me now and I can't turn back the clock. Everything is my fault. Mum and Dad getting killed. David and I breaking up. Even Charlie leaving. I never should have agreed to marry him in the first place. It was a mistake – a huge mistake.

'Thanks for the drink, Carla,' I say, pushing the glass away from me and getting to my feet. I need to go. 'This really helped.'

'No problem.' Carla smiles. 'Are you going somewhere?'

'Yeah,' I say. 'I have a deadline.' And then I hug her and walk out, suddenly knowing what I have to do.

Julie's Blog

8.00 p.m.

Just helped Mr X move all his stuff out of my flat. He begged me to let him stay and I almost caved in. Almost. Until I found a half-written letter that was shoved under one of the piles of anthropology books he had stacked everywhere in the living room. A letter he was writing to his wife, begging her to let him move back in. By the sounds of it, he'd already written her one and she hadn't replied, so this was his second attempt to worm his way back into her affections. It was right then and there that I knew for sure: Mr X never loved me, not ever. He just loved the idea of me. Maybe like he loved the idea of being married, before he actually went ahead and did it. He's just the classic commitment-phobe – wanting what he can't have and then running a mile when he gets it. I almost want to warn UC One about him, because I know that's where he's headed – right to her front door. And she'll probably welcome him with open arms. Yes, I almost want to warn her. Almost. But for the moment they can have each other.

9.00 p.m.

This is complete and utter bliss. Watching trash TV, eating takeout and looking forward to hooking up with the girls later to go clubbing. At last I have my life back.

9.30 p.m.

Text from the janitor:

**Hey you, wanna meet in a cow shed
near you anytime soon?**

Open Forum

From Broken Hearted: Was I right or was I right? I'm so glad she's rid of him. Hopefully she'll have better luck with the janitor. At least he's not married.

From Devil Woman: You hope.

From Hot Stuff: He couldn't be . . . he sounds so nice!

From Sexy Girl: You never know, I guess. Hey, do you guys wanna meet up tonight? Go for a drink?

From Angel: That'd be GREAT. Can we go to Blazin' Saddles again? The cocktail hour is from 5 till 7 p.m.

From Devil Woman: Easy there, Angel. You might start to enjoy yourself if you're not careful. And before you ask, Graphic Scenes: no, there was no HOT SEX.

Eve

Dear Charlie,

This will have to be a very quick letter because I'm getting ready for my grand dinner party. I'm so nervous and I don't know why. Everything is prepared and ready to go: I've peeled the potatoes and the vegetables, I've basted the chicken and I've set the table. I've even remembered to buy some herbal tea, just in case Homer would like some afterwards. Or anyone else too, of course. Maybe his girlfriend likes herbal tea, although from what I hear those cheap and nasty alcopop drinks might be more up her street. Anna says she's definitely a bit dim. Apparently she only reads trashy magazines and she's obsessed with all the WAGs and their giant designer handbags and sunglasses. According to Anna, all she ever talks about are her hair extensions, and even then she can barely string a sentence together properly. I can't imagine what Homer sees in her if that's true – he's so well read and cultured, even though he never rams it down your throat. I remember the look on his face when I caught him reading Chekhov on a tea break – he was almost embarrassed to be found out, it was so sweet. What could he possibly see in someone who only worries about her acrylic nails? I just don't understand it.

I've told Tom that Homer's coming tonight, and I think he understood me because he's licking his fur far more than usual in preparation. I'm convinced he's been pining since the flat was finished – he's definitely been off his food. He even turned up his nose at salmon steak yesterday.

Larry called to say that he's really looking forward to meeting everyone, which was sweet of him. He sent me a massive bunch of roses today. The delivery guy had trouble carrying them in from the van, they were so enormous. It was lovely to get flowers, and very thoughtful of him, but I couldn't help but be reminded of you. Do you remember when we had that terrible row about environmental politics? You were cross because I'd forgotten to buy that eco-friendly washing-up liquid you liked to use, the one that never lathered properly. I said you needed to lighten up, and you said that if everyone took that attitude then the planet was doomed. We ended up sleeping apart for three days, until you sent me an enormous bouquet of pink roses to apologize.

I remember my first thought when I got them was that if you were so devoted to environmental principles then why didn't you go pick me some flowers and give them to me yourself, instead of buying an ostentatious display of out-of-season blooms flown in from Holland? A hand-picked bunch of daisies would have meant so much more to me than an over-priced bouquet. But then I never wanted grand displays, I only ever wanted simple romance. I think it was right then, right at that second, that I saw through you for the very first time, even if I didn't admit it to myself at the time. You couldn't be bothered thinking about what I would really like, you just picked up the phone and used your credit card and you thought that would placate me. I don't even like roses, do you know that? Daffodils are my favourite flower, which is funny because, when I think about it, the shade that Homer chose for my walls is almost exactly the same colour as spring-time daffs.

Anyway, it's unfair of me to compare Larry to you. I need to give him a chance; he seems like a really nice person, even if the thought of kissing him again is not setting my soul alight like Anna says it should. She says I should be thrilled that he seems so interested and doesn't think twice about sending expensive flowers at the drop of a hat, but then she always was more high maintenance than me. She's been training Derek for years to give her exactly what she wants. It's just a pity that now, when he buys her the expensive underwear she loves so much, he can't help trying it on first.

I better go. I want to get a head start on the gravy before my guests arrive.

Eve

Are You Easy to Impress or High Maintenance?

How high are your standards when it comes to love? Take our test and find out!

On a first date you expect a man to:
a) Take you to a fancy restaurant. You also want flowers and chocolates, at the very least.
b) Be kind and make you laugh. Fancy restaurants are usually overrated, so you don't care where you go.
c) Turn up. The last guy you dated stood you up on a regular basis.

Is a man's appearance:
a) The most important thing to you. There's no way you're going to be seen with Will Ugly.
b) Not that important. In the end, looks count for very little.

c) You feel so lucky that any man would ask you out that his looks never come into it. You're just grateful for what you can get.

On a special anniversary you expect a man to:
a) Go all out. You're talking jewellery and you're talking seriously big.
b) Make you a special card. Homemade gifts always mean so much more.
c) You can't imagine your man ever remembering a special date. He never has before.

Results

Mostly As: You're as high maintenance as they get, but you need to examine how your relationship really works at its very core. You and your man may not last unless you set more realistic expectations and focus on what's really important.

Mostly Bs: You and your man strike a healthy balance between caring for each other and setting realistic romantic expectations. You two are set for the long haul!

Mostly Cs: You need to raise the bar, girlfriend! If you have such low standards you'll never find a man who treats you well. You deserve better, so aim high!

Molly

Dear Charlie,

From the outside, you and I might have looked like a perfect couple, but the truth is that things were wrong from the start. I didn't want to admit that to myself, I didn't want to see that we weren't right for each other. I wanted to believe that because you seemed to love me, getting married was the right thing to do. What you didn't know was that I also hoped it would help me forget someone. Just as when Mum and Dad died I hoped that running away would help me escape the guilt and grief. But running away and trying to hide solves nothing, I know that now.

The awful truth is that when you left straight after we got back from our honeymoon I was shocked but I was also relieved. I didn't know why you left then and I don't want to know now, because, if I'm honest with you and myself, it would never have worked between us. We were never meant to be together, not really – you know that as much as I do. I know in my heart that trying again would be a mistake, and I'm sure you do too. Goodbye, Charlie. I wish you happiness and true love in your life.

Molly

'*This* is your feature on why you got married?' Minty finishes reading the letter aloud, scratches her right nipple and frowns.

'Um, yes,' I say.

I'm in trouble – she hates it. I'm going to be fired. I'm going to be given three minutes to clear my desk. Samantha is going to get my job.

'I know it's shorter than we planned, but I think it works.'

'Is all this true?'

'Yes, I'm afraid it is.'

'Well ...' She pauses to search for the right words and I brace myself. 'Good work.' She scratches her left nipple.

Good work? She likes it! She actually likes it.

'It's very ... touching.'

Minty shifts in her seat and blinks hard. I might be imagining it, but there could be a tear in her eye.

'So, this husband of yours – he's gone for good?'

'That's right,' I say.

Saying it out loud is scary, but it also feels like a great weight has been lifted off my shoulders.

'Right.' Minty narrows her eyes at me. 'You seem calm.' She's choosing her words carefully.

'Yes. I am.'

'When my first husband left I was devastated,' she says quietly.

'You were?'

'Yes. That bastard slept with my best friend. I cried for three months.'

'You cried?' I can't imagine Minty ever shedding a tear.

'Of course.' She shuffles some papers on her desk. 'I know everyone thinks I have no feelings, but like I said to Michelle when that ex of hers was sex-texting his old teacher, "Do your crying in private and hold your head high in public."'

Michelle? Michelle from Accounts? Michelle with the teddy bears and love-heart photo frames? My mind is racing.

'She told everyone that you said if she didn't stop snivelling in the office you were going to fire her.'

Minty smiles. 'Ah yes, I asked her to say that. I can't have everyone knowing I have a soft side. They'd all take advantage of me then.' Her eyes are glittering. 'But you go ahead and cry here if you want to.'

She pushes a box of tissues across the table to me.

'Actually I'm fine,' I say.

'You are?' Minty is surprised.

I think about it.

'Well, I will be,' I correct myself. 'I just have one more thing to do.'

An hour later I'm in the graveyard, standing at the spot where Mum and Dad were laid to rest. I can't remember their funerals. Everything from that morning is a blur; all I can really recall is clinging to David and sobbing into his shoulder, sure that nothing would ever be the same again.

I reach across to feel the engravings of their names etched into the marble. There's a potted basket of colourful flowers nestled at the base of the headstone. They're hyacinths: Mum's favourites. Tanya must have put them there before she left for New York. Mum would have loved them. My eyes well at the thought. It still seems so surreal that they're dead. Even after all this time, I can't get my head round the fact that I won't ever see them again. Dad will never again bribe me to smuggle him some of the chocolate the doctor had told him to cut out for the sake of his cholesterol; Mum will never nag me about not wearing a proper coat on a cold day. They're gone and they're not coming back. I have to accept that.

'Hi, Mum. Hi, Dad,' I whisper. 'It's me: Molly.'

I'm talking out loud, but I can't stop myself. It's a good thing the place is deserted: I must look and sound crazy. But that's why I'm here, after all: to tell them everything that's happened. I feel a tear slide down my cheek, then another and another. I wipe my nose on the back of my sleeve.

There's no point looking in my bag for tissues: I never remember to buy any.

'I've made a mess of everything,' I snivel. 'You'd be so ashamed of me.'

'They'd never be ashamed of you, Molly.'

I recognize the voice immediately but I don't move. I must be hallucinating. It can't be him. What would he be doing here? I've finally completely lost it. But somehow it doesn't seem to matter so much any more.

'They thought the world of you. You made them proud.'

His voice sounds so real. If I didn't know better, I could swear he was standing right behind me. I can almost feel the heat of his body.

'Molly?' His voice is a gentle question.

It's only then that I turn around. I'm not hallucinating: it's David. He's here.

'They were great people,' he says solemnly, his face unreadable.

I nod at him, speechless.

'What happened wasn't your fault.'

'Yes, it was,' I croak.

How can he say that? If I hadn't invited them for dinner they'd still be alive and well, playing golf and going to the theatre. If I hadn't persuaded them both that they couldn't miss my roasted lemon chicken then they'd be here. They're dead because of me.

'No, it wasn't. It was mine.' He hangs his head.

'That's ridiculous!' I whisper, my voice hoarse.

Hearing him say that horrifies me. Mum and Dad loved David like a son. They would never think badly of him or blame him for what happened.

'If I hadn't insisted they come over that day, it would

never have happened. I wanted them to be there because I wanted them to see me propose to you.'

'What?' I squeak. He'd never told me that.

'I was going to ask you to marry me, and I wanted them to share the moment. But they never made it and that was *my* fault, not yours.'

'It was an accident, David.' As I say it, I believe it for the first time. Mum and Dad's deaths were nobody's fault. Not David's, not mine. It was just a tragic accident that no one could have prevented. Suddenly it's crystal clear.

His eyes are glued to mine.

'If you believe that, then you have to forgive yourself. They wouldn't want you to blame yourself. They would never have wanted that.'

A wall of emotion hits me full force and before I know it I'm wailing in anguish, like I'm in physical pain. I can feel David's arms around me and I sink into his embrace.

'It's OK, it's OK,' he whispers.

I'm sobbing, great big wracking sobs that make my whole body shake.

'I'm so sorry,' I wail, hugging him so hard that he almost topples backwards. 'I'm so sorry.'

'It's OK, it's OK,' he mutters into my hair, guiding me to a bench on the path and sitting me down. 'You'll feel better in a minute.'

I sob into his shoulder, feeling his solid chest rise and fall. I could stay here wrapped in his arms for ever, but I know I can't. I know he doesn't want anything to do with me. I don't even know why he's here.

I wriggle free and lean back against the bench to try to catch my breath. I'm still feeling very shaky.

'It wasn't your fault, Molly. You have to forgive yourself

and move on. That's what your mum and dad would have wanted. It was an accident; accidents happen.'

Deep down I know he's right. Mum and Dad would be really cross with me for the way I've been thinking.

'What are you doing here?' I ask, hiccupping back my sobs and trying to regain control of my emotions.

'I came to give you these.'

He hands Samantha's oversized sunglasses to me, smiling ruefully.

'You dropped them when you left the photographer's studio. I went to your office and when they told me you were out I just had a hunch you'd be here, I don't know why.'

I take the glasses and shove them into my pocket. Without them on, he can see what I really look like for the first time. There's no point pretending any more.

'Thanks.'

'That's OK. I figured you'd need them – you know, for your photosensitivity.'

I think I see a small smile play around his lips.

'I was lying about that,' I say quickly, the words rushing out in a torrent of truth. 'I don't need the glasses. I only wore them so you wouldn't see how awful I look.'

'You don't look awful. You look amazing, you always do.'

I wipe my nose on my sleeve again. He can't be telling the truth – I know I look a mess – but it still sounds wonderful to hear him say it.

'Molly,' he goes on. 'I lied about something too.'

'You did?'

'Yes. When you asked me if I believed in soulmates I said I didn't, but that's not true. I know I shouldn't tell you this because you're married now, but *you're* my soulmate. You always were.' His voice breaks. 'I'm sorry, I shouldn't be saying this, but I just have to. It's eating me up.'

'But you hate me!' I splutter, astounded.

'Hate you? No, Molly, I don't hate you. I almost wish I did though. It would be a lot easier.' He smiles sadly and kicks the ground. 'When you left you broke my heart and I tried my best to forget all about you. I buried myself in work, I even went out with other girls, but nothing worked.'

'Nothing worked?' I snuffle, hope rising in my chest.

'No, nothing. You're a very hard act to follow.'

'I am?' I whisper, almost afraid to speak.

'Yes, you are.' His eyes meet mine and I hold my breath. 'I've never stopped loving you, you must know that.'

'You never stopped loving me?' My heart soars. David doesn't despise me, he still loves me – I can't believe it.

'I'm sorry. This is totally inappropriate – I know you're married. Please forget I ever said it.' He moves off the bench. 'I'd better get going. I'm sorry about all this.' His head is bowed.

'No!' I shout with joy, launching myself across the bench to him. 'Say it again!'

'I can't. It's not right. You're married now, Molly.' He places his hands on my shoulders to hold me away from him, his face ashen.

'There's never been anyone but you, David,' I say. 'Even when I tried to convince myself there could be. I only left you because after Mum and Dad died I couldn't bear the thought of ever losing you too.' My voice catches in my throat. 'I told you I didn't love you any more to make it easy for you to hate me.'

His eyes widen, the realization of what I've just said hitting him.

'You mean . . .?'

'I mean I never stopped loving you either.'

'But what about your husband? What about Charlie?'

'We're over. We never really began.'

'I don't understand.' His eyes are puzzled.

'I married Charlie to forget you. I never loved him, not really. And it seems he felt the same way because he left me straight after we got back from honeymoon.'

David's face falls. 'This isn't right, Molly. I don't want to be the rebound guy. This has to be for real or it'll never work.'

'It *is* for real, David,' I plead. 'Charlie wants me back. He wants to start again, but I don't. The only second chance I want is with you. Please, David. Please give me another chance.'

My voice is shaking. If he doesn't believe me I don't know what I'll do because I've never been more sure of anything in my life.

He says nothing but his eyes roam my face, questioning, trying to be certain of doing the right thing. He needs to know I'm sure, that I won't run away again.

I nod at him, desperate for him to know that I mean what I say. At last he smiles and reaches for me, my mouth finds his and I know that this is exactly where I was always supposed to be: in his arms.

Julie's Blog

Dear readers,

Thank you for your good wishes – they mean so much to me. As you all know, Mr X and I are no more. On a happier note, I have been approached by no less than four publishers keen to make my blog into a best-selling novel, and there has also been significant interest from Hollywood. Bidding is on-going as we speak, so watch this space!

Thank you all for your wonderful messages of support, and please do keep checking back here. My blogging will continue soon – this time with the kind support of my new Internet sponsors, the Chocolate Chip Cookie Company.

Very best wishes,
Julie

Open Forum

From Hot Stuff: Wow! U rock!!! Can't wait to read the book!

From Devil Woman: That's fantastic news. Keep blogging, we love you!

From Angel: I don't believe it! She's got a publishing deal from this!!!

From Graphic Scenes: Hey, will you sex up the book? The blog was OK, but it was a bit tame.

Eve

Dear Charlie,

So much has happened since my last letter, I don't know where to start.

I had my dinner party. Larry was the first to arrive, with another bunch of flowers under his arm. Anna and Derek were next. I was relieved to see that they were getting on – from what I could ascertain, Derek was even wearing his own underwear. Then Johnny the plumber and his Internet girlfriend arrived, holding hands and mooning over each other in a nicely behaved way. It was all looking good. I'd even got the timings of the meal just right, so I knew the food would be fine. But I was still very fidgety. I just couldn't settle for some reason. I was jumpy and anxious and pacing the floor – even a glass of wine didn't do much to get me in the party mood. I thought it was because I had the gravy on my mind – you must remember how I hate to make gravy. You always used to take over whenever I tried. Remember the Christmas there were so many lumps in my first attempt that you had to throw the entire contents of the saucepan into the bin and start again? That was so embarrassing. Anyway, I was flustered and irritable and definitely not the perfect hostess I wanted to be. But I didn't know why.

And then Homer and his hot date walked in. The minute he came through the door with her on his arm, I started to feel even stranger. I kept criticizing her in my head – her dress was too short, her hair was too blonde, her boobs were too fake. I had turned into my mother, I knew I had, because all I kept thinking was: that girl is not good enough for my Homer. I was thinking about him as *my* Homer. She wasn't smart enough, she wasn't classy enough. She looked like she would enjoy rave music, not Vivaldi. And then it struck me. I was *jealous*. I could barely speak to her and I couldn't even look at him. Poor Larry had no idea what was going on, because I was ignoring him too. All I could see was Homer. The room was full of him, he was everywhere I looked, from the colour of the walls to the classical music playing in the background. It was all him.

So I escaped to the kitchen to check on the meal and to get a grip of myself. It was while I was stirring the gravy that Homer came in behind me. Without saying a word, he handed me a small parcel, wrapped in yellow paper, the exact shade of the walls. It was a portrait: a portrait of me sitting at my writing desk, my head bent in concentration. He had painted it from memory. It was so beautifully and tenderly done that I burst into tears. No one had ever done anything like that for me before.

Then I was crying, great big snotty tears over the gravy, desperate to try to save it, not wanting to think what the gift might mean. Afraid it didn't mean what I wanted it to. And then Homer took the spoon from my hand, pulled me close and told me to stop stirring because he loved lumpy gravy ... and I just knew. He held my face and whispered that ever since I'd hit him over the head and tried to kill him, he knew his life was never going to be the same again. And we've been together ever since.

You see, Homer was right all along: you should never judge a book by its cover. Because he isn't only a painter, he's an artist and a scholar as well. That's why everyone calls him Homer – after the ancient Greek poet, not the cartoon character. Not that I care. I'd love him even if he sat and watched *The Simpsons* all day long. I've been trying to take it slow this time, not to rush into anything, like I did with you. But Homer is really understanding. He doesn't put any pressure on me; he says I can take all the time in the world, that he'll be waiting for me. And he likes me just the way I am, all six-foot beanpole of me.

What else has happened? Oh yes, I told my mother the truth about you, that you didn't just leave me for no good reason, that I caught you in our bed with another woman and that, even when I was stupid enough to beg you to stay and work things out, you left anyway. I realized that the reason I'd always been so afraid to confide in her was because Dad had done exactly the same thing and I didn't want to disappoint her. She has such high expectations for me; I didn't want to shatter her dream that I could have the happy ending she never had. Actually, I shouldn't take the credit for that breakthrough – it was Mary the therapist who pointed this out, but I'm sure I knew it somewhere on a subconscious level.

Anyway, Mum took it much better than I expected. I think she must have already known the truth somewhere inside, she just couldn't admit it to herself. She said you didn't deserve me and you never had, and she was proud of how I'd behaved with such dignity. She's only sorry I didn't tell her sooner so she could have given you a piece of her mind. In fact, she probably still will – she knows where you work, so watch your back. I was nervous how she'd react when I told her about Homer though: I thought she'd feel that a mere painter wasn't good enough for me. But she took it really well. We're so much closer since I confided in her about what really happened with you. Plus the news that Mike is now engaged to Stacey the religion teacher is distracting her. It was visiting the death-row prisoners in Texas that prompted him to propose. Apparently, listening to an inmate called Steve describe the depth of his feelings for his Irish pen friend Samantha convinced Mike that he should make his move. He says he was moved to tears hearing how a condemned man writes love letters to a stranger in Ireland who claims to love him back. Of course, the fact that Stacey is already four months pregnant may have had something to do with his decision. Anyway, Mum's slowly adjusting to the idea of becoming a grandmother ahead of schedule and Anna has already devised a plan to distract her – her next mission is to find Mum a man!

What's next? . . . Oh yes, I've finished my therapy sessions with Mary. My feelings for you are finally dead and I'm ready to move on. I've realized that I wasn't to blame for what happened, that it's you who's broken, not me. The truth is, I've learnt so much about myself and I'm a much happier and more confident person. Which leads me to the best news of all. I've been commissioned to write a women's fiction novel! Do you remember Mum's cruise buddy Leona Merkel? Her daughter Lee, who is Carla Ryan's publicist, has been reading my relationship quizzes in *Her*. She called me and suggested I pitch some book ideas. Homer really encouraged me to do it, and guess what? The publisher loved them! I've just signed a two-book deal and, with the advance, I'm going to Italy with Homer. We plan to see Capri and Mount Vesuvius and wander through the cobble-stoned streets in those tiny white-washed villages on the coast. I have a feeling it's going to be a very special trip.

So this is finally goodbye, Charlie. I never thought I'd say it, but by breaking my heart you've taught me a lot about myself, lessons I needed to learn the hard way. I hope you find true happiness someday, just as I have, but I don't know if you ever will. Somehow I think it's just not your style.

Eve

Are you a Happy Camper or a Blues Bunny?

They say that true happiness is hard to find, but would you know it if it came knocking on your door? Take our quiz and find out!

The last time you felt truly happy was:
a) Today, when the sun shone through the window.
b) You can't remember. Maybe last year, when you were holidaying in that five-star resort in Dubai.
c) Today, when you fired someone. Power is the happiest feeling of all.

In your opinion, to be happy you need:
a) To have an open mind. Happiness is found in all sorts of things if you only look.
b) A big bank balance to fund lots of holidays and shopping.
c) To be driven. Success is a sure-fire recipe for happiness.

What does your man have to give you to make you happy?
a) Breakfast in bed. There's nothing like cuddling up with the papers.
b) A gift voucher for a swanky store – or, even better, his credit card.

c) No man could make you happy, not unless he was working for you.

Results

Mostly As: You know that happiness is found in simple everyday pleasures and you grab them while you can. If only we were all as wise!

Mostly Bs: Deep down you must know that happiness can't be found on a credit card. Put it away and concentrate on the important things in life – that's where happiness really lies.

Mostly Cs: What's the point in sweating the small stuff? You should be working to live, not living to work. Life's too short! You need to grab your happiness where you can – and that means outside the office!

Epilogue

To: Charlie
From: Rex
Re: You fat bastard
Hey Charlie, you fat bastard,
What's this I hear about you and Molly splitting up? If it's true
I want my wedding gift back, mate.
Rex

To: Charlie
From: Lulu
Re: Urgent
Hi Charlie,
Remember me? I have some news for you: you're going to be
a daddy. Before you ask, yes, I'm sure it's yours. The date of your
stag night means there's no mistake. Get in touch. We have a
lot to talk about.
Lulu

Acknowledgements

Thank you to:

The brilliant team at Penguin Ireland: Patricia Deevy, Michael McLoughlin, Cliona Lewis, Brian Walker and Patricia McVeigh. They do the work of thousands!

The equally brilliant team at Penguin UK: Tom Weldon, Naomi Fidler, Ana-Maria Rivera, Tom Chicken, Natalie Higgins, Clare Pollock, Keith Taylor, Caroline Pretty and all the sales, marketing, publicity, editorial and creative teams without whom this book would never reach the shelves.

The wonderful Alison Walsh. Without her wise insight and expert guidance, I would never have crossed the finishing line!

The lovely Simon Trewin and Ariella Feiner at United Agents, who are always there for me.

The booksellers in Ireland and the UK, who have given my novels such great support.

My fantastic family. Your unwavering love and encouragement mean everything to me. What would I do without you?

Darling Rory, Caoimhe and Oliver. The truth is, there would be no books if you three didn't constantly cheer me on and feed me tea and biscuits! I owe it all to you.

My loyal readers. Please keep writing to me! Hearing from so many of you really makes all the hard work worthwhile. I hope you enjoy this book.

Niamh

**And now read a sneak preview from
Niamh Greene's next fantastic novel,**

Rules for a Perfect Life

'This could be the best news ever!' Claire is beaming at me.

'And you think that because?' I take a sip of my wine and try to figure out how she believes that my being made redundant could be a good thing. It certainly doesn't feel that way.

'Because this gives you the freedom to pursue your dreams – you know, reclaim your inner self.'

'Right.' I'd almost forgotten that ever since Claire lost her job with the hedge fund she's been on some ridiculous journey of personal discovery – there's been nothing but talk of reclaiming her inner self for weeks now.

'I'm not convinced you were ever that happy in Hanly and Co.,' she adds. 'I think being an estate agent stifled your creative side.'

'I *was* happy there,' I sigh. 'Perfectly happy.'

'No, you were perfectly *settled*. There's a difference. A very big difference.' Claire eyes me meaningfully. I'm tempted to ignore what she's just said, but curiosity gets the better of me.

'What do you mean?'

'Well, you showed up every day, you clocked in, you clocked out, but what were you really achieving?'

'Um, the highest residential sales in the office?'

'Besides that?' She waves away my achievements of the last five years.

'That's all that really counted, Claire. Commission was always based on sales, you know that.'

'Yes, but what did that commission *give* you?'

'The ability to buy stuff?' I think about my handbag collection. I'll have to stop adding to that now I'm unemployed. The thought makes my heart pound so hard in my chest I can almost feel my breastbone shudder.

'Aha!' Claire slams her fist on the table. I can't help noticing her nails need a manicure.

'What's your point?' I feel weary. Weary to my bones. That can't be a good thing.

'My point is "stuff" can't make you happy.'

Has she lost the plot? Of course it can. My bag collection makes me very happy on a daily basis.

'I beg to disagree,' I say. I know saying 'I beg to disagree' makes me sound like something from the eighteenth century, but Claire is bringing out that side of me. It's not a side I like.

'OK. So you have lots of bags,' she says, 'But how does that fulfil you?'

'They make me feel good. They . . . they accessorize my outfits.' I'm starting to feel defensive. Has she completely forgotten how designer stuff can alter your mood? Her Chanel handbag used to be her prized possession. I look at her now and wonder where that bag is. She's carrying something that looks suspiciously like it has been purchased in a secondhand shop. And not a cool secondhand shop where you might see a Kate Moss-type buying vintage Dior; no, some grubby place that sells mothballed jumpers even the cat wouldn't touch. Claire's bag of the moment is a gruesome patchwork concoction, with multicoloured beading and – horrors – tiny little mirrored tiles stitched to the edges. It's absolutely hideous and if Claire was in her right mind she'd shove it into the pub fire that's glowing nicely in the grate beside us. The old Claire wouldn't have used that bag to put her dirty laundry in. Then again, the old Claire wouldn't have appeared in public without at least six inches of slap on her face and, from where I'm sitting, her skin looks completely devoid of make-up. I'm not sure she's even wearing bronzer. In fact, I'm starting to worry that Claire has let herself go entirely. Maybe she's become depressed since the hedge fund collapsed – that could explain her scruffy appearance. It's really very worrying, especially considering I may end up just like her very soon. I might even start believing that crystals can heal, like she does.

Right on cue, Claire takes a small crystal from her hideous patchwork bag and presses it into my hand. 'Here, take this. Keep it close, it'll help. And promise me you'll think about what I said.'

'OK,' I mumble, quickly shoving the crystal in my pocket before anyone can see it.

'So, what's Robert said about you getting the sack?' she asks, taking a sip of the mineral water in front of her.

'He's, um, been very supportive,' I lie.

She nods approvingly. 'Of course he has – he's wonderful. You're really lucky to have him.'

I force myself to smile at her. The truth is, I haven't told Robert that I'm going to be unemployed. Not yet, that is. I meant to tell him, of course I did, but then he came home the very same day I'd received the news, fretting that his own job might be in danger, so I hadn't the heart to break it to him. I decided to wait a bit longer, just a day or two, until I'd got used to the idea myself. Only now a week has drifted by and I still haven't mentioned it. I'm going to have to find a way to break it to him though, because soon I'll be sitting at home looking up the wanted pages and he's bound to notice that.

'Have you decided what *you're* going to do next?' I ask to change the subject.

'I have, actually.' Claire looks at me levelly. 'I've decided to do a course in holistic therapy. I'm going to set up my own practice – in the country.'

I splutter my white wine across the table, narrowly missing spraying her in the eye. 'You're *what*?'

Claire is going to become a holistic therapist and live in the country? This is insane! Claire has an addiction to caffeine. She smokes. She thinks water is for sissies. I thought this whole detoxing thing was just a phase. I fully expected her to snap out of it.

'Yes,' she says carefully, 'I've been feeling so fulfilled since I started this journey that I want to move it to the next level.'

Oh, God. She really is talking like a lunatic. Maybe she *has* lost the plot since she was made redundant. Maybe I haven't been paying enough attention.

'I don't want to get sucked back into the rat race. I realize what's important now – and it's not money or possessions.'

I'm speechless.

'I've even applied to go to an ashram in India.'

'An *ashram*?' I squeak. This beggars belief.

'It's a hermitage – where you can practice yoga and meditation.'

'I know what an ashram is. I just never imagined you'd ever go to one.' It sounds like the sort of thing Claire would have laughed about only a few months ago – didn't she used to say yoga was a useless waste of time?

'Well, neither did I, but that was before . . . '

Her voice trails away while she tries to compose herself. I think I see a tear glinting in her eye. This is too much. Claire never cries. She's been known to thump people who cry in public. She whacked me once when we were watching a sad movie after I broke down when the heroine died in a tragic accident. The bruise lasted for well over a week.

'Anyway,' she goes on, 'I may not even get a place in the ashram – it's so popular that it's really difficult to get into. But, either way, I've decided to leave the city. And that's where you come in.'

'Where *I* come in?' What's she talking about? What do I have to do with this harebrained idea?

'Yes. I want to leave the city – and, Maggie, I want you to help me.'

Rules for a Perfect Life will be published
in Summer 2010